S0-AFC-140

GENTLE YEARNING

ROCHELLE ALERS

Genesis Press, Inc.

Indigo Love Stories

An imprint of Genesis Press, Inc.
Publishing Company

Genesis Press, Inc.
P.O. Box 101
Columbus, MS 39703

All rights reserved. Except for use in any review, the reproduction or utilization of this work in whole or in part in any form by any electronic, mechanical, or other means, not known or hereafter invented, including xerography, photocopying and recording, or in any information storage or retrieval system, is forbidden without written permission of the publisher, Genesis Press, Inc. For information write Genesis Press, Inc., P.O. Box 101, Columbus, MS 39703.

All characters in this book have no existence outside the imagination of the author and have no relation whatsoever to anyone bearing the same name or names. They are not even distantly inspired by any individual known or unknown to the author and all incidents are pure invention.

Copyright© 1998, 2006 by Rochelle Alers. All rights reserved.

ISBN: 1-58571-216-7
Manufactured in the United States of America

First Edition 1998
Second Edition 2006

Visit us at www.genesis-press.com or call at 1-888-Indigo-1

*When a man seduces a virgin who is not betrothed,
and lies with her, he shall pay her marriage price
and marry her* -- Exodus 22:16

CHAPTER ONE

A cold, biting early March wind searched through layers of wool, invading the natural warmth of Rebecca Williams' body. It stung her eyes, whipped her coifed hair around her face, and stabbed her cheeks like hundreds of tiny razors. She stood motionless, staring down at the mound of dirt on the grave.

Everyone who had attended the burial had left to escape the fast-moving storm that was predicted to leave more than a foot and a half of snow along the Mid-Atlantic and New England coasts.

Rebecca's parents had left the cemetery to make it to the airport for their return trip to Florida before all outgoing flights were canceled, her sister and brother-in-law were on their way to New Jersey, and the thousands of law enforcement officers who had come to pay their last respects to a fallen comrade had filed silently out of the cemetery to return to their home cities and states.

Only Rebecca Williams and Daniel Clinton remained.

She felt her late-husband's, ex-partner's warm breath on the nape of her neck as he moved behind her. Closing her eyes, she leaned back against his solid body. His arms curved around her waist and she sank into his warmth and strength.

Daniel Clinton had promised Michael Williams that he would always be there for Rebecca if anything happened to him, and he was. He was with her within an hour after the news had come that sixteen-year veteran New York City Police Detective Michael Williams had been shot and killed during an undercover narcotics buy and bust. Highly decorated Detective Williams had succumbed to a single bullet from a nine millimeter handgun. He had been shot at point blank range in the back of his head, and died instantly.

Daniel had come to Rebecca as soon as he had received the telephone call from an officer at the station house where Michael had been assigned, encountering several uniformed men who had already come to offer their condolences to the widow.

It was he who had driven her to the morgue to identify Michael's body. It was he who had helped her with the funeral arrangements. And it was he who had stood by her side while she graciously accepted the sympathy of the Governor, Mayor, Police Commissioner, and the many other officials who represented the City and State of New York.

She was stoic, her voice soft and controlled, her posture straight and elegant. She hadn't cried, but she hadn't smiled either. It was as if Rebecca Williams was playing a role that she had been born to play. She was the wife of a man who had died in the line of duty.

Swirling white flakes began falling, softly at first, landing and melting quickly on the withered grass and on any other dry surface. And still she did not move.

Daniel waited, feeling the chill penetrating the soles of his shoes and temporarily numbing his toes. Another quarter of an hour passed and the falling snow picked up in intensity, obliterating the lead-gray skies and everything within three feet from where they stood.

"It's time to go, Rebecca." Daniel's baritone voice rumbled softly in her ear.

Rebecca shook her head. "I haven't said good-bye to him."

"You don't have to say good-bye now. You can always come back and do it later." His gloved fingers curved around her upper arms. "We'll come back after the snow stops."

Her shoulders slumped in resignation. "You promise, Daniel?"

Burying his face in her damp hair, he whispered, "I promise."

Nodding, she permitted him to lead her out of the cemetery and to the winding path where he had parked his car. He opened the door to a racy black two-seater sports car and helped her into the low-slung bucket seat, waiting until she had secured her seat belt before he circled the Porsche. He removed his top coat and suit jacket, tossing them into the small space behind the seats, then slipped in behind the wheel.

Daniel turned on the ignition, shifted into gear, and with a thrust of power, left the Long Island cemetery. He drove quickly, expertly, keeping his gaze on the road. The small car heated up within minutes, the warmth seeping back into his limbs.

Rebecca's soft sigh resounded in the confined space as she settled back against the leather seat, closing her eyes. It was over. Michael was gone.

She'd told Daniel that she hadn't said good-bye even though she had. She told Michael good-bye each time he picked up his gun and shield to go on duty. It was as if she held her breath when he walked out the door, not letting it out until he returned hours later. And if he hadn't come home when his shift ended he always called the first chance he got, reassuring her that he was alive and well.

But when the two uniformed officers had shown up at her apartment four days before, she knew without their saying anything. Their strained expressions and the sadness in their gazes told her all she needed to know. Michael Harrison Williams was dead.

"Do you need more heat, Becky?"

Daniel's deep, soothing voice pulled her out of her reverie as a slight smile softened her lush mouth. Daniel Clinton was the only one she knew that shortened her name. "No, thank you. I'm fine."

Daniel chanced a quick glance at Rebecca's profile. Her dulcet voice was totally incongruent to her fragile face. Looking at her one would have thought she would claim a light, whispery voice, not the low, husky one that never failed to send shivers up and down his spine.

It was her voice that had attracted him to her eighteen years ago. He had been sitting in a restaurant and he heard her laugh from the booth behind his. The sound was like velvet full and lush, cloaking and erotic. It had taken all of his willpower not to stand up and match a face to the sensual voice.

But he did see her face when she walked out of the coffee shop near the campus where they both attended classes. He later discovered that she was an incoming freshman, majoring in early elementary education, while he was a graduating senior. He had been on the New York City police force for four years, and he was scheduled to earn an undergraduate degree in criminal justice.

Rebecca was more beautiful now at thirty-six than she had been at eighteen. Her skin was flawless, a shimmering rich fawn-brown; her curling dark auburn hair, dark-gray eyes, delicate features, and the pale blue veins showing through the burnished skin she had inherited from her father. The full lushness of her exceptional mouth, and her slimness was her mother's. Her parents were complete opposites in looks—light and dark, but their genes had compromised and had given their offspring the best of two races.

Two months before his graduation, Daniel met Rebecca at a lecture, the attraction was instantaneous, and it was only after they'd dated for a year and he met her father that he realized why Rebecca was drawn to him. He and James McDonald shared similar physical characteristics—height and overall physique. Her father was also in the same field. He was a criminal court judge.

Daniel had been the one to introduce Rebecca to her dormant sensuality, and from the first time their coming together was passionate and erotic. She wanted marriage and a family, but he didn't. Not as long as he was a police officer. During his short tenure on the force he had attended three funerals, calmly observing the reactions of the grieving widows and their children. The images of their stricken faces haunted him in his sleep. This was not the image he wanted for Rebecca. But she did eventually marry, not him, but it was to a cop.

They'd parted as friends, and when they met again he was on duty, sitting in a cruiser with his partner Michael Williams. Michael took one look at her and fell hard. It was six months before Michael revealed that he and Rebecca were dating, and another six months before they became husband and wife.

Daniel was happy for the both of them, because he loved Michael like a brother and his love for Rebecca had never waned, and he consented to be best man at Michael's wedding.

Over the next eight years he got to see a lot of Rebecca and Michael whenever they met socially. It was at these events that he came with whatever woman he was dating at the time. A little piece of him always regretted his decision not to marry Rebecca when he saw how happy she was as a wife. Some women were born to be wives, and Rebecca McDonald-Williams was one of those women.

But her world had come crashing down with a single bullet. The buy and bust had gone down and so had Michael, leaving Rebecca alone and without the protection of a husband.

She may not have a husband now, but she wasn't alone. Daniel was there. He had always been there for her. Only moments before they entered the church where a minister was waiting to preside over the ceremony that would join Rebecca and Michael as husband and wife, Michael had made him promise that he would take care of Rebecca if anything happened to him.

The look of panic in Michael's eyes and the strained timbre of his voice had frightened Daniel, and he knew what Michael was feeling at that moment. It was fear. The same fear he had experienced when Rebecca had broached the subject of marriage. The fear and risk every law enforcement officer experiences when they commit to marriage, knowing that his or her life and future are not promised to them once they go on duty.

Daniel had encountered the fear and the risks firsthand when a serial rapist almost ended his own life. The crazed man's hunting knife found its mark, sinking deep into his shoulder blade, severing muscles and tendons and causing extensive damage that prevented him raising his left arm above his head for months. It had been the first and only time he'd drawn and discharged his weapon at another human being. Despite losing copious amounts of blood and being left-handed, he had brought the perpetrator down with a bullet in his leg, ending a reign of terror from a man who had preyed on women in New York City's Harlem community for more than a year.

The dreaded 10-13—police officer needs assistance— call went out and he woke up hours later knowing that his career as a police officer was over. He was thirty-five years old and he had to look for an alternate profession.

He combated depression by returning to college, where he earned a Masters in Communications, and at thirty-seven set up his own security company. The next three years were very good to him, and now he looked forward to his fortieth birthday with a confidence he hadn't thought possible. He had not married or fathered children, but his company was solvent, and he was in excellent health. But all of that paled when he realized his promise to Michael and his commitment to Rebecca.

Adjusting the speed of the wiper blades, he concentrated on the taillights of the car in front of his. What he did not want to do was think too much about Rebecca. He did not want to consciously acknowledge that his feelings for her hadn't changed, because he knew they had. It wasn't the profound need to be with her, to share a bed with her, but a soothing, gentle yearning to take care of her. He'd promised that he would protect her—and he would.

A blowing wind intensified the falling snow as it slashed against the windshield, obscuring visibility until he slowed the car to less than twenty miles per hour. A driver in the left lane signaled, then skidded without slowing and spun out in front of his car. Daniel downshifted and maneuvered off to the shoulder to avoid a collision.

"Fool," he mumbled under his breath while silently adding a colorful expletive. He chanced a quick glance at Rebecca; she hadn't moved. She stared ahead with unseeing eyes.

Waiting a full minute, he peered into his side view mirror, then pulled out when he saw an opening. He wanted to turn on the radio or slip in a tape or CD to counter the swollen silence, but didn't. He wanted to hear Rebecca's voice. He needed for her to say something, anything.

What bothered him more than her silence was the fact that she hadn't exhibited any outward signs of grieving. It was as if the shock of Michael's death had numbed her. She reacted mechanically, responding only when addressed. He wanted her to scream, cry, throw objects. He wanted her to let out her grief so that she could begin the process of healing.

He exited a parkway along Long Island's south shore without further mishap, driving slowly down the wide avenue that led to the building where Rebecca had shared an apartment with Michael for the past eight years. They'd moved into the apartment, saying they would buy a house once they started a family. Daniel knew that his two best friends wanted children, but it had not become a reality. The last time he had shared dinner with the Williamses, they talked about adopting and asked if he would be the godfather. He agreed, tightening the invisible bond which would bind the three of them together for a lifetime.

But now there would be no adoption because the circle was broken. Michael Williams—husband, ex-partner, best friend, brother was gone forever. Michael was gone and only he and Rebecca remained.

Chancing a surreptitious glance at her profile, Daniel saw the quivering muscle in her delicate jaw. What he wanted to do was stop the car and shake her until she let go of the heroic pretense. It was over. Michael was dead, buried and it was all right for her to act out—let go. She was young, beautiful, widowed *and* alive. Breathing alive! Flesh and blood alive! Pulling into her building's parking lot, he maneuvered beside Rebecca's snow-covered Honda, not bothering to turn off the ignition.

Large, dark-brown, deep-set eyes under sweeping black silken eyebrows searched the impassive expression of the woman sitting beside him. Her leather-gloved hands were curled into tight fists on her lap, and Rebecca looked rigid enough to shatter into thousands of tiny pieces if he touched her.

Still not moving, Rebecca made no attempt to get out of the car. She couldn't; she did not trust her legs to support her body. She had held everything together for four days and now she didn't have to be brave any longer.

She did not *want* to be brave and she did not *want* to be alone. As long as Michael's body had remained above ground she felt that she wasn't alone. Now he truly was gone, his remains sealed in a box and lowered into the cold, frozen earth. She would never hear his distinctive laugh or see his sparkling, laughing eyes again. And she would never languish in the comfort of his protective embrace. For the first time in her life she was afraid of being alone; she couldn't bear to face the loneliness of staying in the apartment without Michael.

"Please come up with me, Daniel." Her low, husky voice floated through the car like a thick, cloaking fog.

Daniel nodded, shutting off the engine. Opening his door, he stepped out and reached for his top coat. He pushed his arms into the sleeves at the same time he circled the Porsche and opened the passenger door for Rebecca. The snow was now falling heavily, quickly coating his bare head. She placed her gloved hand in his and he pulled her to her feet. Curving an arm around her waist, he led her across the parking lot and into the warmth of the vestibule in the four-story apartment building. In her heels Rebecca's head came above his shoulder. She was five-nine in her bare feet, and he stood six-four.

"Give me your keys, Becky."

Rebecca opened her purse, searched the depths for her keys, then gave up, handing the leather handbag to Daniel. She couldn't control her trembling hands.

Daniel found the keys and opened the door leading to the lobby. His right hand went to the small of her back as he steered her toward the elevator. He had come to the apartment building countless times, but it seemed as if this was the first time that he noticed the tasteful furnishings in the lobby. It was an indoor oasis, warm and welcoming, with natural rattan love seats and colorful seat cushions. A waterfall in a corner gurgled softly, the water floating over rocks into a pool. Live plants surrounded the man-made waterfall, adding a tropical ambience to the space.

The elevator doors opened and they entered. He pushed a button and, within seconds, it stopped at the top floor. Their footsteps were silent along the carpeted hallway as they walked side by side. Daniel inserted the key in the lock of a door bearing the name of Williams. It opened to a spacious foyer, then out to an L-shaped living/dining area radiated warmth and comfort. He placed Rebecca's keys and handbag on a small round table in the foyer before reaching over and removing her coat.

She stood in front of him, her gaze fixed on his mouth. He saw what had attracted him to her—her face and more. However, the more was not reflected in the sadness of the dark-gray eyes or the unsmiling mouth. What he wanted to do was replace her pain with joy. He needed to hear the laugh that had drawn him to her when he hadn't yet seen her face; a face that was heart-stoppingly beautiful.

"Have you eaten today, Daniel?"

He smiled, his straight, white teeth showing beneath the thick brush of a neatly barbered mustache. It was the first time in days that she had spoken without someone prompting a response from her.

"No, I haven't. And I suspect neither have you."

The beginnings of a smile touched her full mouth. "I'll fix us something."

His hand went to her shoulder, stopping her from walking away. "Let me help you. Why don't you go and change while I start."

Rebecca decided not to argue. It was her house and her kitchen, but she did not have the energy for a confrontation, especially not with Daniel. What she did not want to do was have him leave. Not now. Not when she was afraid to be alone.

She had always been extremely persuasive with Michael. Daniel Clinton was very different. It wasn't that he never conceded. It was just that when he took a stand he stood firm. There had been very few times when she had gotten him to relent.

Heading for her bedroom, she thought about the man who had been her first love and her first lover. They had been sleeping together for more than a year when she realized she wanted to marry him. When she'd mentioned the word he stared at her as if he had never seen her before. Slowly and methodically he enumerated all of the reasons why he would not marry as long as he remained a police officer. Her pleading and tears did not sway him when he gathered his clothes, gun and shield and walked out of her apartment.

They saw each other the following day, and he announced quietly that he could not sleep with her any more. They would remain friends without the intimacy. She continued to date Daniel for another six months before ending it. There was no way she could see him, kiss him, and not share her body with him. His possession and passion were stamped on her like an invisible tattoo. She never forgot him or stopped loving him, even after she had married Michael.

Rebecca moved as if she were in a trance. She slipped out of her heels, and out of the hated black dress. The black underwear followed until she stood in front of a Cheval mirror completely naked. She stared at the reflection staring back her. Her eyes looked larger, vacant, while all of the rich natural color in her face had disappeared. What had been professionally coifed hair, blown out and curled softly at the ends, now curled naturally over her forehead from the wet snow.

She refused to acknowledge her flat belly; a belly that had remained flat despite her many attempts to conceive. The love of a man meant marriage, and marriage to her was children, children she would never have now that her husband was dead. They'd waited three years into their marriage before trying to start a family. There were highs when her period had not made its usual appearance, then there were the lows when it did. It had taken five years before she and Michael decided to adopt, because he was unwilling to go through testing and invito fertilization.

It was only three weeks ago that they had invited Daniel for dinner and asked that he be godfather to their child.

Daniel had merely raised his expressive eyebrows, smiled, then given his consent. His only stipulation was that the child's middle name be his. Daniel for a boy or Danella for a girl. She and Michael quickly agreed. The three of them lifted their champagne-filled flutes in a rousing toast. It was the last time they were all together.

Pulling her tortured gaze away from the mirror, she walked over to her lingerie chest and selected a pair of rose-pink panties and matching lace bra. The color seemed to warm her flesh, and actually lifted her spirit for the first time in days.

She covered her underwear with a pair of well-washed jeans and an oversized navy-blue T-shirt. The shirt had been Michael's and bore the insignia of the NYPD. Even though every room in the one bedroom apartment was carpeted and well heated, she still pulled on a pair of socks. Her feet and the end of her nose remained cold until the hot summer weather. Even then they were cool.

She left her bedroom and made her way into the narrow utility kitchen, stopping short. A fist of breath was knocked out of her lungs at the sight of Daniel Clinton taking up more space than she could have thought possible. He stood at the sink rinsing two steaks he had defrosted in the microwave oven.

His height, the breadth of his wide shoulders, slender waist and hips, and his large capable hands brought back memories she had buried when she pledged her life and future to another man. She did not want to remember the hypnotic feel of his hands on her naked flesh or the crushing weight of his heavy body on hers after their passions were sated.

He had rolled back the cuffs to his white shirt and removed his tie. The pristine laundered garment was tucked neatly into the waistband of his tailored slacks, which fell at the precise break above his Italian-made loafers. It had been Daniel Clinton's body that had garnered her attention first, then his face. She initially thought that the angles in his face were too sharp, too severe, to label him as handsome. But it was his eyes—bedroom eyes—that changed her first impression of him. Large, deep-set, dark eyes under half-lowered lids said all that his mouth hadn't, and she suspected Daniel knew that because he used his eyes to their maximum advantage. All he had to do was glance at her and she knew exactly what he wanted.

Heat scorched her face when she realized the direction of her thoughts. She had just buried her husband, while something within her called out for her former lover, and she knew in that instant that it had been a mistake to invite Daniel to come home with her.

Her gaze moved up to his head, noting the liberal sprinkling of gray in his close-cut hair. The gray contrasted softly with the deep, rich sienna brown of his face. She'd loved the color of his skin. It always reminded her of the vibrancy of a leaf turned brown by the colder weather, yet still glossy before it floated gently to the dark earth to wither. It was now March fifth, and in another three weeks Daniel would celebrate his fortieth birthday. He was approaching middle age as a magnificent male in his prime.

Daniel had sensed Rebecca's approach, refusing to acknowledge her. She had come into the kitchen like a wary cat, not trusting herself. Out of the corner of his eye he saw that she had changed her clothes. The jeans he had seen her in so many times before no longer outlined the curves of her slender body. They hung loosely around her thighs, and he doubted whether she had had more than the countless cups of coffee he had seen her drink over the past four days. It was no wonder that she was non-responsive. She was probably too malnourished to exhibit any energy.

"I've got everything under control here," he said softly. "Go sit in the living room and I'll bring you something to drink."

Rebecca crossed her arms under her breasts. "I need to do something."

His gaze lingered briefly on her mouth before his own lips parted in a smile. "Sit down and put your feet up, Becky. You'll have plenty to do later."

"You're right about that," she agreed. She had to pack Michael's clothes and go through all of his personal belongings. And there were still a lot of legal documents she had to read, decipher and sign.

She left the kitchen and made her way into the living room. She didn't sit, but stood at the wall-to-wall window, staring down at the street. The falling snow had all but obliterated the sidewalks. The meteorologists were right with this prediction. The northeast would be hit again by a crippling winter storm. This storm would be the tenth of the winter season. In another two weeks it would officially be spring. A time for renewal and rebirth. Unfortunately it would signal the opposite for her.

"I thought I told you to sit down and put your feet up."

Rebecca turned at the sound of Daniel's voice, hearing the censure in his tone. He stood several feet from her, holding a glass filled with a deep, rich red wine. She closed her eyes, then opened them. A slight frown furrowed her smooth forehead.

"Please don't fight with me, Daniel."

He placed the wineglass on a side table and closed the distance between them. Cradling her face gently between his large hands, he flashed a gentle smile. "I'm not fighting with you, *Love*." Rebecca's luminous eyes widened and he knew he made a grievous mistake. The endearment was one he hadn't used since they parted, and he had never called another woman *Love*. That was an epithet he had reserved for Rebecca and only her.

His fingers tightened slightly on her silken flesh. "I promised Michael that I would take care of you, and I intend to do just that," he said quickly, arching a sweeping eyebrow. "I'm going to feed you, and before I leave here I am going to make certain you get some sleep. I see you falling apart right before my eyes. We can't have that, Becky Williams, can we?"

She managed a sad smile. "No, we can't, Daniel Albert Clinton."

Daniel winced, shaking his head. For a reason he could not explain he felt uncomfortable with his middle name. Perhaps because it was his father's name, and at one time he had been estranged from Albert Clinton for many years.

His father left him and his mother a week after his tenth birthday, and in the ensuing years they had interacted with each other less than a dozen times.

"I knew I never should've told you my middle name."

Lowering his hands, he led her to an armchair and eased her down to it. Bending slightly he raised her sock covered feet to a matching ottoman.

He sat down on the edge of the ottoman and reached for the glass of wine. He held the glass to her lips, saying, "Drink."

Rebecca took a sip of the fragrant wine, peering at Daniel over the rim. He was the most masculine man she had ever encountered, and she wondered why he hadn't married now that he wasn't a police officer. Whenever she and Michael invited him to their home for a social gathering he usually brought a woman, but never the same woman twice. She had stopped asking herself why.

After three sips of the rich, full-bodied wine, she felt lightheaded and pushed the glass away. "I can't drink anymore until I eat."

Daniel set the glass on the table. He brushed her hair away from her cheek with the back of his hand. The dark red silken strands curled around his fingers with a life of their own. Leaning over, he pressed his lips to her forehead.

"Try to relax."

Closing her eyes, she nodded. What she wanted to do was sleep and wake up to find everything the way it was before the two uniformed officers had come to her door. Before the day Michael walked out of their apartment for the last time, and before the news report blared across the television screen that a police investigation had been set up to uncover why an undercover narcotics detective did not have adequate backup for a buy and bust procedure.

Taking Daniel's advice, she willed her mind blank and, within minutes, everything around her vanished as she offered herself up to the comforting arms of a dreamless slumber.

CHAPTER TWO

Daniel retreated to the kitchen and took several sips from his own wineglass. The dark-red room temperature liquid slid easily down the back of his throat, warming his chest.

He did not like issuing demands, but Rebecca hadn't offered him a choice. There was only a four year difference in their ages, even though he'd always felt older, yet there had never been a time when he'd raised his voice to her or exhibited what he thought of as a display of masculine superiority. With her that was never a thought or necessity.

Rebecca McDonald had come to him untouched, a virgin, and he had treasured the gift of her chaste body. She had also given him what no other woman had given him up to that time and since: all of herself.

She had loved him unconditionally while he had set up barriers and prerequisites for their future. When they began dating he had been too much of a coward to tell her that he would never marry as long as he was a law enforcement officer. In the end he still had been unable to protect her; she became the widow of a law enforcement officer.

Taking another swallow of wine, his eyes narrowed in concentration as he remembered his shock when hearing Michael's admission that he was involved with Rebecca. His facetious smile had not betrayed the burning rage rendering him motionless and speechless. It took Herculean self-control not to punch out the man he had come to think of as a brother. What he hadn't wanted was for Michael to have what he'd had, what he knew Rebecca was capable of offering a man. It would have been easier for him to accept her involvement with another man; anyone except Michael.

It took several months for him to work through his feelings of betrayal, realizing that he had not been betrayed. It was that he had not let Rebecca go. He hadn't married her while he still wanted her. His dilemma was resolved the day he agreed to be Michael's best man. Outwardly he had let Rebecca go, inwardly he would love her forever.

Refilling his glass, he went through the motions of preparing a marinade for the steaks, washing two baking potatoes, and dicing vegetables to accompany the green salad.

Daniel turned on the eye-level oven, adjusting the temperature to a medium setting, then, using a sharp knife, made a half-dozen slashes in the potatoes. He was very careful not to cut completely through each one, filling each slot with thinly sliced Vidalia onion rings, and sprinkling them with an herb seasoning, followed with a light cover of butter-flavored cooking spray, before securing them tightly in foil. They would bake slowly while the steaks marinated.

Retrieving his glass of wine, he returned to the living room and sat down on a comfortable sofa. Rebecca lay less than six feet away, her chest rising and falling gently in sleep. He would let her get in an hour's sleep before he woke her to eat.

He flicked on the television, utilizing the remote. Pressing the MUTE button, he sat staring at the screen sipping wine. Silent images flickered with constant news bulletins updating the storm while Daniel's gaze was fixed on the mouths of the newscasters. Camera shots of abandoned vehicles along the highways and local roads indicated that he would be forced to spend the night on Long Island instead of in his own apartment in the Westchester County suburb of New Rochelle.

Slowly and methodically he began changing channels until the identifying logo for the sports channel appeared, then spent the next hour watching the highlights of the prior evening's basketball game between the New York Knicks and the Chicago Bulls. A smile curved his mouth when he relived the last second three-point shot that won the nail-biting, heart-pounding game for the Knicks.

He had courtside tickets to the game, but gave them away to two of his employees. When he apologized to the woman he had promised to take to the game, explaining that he had to be with Rebecca during Michael's wake, she hung up on him, but not before she offered a few choice words about how he was taking his role as Rebecca's protector and confidant too far.

He replayed her verbal assault once he sat in one of the viewing rooms at the funeral home, watching Rebecca as she thanked each person who had taken time from their busy day to pay their respects. Her voice, soft and even, was soothing and the sad smile she affected had not slipped. And not once had she shed a tear. The fact that she hadn't unnerved him. When, he wondered, was she going to grieve so that she could heal? Then he questioned whether he really was overcompensating with his safeguarding of his ex-partner's widow. What he was unable to do was come up with a plausible answer.

Rebecca stirred restlessly on the chair. Opening her eyes, she saw the flickering images from the television, but no sound coming from it. The table lamps were not lighted and the drawn vertical blinds gave her no indication of the hour.

The smell of broiling meat reminded her how hungry she was. She couldn't remember the last time she'd eaten a full meal.

The chandelier in the dining area was dimmed to its lowest setting; the fragile lights cast an ethereal glow on the china, silver, crystal, and an antique-white lace tablecloth. Daniel had set an elegant table.

A wry smile softened her mouth. That was one of the differences she noticed immediately about the two men who had had a profound effect on her life. Daniel would set a full table even if they sat down to eat peanut butter and jelly sandwiches, while Michael preferred eating a standing rib roast dinner on a lap tray in front of the television. Michael had been laid-back, easygoing; Daniel traditional, conservative.

Michael had always made her laugh, while Daniel always elicited a smile. Her husband had made her sizzle and her first lover had made her burn. The two men had been her lovers, but one man had become lover and friend, the other lover and husband.

A husband who was to be her life partner, even though that partnership was dissolved by the firing of a single bullet; husband who, when he died had taken a piece of her with him; and a husband whom she had grown to love more than she thought possible. This was the first time in more than eight years that Michael and Daniel occupied her thoughts simultaneously.

It had taken more than a year of marriage for Michael to erase the passionate memories of the man to whom she had offered her innocence. The two men were similar, yet so different.

Both were an only child—Michael reared by a dowager aunt after his parents died in a fire, and Daniel, who was doted upon, by his divorced mother. The day Eunice Clinton died was the same day Rebecca told Daniel that their relationship was over. She did not know that he had grieved twice.

She closed her eyes again, nearly sinking back into the arms of Morpheus before she shook herself awake. She wanted to sleep—forever if that were possible, but knew she couldn't. Opening her eyes, she forced herself off the comfortable chair and stood up.

Making her way silently across the carpeted floor, she walked into the kitchen, bumping into Daniel, who was carrying a bowl of salad to the dining area. The solid wall of his large body stopped her approach, jolting her while she struggled to regain her footing.

Daniel's right hand moved with amazing speed, his fingers curving around her upper arm and righting her. The bowl cradled in the crook of his left arm tilted dangerously in the direction of the floor.

"Sorry," she gasped, reaching out and managing to balance the wooden bowl.

Daniel's hand lingered on her warm flesh before dropping. "My fault. I should've been more alert," he apologized. The warmth and the sensual fragrance of Rebecca's perfume wafted in his nostrils, making it impossible for him to move.

He couldn't pull his gaze away from the delicate face flushed with high color, hypnotic soft dove-gray color eyes framed by charcoal-gray lashes, or the glossy silkiness of her dark red curling hair falling in seductive disarray over her forehead.

In the time that she had been married to another man Daniel had dismissed Rebecca's beauty and the silent, sensual power she wielded. He had successfully concealed the lust she always elicited in him. Even after had stopped sleeping with her he had still wanted her. It was everything, the total woman—voice, face, and body that had pulled him in and refused to let him go.

But she had let him go. Quietly, calmly she had told him that she could not continue to date him. She confessed her love for him, offered him friendship, then stood up and walked away. He let her walk away, and within seconds of the door closing behind her departing figure the phone rang. It was his great-uncle, informing him that his niece, Daniel's mother, had passed away. That day was the longest and darkest one in his life, wherein for the first time he drank himself into a stupor, blotting out the pain of losing the only two women he had ever loved.

Reluctantly he dropped his gaze. A slow, warm smile parted his lips under the silken black mustache that concealed much of his strong masculine mouth. He had grown the mustache, along with a beard, during his convalescence following the stabbing. After his official retirement from the Department he shaved the beard, but the mustache had remained. It seemed to soften the sharp angles of his high cheekbones, while adding another dimension of character to his face.

"You woke up just in time," he informed Rebecca, his deep voice reverberating, like distant rolling thunder, from the bowels of his chest. "The steaks are just about ready." His smile widened. "Do you still like yours well done?"

She returned his smile, savoring the wonderful sound of his voice. There were times, years before, when she'd sat silent, eyes closed, listening to him read. She never understood Shakespeare unless she heard Daniel reading his work. Hearing him recite The Bard's sonnets was always a breathtaking, heart-stopping experience.

"Yes," she replied softly. He'd remembered her food preferences. "I'll be right back."

What she wanted to do was splash cold water on her face and wash away the remnants of sleep. Her mind and body were past exhaustion and she was unsure whether she would be able to even keep her eyes open long enough to eat.

Once in the bathroom, she bathed her face with cool water, patted it dry with a thick, thirsty towel, then ran a large-tooth comb through her curling hair. Minutes later she returned to the dining area to find Daniel placing a succulent steak on a plate. Juices from the broiled meat pooled onto the china dish and she knew the steak was not hers.

"Yours will be out in a minute," Daniel said, following the direction of her gaze. He pulled out a chair at the opposite end of the table from his place setting. "Come sit down," he urged in a soft tone.

Rebecca permitted him to seat her, the warmth of his large body and the familiar fragrance of his aftershave sweeping over her where she found it difficult to draw a normal breath. Guilt assailed her. Michael hadn't been in the ground a day and her traitorous thoughts were racing dangerously to a place that made her think of herself as an adulteress; but she wasn't an adulteress because she was no longer married; she had married a police officer, and now she was alone because he had been killed in the line of duty. It was the scenario Daniel had sought to shield her from, and he had been unsuccessful. She hadn't married him yet she was still a police officer's widow.

Daniel walked into the living room, turned on a state-of-the- art stereo unit and selected a station featuring easy listening jazz; melodious music floated out of the speakers from the powerful component, filling the space with the haunting sounds of David Sanborn's distinctive saxophone.

The familiar haunting theme from the movie "American Gigolo" made him want to ease Rebecca from her chair and crush her to his body while they swayed to the sensual music. There had been a time when they'd danced together every chance they got. Often times the dancing led to other pleasurable pursuits where they ended up in bed together.

Of all the women he had slept with Rebecca was the most indelible. Not only had she come to him untouched, but she had been the only one most attuned to his needs and desires. Her untutored body had responded to his as if they had choreographed every move. And she'd always left him weak and gasping for his next breath.

Still, it had taken her almost three months before she felt comfortable enough with the act to let go of all of her inhibitions. It was only then that he introduced her to different positions and other ways of pleasuring each other. She was a quick study and the result was optimum sexual gratification for both.

His body reacted sharply to the images of his making love to Rebecca and he waited in the living room until the apparent evidence of his arousal diminished.

Several minutes later, nothing in his demeanor indicated that he was anything but relaxed when he returned to the kitchen and removed her steak from the broiler. The aroma of seared meat filled the kitchen when he placed it on a plate. Returning to the dining area, he pressed the dimmer switch, flooding the area with golden light.

Rebecca glanced up at him, giving him a gentle smile. "It smells wonderful."

He placed the plate in front of her. "I'd like for you to eat most of it."

She nodded. "I'll try."

A moment later, Daniel returned with the platter with the potatoes, methodically unwrapped them and placed one on her plate. "This too," he said quietly.

"I'll try," she repeated.

He sat down across from her, watching her for a full minute before turning his attention to his own plate. He suspected Rebecca was hungry, but he was also very hungry. It was nearly four o'clock and the only thing he had consumed all day was a single cup of coffee earlier that morning. At six-four and a solid two hundred twelve pounds he needed more than a cup of coffee to keep up his strength.

Rebecca took a bite of the baked potato, and, finding it extremely palatable, quickly devoured it. She was slower eating the steak and the accompanying salad made up of red-leaf lettuce, julienne red, green and yellow peppers, carrots and marinated hearts of palm and artichoke with a honey-lime vinaigrette dressing. It took nearly an hour, but she managed to eat most of what had been on her plate while ignoring the glass filled with wine.

She smiled across the table at Daniel. "It was delicious. Thank you."

He nodded in acknowledgment. "Aren't you going to drink your wine?"

Rising to her feet, she shook her head. "As it is I can't keep my eyes open, and if I drink any more wine I'll fall flat on my face."

Daniel stood up and circled the table. He stood over Rebecca, his dark gaze seeing what she refused to concede. She was in pain, hurting, and still she refused to let go of her grief.

"Why don't you go to bed. I'll clean up here."

"No, Daniel," she retorted. "You've done enough for me. You'd better go before you get snowed in."

"It's too late for me leave."

She glanced at the clock over the kitchen sink. "It's only a little after five."

"It's too late for me to leave, because I'm already snowed in. Most of the parkways are closed, except to emergency vehicles."

Her gaze swung back to him. "I shouldn't have asked you to come up with me. If you'd left right after the burial…"

"Enough, Becky," he said in a quiet tone, interrupting her. "Stop beating yourself up over nothing. I'll sleep on the sofa."

Her eyes glistened with unshed tears. Inhaling audibly, she tried bringing her fragile emotions under control. "How can I thank you for being here these past few days?"

Pulling her into a close embrace, Daniel pressed his mouth to her perfumed hair. "There's nothing to thank me for. I promised Michael that I would take care of you if something happened to him, and I'm doing just that. You need me and I'm here for you."

Burying her face against his warm throat, she breathed in the masculine scent that was exclusively Daniel Clinton's. Her arms moved up and circled his strong neck, she clinging to him like a drowning swimmer. Why did she need him so much? Why couldn't she let him go? Was it because she didn't have Michael? Because she was alone?

"I miss him so much, Daniel."

His hands made soothing motions over her back. "I know, Becky. I miss him, too."

He held her, feeling her heart flutter wildly under her full breasts, feeling her flat stomach pressed against his middle, and feeling the slight trembling she was unable to control.

Her pulse slowed as she melted against Daniel's unyielding strength. He was there for her; he had always been there for her; if it hadn't been for him she never would've met and married Michael.

Sighing softly, she smiled and pulled away in his loose embrace. "I'll get you what you need…"

"I don't need anything," Daniel interrupted again.

She arched a delicate eyebrow. "You're going to need linen for the sofa bed, towels and a toothbrush."

He nodded. "Get whatever it is I'll need, then I expect you to be in bed within the hour." The thumb of his right hand grazed the delicate skin under one eye. "The last I heard fashion experts still haven't sanctioned dark circles under the eyes as fashion chic."

Rebecca couldn't help smiling. "You've never been one to bite your tongue."

Patting her affectionately on her bottom, he said, "That's because being honest is always best. Go, Rebecca."

She did not hesitate. Whenever he addressed by her given name she knew he was either very serious or angry. And she had seen his anger only once to know enough not to test his temper.

Turning, she walked through the kitchen to an alcove that separated her bedroom from the full bath. Opening a closet, she withdrew pillows, sheets, towels, toothbrush, and a thermal blanket. She removed a goose-down quilt from an upper shelf, adding it to the pile.

She heard the sound of running water coming from the kitchen as she returned to the living room. She caught a glimpse of Daniel standing at the sink rinsing dishes before he loaded the dishwasher. A slight smile curved her mouth. One thing she had learned about Daniel Albert Clinton was that he was as secure in the kitchen as he had been in the bedroom.

His confidence was apparent from the first time they were introduced. He had just turned twenty-three, but somehow he seemed so much older to her. And it was his quiet self-assurance that had attracted her to him. Everything he said or did was gentle and unpretentious. Even when he'd refused to marry her he sought to soften her disappointment with carefully chosen words that soothed rather than rejected, and for a fleeting moment she wondered how different her life would have been if she had married Daniel instead of Michael.

She knew the answer to her own musings. She would've still been Daniel's wife instead of Michael's widow.

She returned to her bedroom, turned on a lamp, closed the door, then made her way to the adjoining half-bath. Stripping off her jeans, T-shirt and underwear, she walked into the shower stall and turned on the water. She sat on the tiled floor, her back pressed against a wall. She wanted to cry, scream, but couldn't. All of the pain that had built up over the past four days refused to come out. She he'd her breath until she thought her chest would explode, and still the tears wouldn't flow.

"Why?" she moaned. "Why did you leave me, Michael?" Her fist pounded the tiles when she realized what she felt was anger. She was angry at Michael for going undercover, but more than that she was angry because he'd left her alone. He knew she did not like being alone.

Her fear of being alone had begun when she was just six. Her family had attended an annual state fair in Connecticut, and she, lingering too long at the petting zoo, became separated from her mother, father, and sister. She wandered around frantically for more than half an hour until a woman—a plainclothes detective who had observed a strange-looking man following her. She was reunited with her family and the reunion was emotional for everyone. Rebecca was lectured sternly about what *could* have happened to her. Fears she hadn't thought of were imprinted on her brain forever. Now, whenever she experienced a nightmare it was always of her being alone, alone to face whatever dangers waited for her.

She had no idea of how long she sat on the floor before she finally rose to her feet. Slowly, mechanically she washed her body, then went through the motion of rinsing away the soap before she turned off the water.

The nerve endings along her legs quivered uncontrollably, the sensation reminding her of an insect crawling over her flesh. Drying the moisture from her body, she returned to her bedroom, pulled back the comforter on the bed, turned off the lamp, and collapsed atop the sheets. Within thirty seconds she was asleep, all of her fears momentarily at bay.

Daniel finished the dishes, pulled out the convertible sofa bed and made it up with the bedding Rebecca had left on a side table. Glancing at the watch on his wrist, he winced. It was only six-thirty, and much too early to retire for bed.

If he had not been in Rebecca's apartment he probably would still be at his office, signing payroll checks. His company had grown steadily over the past three years. He started out with four employees, and now he had nearly twenty.

Picking up the telephone, he dialed his office manager's home. The call was picked up after the first ring. He heard several "I got it," before he registered a familiar female voice.

"Hang it up! Now!" The distinctive sound of a receiver settling on a cradle followed. "Hello. Robinson residence."

"Hello, Faith."

"Daniel Clinton, where are you? You've had me worried sick. I've been calling your house and your car phone for the past two hours. Oh, Daniel, don't do this to me. I thought something had happened to you—with the weather and all."

He managed a smile. Faith Robinson worried as much about him as she did her teenage son and daughter. "I'm okay. I'm still out here on the Island."

"You're not thinking of trying to drive home tonight, are you?"

"No. I'm going to stay over. I'm calling to let you know that if I don't get into the office before eight tomorrow morning, you can use the rubber stamp to endorse the paychecks."

There was a lingering silence, then Faith's voice came through the wire again. "Derek did not show up at his post again."

A muscle ticked nervously in Daniel's jaw as he clenched his teeth. "Don't pay him."

"What if he gets ugly?"

"Tell him I have his check. Let him get ugly with me. Who's been asking for overtime?"

"Tony Colon."

"Have him fill in for Derek. I'm going to try to get out of here as soon as the roads are plowed."

"How is she?"

Daniel knew who Faith was referring to. Faith and her husband had come to the wake. The two women had met when Daniel hosted a Christmas party for his staff the year before. He invited Rebecca and Michael, but Michael was unable to attend because he had been placed on special assignment. The President had come into New York City for a political fundraising gala and Michael was selected to be a part of a security detail to assist the Secret Service.

"She's about the same."

"That girl better let it all out before she loses herself."

He silently agreed with Faith, unable to verbalize his own fears for Rebecca. "Thanks for taking care of everything on the home front this past week."

"Think nothing of it, Boss Man."

He smiled. Faith had given him that title the first week she had come to work for him. She had returned to the workplace after her children entered high school, claiming she needed to save money for their college tuition. She organized his office, developed a respectful relationship with his clients and employees, while becoming an invaluable employee herself. He paid her well and respected her suggestions.

"Good night, Faith. I hope to see you in the morning."

"Good night, Daniel."

He hung up, his thoughts lingering on Derek Grady. Derek's father had asked him to give his son a job. The older Grady had issued an ultimatum—college or work. Derek opted for work, and Daniel, doing his father a favor, had hired him. He had personally seen to the young man's training, yet it appeared as if Derek did not want to attend college *or* work. He either showed up at his assigned post late or failed to appear at all. Verbal warnings hadn't worked. Daniel knew the next step would be termination. He could not afford to lose a client because his company's security personnel failed to show up as scheduled.

Walking over to the window, he peered around the blinds. The shadowy glow from the streetlights highlighted the still-falling snow. There was a strange stillness, indicating the absence of vehicular traffic. The storm had silenced Long Island, turning it into a winter wonderland.

Retracing his steps, he sat down on the sofa bed, feeling as restless as a large caged cat. He turned off the stereo and flicked on the television. The familiar face of Humphrey Bogart filled the screen, and Daniel soon found himself totally engrossed in the classic black and white film.

He hadn't realize he had drifted off to sleep when something woke him; sitting up quickly, he glanced around the room. The Bogart film was over and in its place was one featuring Bette Davis. Peering at his watch, he saw that it was after eleven.

Easing his long legs off the sofa bed, he stood up and removed his watch, shirt and slacks, placing them on a chair. His socks followed. He would shower, then try to get back to sleep, so he could be up early and on the road as soon as they were plowed. Picking up his toothbrush and towels, he headed for the bathroom.

Daniel walked out of the bathroom, a large towel wrapped around his waist, and returned to the living room. A frown creased his smooth forehead when he heard the sound of weeping. Glancing at the television, he saw that the characters on the screen were laughing, not crying. Picking up the remote, he lowered the volume, listening carefully. His ears had not deceived him. Someone was crying, and he knew immediately that it was Rebecca.

Even though he had wanted her to cry, it pained him to hear it. Making his way to her bedroom, he stood outside the closed door. His hand went to the doorknob, gripping it tightly. He had no right to intrude. She had the right to grieve in private.

He wanted to walk away, but could not. Rebecca was in pain and he wanted to help ease that pain. Counting slowly to ten, he gently turned the knob.

Heart-wrenching sobs filled the large space as he moved closer to the bed. Streams of light from the partially closed blinds revealed a naked form, facedown, slender shoulders heaving with the deep, shuddering sobs.

Daniel had seen Rebecca cry only once, and he'd hoped never to experience it again. It was when he told her that he could not marry her.

Sitting down on the side of the bed, he pulled her effortlessly across his lap. She pressed her body to his like a trusting child, her arms circling his neck in a tight grip.

"Don't—don't let him get me," she whispered, her voice breaking.

Cupping the back of her head in his large hand, Daniel buried his face in her fragrant hair. "Shh-hhh, Love. It's all right. I'm going to take care of you. I won't let anything or anyone hurt you."

The scent of Rebecca was everywhere in his nostrils and on his flesh. The soft crush of her breasts brought back vivid and erotic memories of their lovemaking, and he felt his body react with a violent explosion, hardening and surging against the terry cloth fabric concealing his own nakedness.

"I want to die," she whispered close to his ear. "Let me die."

"No, Becky." He shook her gently. "You don't want to die. You're going to live. You're going to laugh, and you're going to fall in love again."

A violent trembling shook her. "I'm cold, Daniel. I'm so-oo cold. I want to die."

He eased her down to the bed, his body following and offering his body's heat, while Rebecca continued her litany that she wanted to die.

"Becky, Becky," he crooned, repeating her name, and punctuating it with soft kisses on her wet cheeks. "You're alive, Love."

She heard his deep, soothing voice, her arms tightening around his neck. All of her childhood fears rushed back, eliciting another flood of tears. The vivid image of Michael, lying on a metal table, so still and cold was fixed behind her closed lids. She wanted to run away, away into the warmth of the sunlight where she would not have to feel the same icy coldness that had invaded Michael's lifeless body.

She wanted to feel Michael's arms around her, taste the sweetness of his mouth, and feel his hardness inside her. She wanted and needed him to make her feel alive.

"Love me," she demanded. "I want you inside me," she continued. Her hands moved from Daniel's neck to his wide shoulders and down to his ribs. Her delicate hands searched under the towel and cradled his heavy sex.

Daniel groaned deep in his throat, his fingers snaking around her wrist. "Becky!"

"Please, please," she pleaded.

"I can't…" Whatever he wanted to say was cut off when her fingers tightened around his maleness, squeezing gently. It swelled to its full length and width, and Daniel knew he was lost.

Lowering his head, he captured her mouth, healing her and himself. It was more than sixteen years since he had touched Rebecca, but it could have been sixteen seconds. Everything he remembered about her came rushing back as he raised his hips and removed the towel, it falling to the carpeted floor.

CHAPTER THREE

Daniel wanted to take her—hard and fast, but decided not to. She needed to be loved, to know that she was loved. Cradling her head between his hands, he increased the pressure of his mouth on hers until her lips parted. He was not disappointed when her tongue met and curled around his, eliciting another surge of desire that heated his throbbing groin.

One hand moved from her head downward to a satiny shoulder and still further to a full breast. It filled his hand, the nipple tightening against the palm. His thumb circled the areolae, its pebbling increasing his own desire and arousal.

Rebecca's mouth was as busy as Daniel's, slanting across his lips, jaw and ear. Her teeth nibbled at his exposed throat, staking her claim at the same time a deep moan rose from the valley of his deep chest.

Shifting slightly, he raised his body, while hers writhed with an escalating awakening. Slowly, methodically, he held her hands at her sides while he slipped down the length of her silken body until his face was level with the juncture of her thighs.

The erotic scent of her body filled his nostrils when he buried his face against the silky down concealing her femininity. His hot breath seared her delicate flesh before it cooled with a sweep of his moist tongue.

Rebecca arched in shock. The sensual fog cleared; she knew she wasn't in bed with her husband. Her lovemaking with Michael had been satisfying and very traditional. He would kiss her breasts and belly, but never ventured to the area between her thighs, whereas Daniel kissed and tasted all of her everywhere.

She wanted to tell Daniel to stop, but couldn't. Not when his rapacious tongue made every nerve in her body scream; not when she felt herself falling over the edge.

Waves of ecstasy throbbed through her, bringing a moisture that bathed the delicate folds around her sex and Daniel's tongue. Gasping in sweet agony, her fingers tightened on the sheet, twisting and pulling it from the confides of the mattress.

She breathed in deep soul-drenching drafts at the same time the ripples of fulfillment gripped her. Arching higher, unashamed screams exploding from her parted lips, she gave herself up to the passion hurtling her higher than she had ever soared before.

The explosions continued, faster and stronger until she abandoned herself to the liquid fire sweeping her into a vortex of sweet, burning fulfillment.

The flames of passion had not subsided entirely when she felt Daniel's hardness easing into her. She took him in, inch by inch. He moaned as if in pain, then began a slow push, preparing her body to accept all of him.

Rebecca gasped, her body opening and giving him the advantage he needed as he rolled his hips, burying himself up to the hilt of his manhood. Her hot, wet flesh closed around him like a tight glove, and he knew he couldn't hold back any longer.

He rolled his hips again, each thrust deeper, harder. The sensation of her body opening and closing around him, pulling him in where he did not know where he began and Rebecca ended, hurled him to a dimension he did not know existed. Blood rushed to his head, making him faint and lighthearted. He had to let it go; he couldn't continue to hold back.

Rebecca's soft sighs of satisfaction were his undoing. Listening to the throaty moans coming from her forced him to let go of the obdurate control on the passions he had kept in check since she left him. Inhaling deeply, he freed his dammed lust, filling her womb with his passion, love and his hot seed.

Collapsing heavily on her slender body, he gasped painfully, trying to fill his lungs with much needed oxygen. He didn't know where he found the strength, but he managed to roll off her body, while savoring the pulsing aftermath of his explosive release.

The bedroom was silent, except for the raspy sounds of heavy breathing. Rebecca and Daniel lay side by side, eyes closed, reliving the raw act that had not been lovemaking, but mating. They had taken all that the other offered, and then some.

Tears filled Rebecca's eyes and rolled down her moist cheeks.

What had she done? She had just buried her husband and, twelve hours later, she lay with his best friend. It did not matter that Daniel was her first lover. What did matter was that she'd sullied her husband's honor by opening her legs to another man while his memory, and the love she had for him, still burned brightly within her.

Turning over, she buried her face in a pillow and cried silently. This time the tears were not tears of pain and loneliness; they were tears of shame.

Daniel felt Rebecca withdraw from him, making no attempt to touch or console her. He knew what she was feeling, because he felt the same. Gritting his teeth in frustration, he silently cursed himself for his lack of self-control. How could he have taken advantage of her? Especially during her time of need? She was mourning her husband, while he had taken what belonged to him.

Was that what he meant by taking care of her? By protecting her? How could he equate taking care of her by sleeping with her?

He lay on his back, motionless, wanting to leave the bed, the apartment. But he was trapped—by the weather and by his emotions. He knew he could walk away from Rebecca; what he did not know was if he could walk away from his feelings. He loved her; he had always loved her, and would continue to love until he drew his last breath.

Turning to his right, he curved an arm around her waist, pulling her against him. She moved fluidly into his embrace, her hips pressed against his groin. Sighing softly, she closed her eyes and slept. It took a lot longer before Daniel found solace in the comforting sleep of a sated lover.

Daniel woke before Rebecca. Pulling a sheet over her body, he slipped quietly from the bed. He walked over to the window and glanced out. The snow had stopped and rays from the rising sun glinted off the startling white powder.

The building's manager had plowed the parking lot, leaving mounds of snow against a wrought-iron fence. He noticed a slow, lumbering trunk navigating its way down the street, spewing salt and sand on the icy roadway.

Backing away from the window, he looked over at the clock on one of the bedside tables. It was seven-ten. He would never make it into his office before eight. He had to drive back to New Rochelle, shave, shower, and change his clothes before he drove down to the Bronx. He had decided to set his company up in the New York City borough rather than in Westchester County, because he couldn't afford to pass up the incentives offered by a developer who wanted to revitalize the once burned-out neighborhood. He had secured a five-year lease in a newly renovated six-story office building, while employing and training people who lived in the neighborhood.

He returned to the bed, staring down at a sleeping Rebecca. Her face, though relaxed in sleep, bore the result of her weeping. Her eyelids were swollen and her cheeks stained by red splotches. What he wanted to do was slip back into bed with her and tell her that she had nothing to fear. That he would always be there for her. That he still loved her.

Successfully curbing the urge to kiss her, he made his way out of the bedroom. He returned to the living room and dressed quickly. He was tempted to leave her a note, but decided against it. He would wait, then call her. A telephone call was less impersonal than a note. Retrieving his top coat from the foyer closet, he opened the door to the apartment and closed it quietly behind him, unaware that Rebecca was awake and had heard his departure.

She shifted on the bed, wincing slightly. The dampness and tenderness between her legs was a vivid reminder of what had happened the night before. There was no doubt that she had slept with Daniel Clinton. Not only did he weigh more than Michael had, but he was also larger than her late husband. The heat flared in her face, bringing back a rush of shame. She wanted to get up and wash away the scent of Daniel's body and rid the bedroom of the evidence of their night of passion; her body, however, would not follow the dictates of her brain.

She was tired, more than she had ever thought she possibly could be. Closing her eyes, she gave into the lethargy that made it impossible for her to move, and fell asleep again. The sun had passed its zenith when she woke for a second time.

Rebecca began her day at two o'clock in the afternoon. She took a leisurely bubble bath, went through her grooming routine of moisturizing her body, then slipped into a red sweat suit with a pair of matching cotton socks.

She had just secured her chin-length hair in an elastic band on the top of her head when the telephone rang. She stared at the noisy instrument, debating whether to let the answering machine pick up the message. She decided to let the machine take the call.

"Hello, Rebecca. This is your mother. If…"

She snatched up the receiver. "Hello, Mom."

"I was hoping that you hadn't returned to your classes," came the beautifully modulated voice claimed by ex-model Linda McDonald.

"I haven't listened to the news, but I'm certain schools are closed today. I'm scheduled to go back on Monday."

"How much snow did you get?"

She peered out the bedroom window. "At least a foot."

"Now I know why we relocated in Florida for our retirement. Enough about the weather. How are you doing, baby girl?"

Tears filling her gray eyes, Rebecca wondered if she would ever stop crying. Her mother's endearment was her undoing. "Hold on a moment, Mom." She put down the receiver, retreating to the bathroom where she blew her nose and splashed water on her face. She returned to the bedroom in control once again. Picking up the receiver, she resumed the call.

"I'm doing well," she lied smoothly.

"You're very blessed to have Daniel Clinton as a friend. James and I are eternally grateful to him that he saw to your needs and took care of all of the arrangements."

He was my friend, she said to herself. *Last night he became my lover again.*

"I'm grateful too, Mom," she said instead.

There was an obvious pause before Linda spoke again. "I was thinking about you and Daniel," she said slowly.

Rebecca's pulse accelerated. "What about us?"

"Well—now that Michael's gone, do you think that you and Daniel will…"

"No!" she shouted into the receiver. "Please don't say it. Michael's death will never change anything between Daniel and me. Remember, I knew Daniel years before I met Michael."

"I meant no harm, Rebecca. I was just asking."

Feeling contrite that she had raised her voice to her mother, she apologized, saying, "I'm sorry."

What she had not told her mother, or anyone else, was the reason why she and Daniel had not married. She knew how taken her parents were with Daniel when they met him for the first time. He and her father had gotten along well. They both were fascinated by the law, Daniel admitting to James that he wanted to put in his twenty years on the force, then attend law school. He did not want to practice law, but teach it. He confessed that under his bulletproof vest beat the heart of a frustrated teacher. What no one knew was that beneath her breasts beat a heart of a woman who would love Daniel for an eternity.

You love him, a silent voice taunted her. And she did. She would always love him.

Her conversation with her mother continued with Linda urging her to come to Florida during her spring recess. She was noncommittal as she rang off. What she did promise was to call her parents more often than she had done in the past.

The remainder of the afternoon found her removing the linen from her bed and the sofa, washing them in the laundry room located on each floor of the building, then preparing a light dinner of a tossed salad with a bowl of creamed potato soup.

The scent of Daniel's aftershave lingered in the apartment, reminding her of his existence and what they had shared. Each time her traitorous thoughts turned to Daniel, her body reacted violently to his powerful and unrestrained lovemaking.

She relived the feel of his hands, the comforting masculine possession of his mustached mouth, and the worshiping probing of his tongue in her body's most secret, hidden place. Biting down hard on her lower lip, she bit back the whimpers of desire threatening to escape. How was it she remembered Daniel's lovemaking more vividly than the ones during eight years she spent with Michael? Was it that she loved Daniel more than Michael?

"No," she whispered in the semi-darkness of the living room. It wasn't that she had loved Daniel more; it was that she had always craved him more. Her relationship with her husband was more balanced and analytical, while the one with Daniel was lustful and carnal. Daniel, as her first lover, had introduced her to a world of sensual delights she wanted to repeat over and over, even after she married Michael.

She had asked Michael to kiss her between her thighs and he had looked at her as if she had taken leave of her senses. He explained quietly that he couldn't, because he didn't feel comfortable doing it, thereby setting the stage for what was to become a marriage steeped in traditional lovemaking.

She matured, as did her body, and as she became more comfortable with her sensuality she knew something was missing in her marriage. She refused to acknowledge what it was until now, now that she had slept with Daniel again.

Leaning over, she turned on a table lamp. The stack of letters and cards on the table had increased steadily over the past four days, and she knew she had to face the inevitable. She prepared a cup of instant coffee, then sat down on the floor and began opening the envelopes.

She was interrupted once by the ringing of the telephone, but refused to answer it. What she wanted to do was finish reading her mail.

Daniel sat on the chair behind his desk, listening to the recorded message on Rebecca's telephone. A chill swept up his spine when he registered Michael's voice on the tape. It was as if his friend was still breathing, still alive.

Taking off the oval, black-wire rimmed reading glasses, he ran a hand over his face and hung up. A wave of guilt washed over him. Hearing Michael's voice reminded him of what he had done with the man's wife. No, not his wife, but his widow.

What had gotten into him? Why hadn't he been able to control his lust for Rebecca?

Once she married his best friend he had consciously dismissed all he had shared with her. He would not allow himself to covet another man's wife.

But she wasn't another man's wife now. She was single. He was single. And he no longer was a peace officer. He was not required to carry a firearm or place his life on the line when he left his home to go to work.

Propping his elbow on the desk, he rested his forehead on his left fist. Conflicting thoughts warred in his head. If he proposed marriage would she accept or would she reject him the way he had rejected her? Would she be willing to spend the rest of her life with him and give him the children he wanted as much as she?

He thought of the other women he had dated over the years; none of them had come close to Rebecca and it took many years before he realized none of them could replace Rebecca. She instilled a calmness in him that was comfortable and peaceful. What she elicited was a gentle yearning for all that life offered. His head came up quickly with a light tapping on his door. Rising to his feet, he recognized Derek Grady.

Nineteen-year-old Derek affected a wide-legged stance, his arms crossed over his muscular chest. Intelligent dark eyes glowed from an equally smooth dark face. The overhead recessed lights gleamed on his shaven head.

"Mrs. Robinson said that you have my check."

Daniel walked around the desk and leaned against a corner, one black wool trousered leg crossed over the other. He assumed a similar position, crossing his arms over a matching black turtleneck sweater.

"Mrs. Robinson is right about that."

"Well—can I have it?"

Daniel surveyed the young man whose body was as muscular and compact as Mike Tyson's. What bothered him was that Derek's intelligence equaled the perfection of his well-toned body. An intelligence he refused to use other than for manipulation and guile.

"I'm going to give you more than your check, Derek. What I'm going to give you is your walking papers. You're terminated."

"You can't!" The two words exploded from his mouth.

"Why can't I? It's my company, and in case you haven't noticed it's my name on the front door, not yours."

Derek dropped his arms and took a half dozen steps, his hands curling into tight fists. He swung at Daniel. "You son-of-a…"

Before the last word was out of his mouth Daniel caught him in a headlock, one arm high on his throat, the other holding one of Derek's arms in a grip which threatened to pull the limb from its joint.

Daniel shook him as if he were nine instead of nineteen. "Don't ever swing at me again, or I'll cripple you where you'll have to learn to use your left hand." He tightened his grip. "Do I make myself clear?"

Derek nodded frantically as he struggled to force air into his lungs. He had underestimated the older man's age and agility. Daniel released him and Derek quickly placed a hand over his bruised throat.

Sobering, he made his way over to a leather chair and sat down heavily. Blinking back tears, he dropped his head. Daniel saw resignation in the youth's body language. Resignation and meekness.

"What's going on, Derek? Why don't you want me to fire you?"

His head snapped. "If I don't have a job, then my father is going to put me out on the street. Where am I going to go?"

Daniel sat down on the edge of the desk, staring at the boy who could've been his son if he had married in his early twenties.

"It doesn't sound as if you have much of a problem."

"Who are you kidding, Mr. Clinton? Being homeless is no joke."

"You wouldn't be homeless if you worked steadily. You can earn enough money to take care of your own lodging."

"I work…"

"One or two days a week when you're scheduled to work five," Daniel countered angrily. "When I was your age I had a job and earned enough where I rented my own place. So did your father."

"My father's nothing but a flunky cop who thinks he's THE MAN."

Daniel felt his temper rise. "If he's a flunky, then he's a damn good flunky, because he's kept a roof over your head all of these years. You were never hungry nor were you ever denied clothes or shoes because he wasn't there or couldn't give you the basics. The man has busted his hump to make it to lieutenant in a system that hasn't always been equitable when it comes to our folks.

"You're a bright young man, but you refuse to use your brain. If you were my son I probably would've taken you to the gym, put a pair of boxing gloves on you and let you go a few rounds with this ex-flunky cop. After being knocked on your ass a couple times, you'd probably see things my way. Like my mother once told me, 'my way or the highway.' She stood all of five-two, and I never challenged her."

Derek's jaw dropped. "You were a cop?" he said, finding his voice. "My father never mentioned anything about you being a cop."

Daniel nodded. "I spent sixteen years on the force."

"Why aren't you a cop now?"

"Some rapist tried to cut my arm off."

"What happened to him?" Derek's eyes now glittered with excitement.

"I'm not proud to say it, but I shot him."

"Did you kill him?"

"No, Derek. I shot him in the leg. The bullet went through his kneecap and shattered it. It left him with a limp."

"That move you used on me—did you learn it being a cop?"

He shook his head. "I took a little extra training in the martial arts."

"How much training, Mr. Clinton?"

Daniel glanced at his watch. It was after six-thirty, and he was ready to go home. "Why don't we continue this conversation at another time. It's dark and the roads where I live get icy at night."

Derek nodded, rising to his feet. "I guess we can't talk about this later, because I won't see you after tonight."

"Why not?"

"Because I don't have a job, and I won't be living at my house if you come to visit my dad."

Running a hand over his graying hair, Daniel let his breath out slowly. "Look, Derek, let's try to come to some agreement right here—tonight. You can keep your job if you promise me that you'll show up at your post on time."

The younger man's face brightened. "I'll show up on time if you'll teach me some of those martial arts moves."

"Show up for work on time for a month and you have a deal." He extended his right hand. Derek shook his hand, a wide smile creasing his handsome face. Daniel handed him an envelope, saying, "You'll find only three day's pay instead of two weeks."

"But I was sick two days last pay period."

"You didn't call in, so that adds up to you being AWOL."

"Damn, a brother can't even take a *sistah* to the movies with this chump change," Derek mumbled under his breath.

Daniel hid a smile. "If you're going to be as good in the martial arts as I expect you'll be, then I'll probably let you assist me with a group of kids I work with on Wednesday nights." He knew the young man worked out regularly in a neighborhood gym.

Derek gave him a skeptical look. "What color belt do you have, Mr. Clinton?"

"Go home, Derek."

"It's black, isn't it?"

Daniel walked around the desk and sat down. "Good night, Derek," he drawled.

"Don't front on me, Mr. C. I know it's black."

Waiting until the door closed behind Derek, Daniel glanced up. It had worked. He'd promised Otis Grady that he would give his son one more chance. His *last* chance.

"Yes, Derek," he whispered softly. "It's black."

Temporarily dismissing Derek Grady, he picked up the phone and dialed Rebecca's number, hoping he would hear her voice and not the recorded message. He was disappointed when he heard the constant ringing and hung up before the machine clicked over.

What he wanted to do was talk to Rebecca, apologize to her for what had happened the night before. He needed to clear his conscience, have her forgive him; hearing Michael's voice on the tape had compounded his guilt.

How could he have exercised so little self-control? Why had he waited until he was almost forty to engage in what he considered an act of betrayal?

Daniel knew the answers to his troubling questions before they were formed in his mind. If it had been any other woman he would not be sitting in his office mentally beating himself up. It had happened because the woman was Rebecca. A woman he had fallen in love with before seeing her face. A woman, a siren, who had called out to him, captured his heart, and refused to give it back.

He sat at the desk for another quarter of an hour, reading a bid proposal, then decided to go home. Standing up, he reached for a dark brown leather bomber jacket on a brass coat tree and slipped his arms into it. He walked out of his office to the reception area. Faith had left at five, her desk cleared of paperwork.

A slight smile curved his strong mouth under the mustache. Faith Robinson had answered his ad for an office manager, and the moment she walked through the door he knew he wanted to hire her. He found her mature, intelligent and no nonsense. But she was also fair and compassionate, and he had hired her on the spot. Faith thanked him at the same time the phone on his desk rang. She'd reached over, picked up the receiver, saying, "Good morning. Clinton Securities. Mrs. Robinson speaking. May I help you?" It was the first of her many greetings over the past year and a half that they had come to work together. Their relationship was cemented from that moment, and Daniel could not deny Faith any request. It had become the same for her.

Walking to the door, he pushed several buttons on the sophisticated security system and a tiny red light blinked a warning signal. He had all of ten seconds to flick off the overhead lights and lock the front door to Clinton Securities. He usually was able to accomplish the procedure within half that time. The moment the tumblers turned in the lock beams of light criss-crossed the space.

Daniel pushed the button for the elevator, and the doors opened. If he had left at five he normally would have to wait more than three minutes for the elevator because most of the offices closed at that time, and he usually ended up taking the stairs down. The elevator arrived at the lobby without stopping, and he waved to the night guard seated behind a table in the lobby. The guard had come to work for his company earlier that week.

The cold, frigid air stung his face the moment he walked out of the building. Ducking his head into the wind, he walked the block to the corner parking lot. Three minutes later he sat behind the wheel of the Porsche, turned on the ignition, put it in gear, and pulled out of the lot with a thrust of power. He maneuvered expertly through the dark, deserted streets toward the bridge that would take him north to Westchester County.

The soothing music coming from the radio's speakers garnered his attention so he did not have to think about Rebecca Williams. Losing himself in the smooth rhythm of a jazz riff, he forgot about her—for the time being.

CHAPTER FOUR

Rebecca stacked the condolence cards in one pile, bills in another, and junk mail in still another. The cards had come from her colleagues, students at the middle school where she taught language arts, family members, friends, and many of Michael's fellow officers.

Sighing heavily, she stared at the letters. She would give herself a week before replying to the people who had been so supportive when she needed them most. But how could she thank Daniel? He had been by her side before she was given the opportunity to react to what had happened to Michael. Not once did she have to make a decision because he had taken care of all of the arrangements.

Her mother's words came rushing back. *You're very blessed to have Daniel Clinton as a friend.* A wry smile softened her mouth.

She was blessed to have known Daniel.

Reaching for the telephone, she dialed his number. His phone rang twice before his answering machine clicked on. Her heart thudded against her breasts as she listened to his deep, powerful voice telling her to leave a message after the beep.

"Daniel, I..."

"Hello," came an in-person greeting through the wire.

Her pulse quickened, causing a flush of heat to sweep over her body. "Daniel, it's Rebecca."

There was a noticeable pause. "Good evening, Becky."

A smile stole across her features. He'd called her Becky. "Daniel—I just wanted to thank you again for everything, and I also wanted to apologize for what happened last night." The words rushed out before she lost her nerve. "I—I didn't mean for it to happen, but…"

"That's all right," he interrupted, his voice low and comforting. "You're not to blame. If anyone's going to take the blame, then it should be me. I took advantage of you and your grief."

"No, Daniel!" she shouted into the receiver. "You didn't take advantage of me," she continued, this time her voice softer, calmer. "It just happened, and I'm not sorry it did. Maybe the timing was wrong, but now that I think back I don't regret it. Our love making has helped me want to live, to go on. Michael's dead, but my love for him will never die. I thought I wanted to die with him. I thought I had nothing to live for, and that was wrong. And you helped me to see how wrong I was. I have my whole life ahead of me. I have a career I love, family and friends that I cherish. For this I thank you from the bottom of my heart."

There was another pregnant pause. "You're very welcome."

Sighing audibly, she was relieved that she had unburdened herself. "My parents also send their gratitude."

"It was nice seeing them again."

Rebecca's gaze was fixed on her sock-covered feet. Suddenly she felt like eighteen again, meeting Daniel for the first time. There was so much more she wanted to say, yet the words wouldn't come.

"Good night," she whispered softly into the receiver.

"Good night, Becky."

She heard the soft sound of Daniel's breathing, and still she did not replace the receiver. It was as if both of them were waiting for the other to break the connection.

Biting down hard on her lower lip, she lowered the receiver, her hand shaking slightly, and placed it down on the cradle. The motion reminded her of the time she'd turned her back and walked out of Daniel Clinton's Greenwich Village apartment for the last time. Her hand had trembled slightly on the doorknob before she turned it and opened the door, walked out and closed it softly behind her.

She hadn't cried when she told him she could not continue to see him, as she had the night he told her that he could not marry her. She hadn't even rehearsed what she was going to say to him, because she had had six months to tell him that she could no longer be a part of his life.

Closing her eyes, she lay on the carpeted floor, remembering his apartment. It was where Daniel had made love to her for the first time. Where she had become a woman in the true sense of the word.

She'd celebrated her nineteenth birthday in Daniel Clinton's arms and in his bed.

She'd had a birthday dinner with her parents and older sister earlier that evening at her favorite restaurant. Her parents had given her a pair of large pearl stud earrings, while her sister Cynthia had presented her with a silver barrette inlaid with blue topaz and amethyst. Her youthful delight bubbled over when she removed the small gold hoops from her pierced lobes and inserted the studs. She then undid the single plait flowing down her back to her waist to secure her curling hair with the barrette.

"What's Daniel going to give you?" Cynthia had questioned, teasingly.

"I don't know," she said as heat scorched her face. "I'm supposed to meet him after he gets off duty."

"What time is that, dear?" James McDonald asked.

"Ten."

"Where are you meeting him?" It was now Linda McDonald's turn to question her.

Rebecca's dark gray eyes danced with excitement and anticipation. "At his apartment. We're going to a jazz club in the Village." Daniel had confessed to having two passions: her and jazz.

A slight frown creased Linda's beautiful face, a face that had graced the pages of many of Europe's fashion magazines before she left the world of modeling to marry James McDonald. "You know I don't like you hanging out late at night."

James placed a hand over his wife's. "Don't, Lin," he warned in a quiet tone. "Daniel will take care of her. Remember, he's a cop," he reminded her.

Linda shot him a look of annoyance. Her husband never sided with her when it came to chastising their children. "How are you getting to his apartment?"

Rebecca smiled at her mother. "I'm taking a taxi." Reaching into her purse, Linda withdrew her wallet. "I don't need any money, Mom. I have enough."

"Case closed," James whispered under his breath.

Rebecca glanced at her watch and knew she would have to leave soon. It was almost nine forty-five and Daniel would be off in another fifteen minutes. It took him only twenty minutes to travel between his apartment and his assigned station house.

She lingered long enough to eat a slice of cake and gulp down a cup of coffee. Standing, she circled the table and kissed her sister, father, and mother. James walked her to the restaurant's entrance and flagged down a taxi. He waited until she was safely seated in the back of the cab before he returned to the restaurant and his family. A slight smile crinkled his bright blue eyes. His baby had grown up to become a secure, beautiful woman.

The taxi stopped in front of the brownstone building in the West Village where Daniel rented an apartment on the top floor. He was waiting at the curb for her. Reaching into the pockets of his jeans he withdrew enough money to pay the driver the fare on the meter. He gave the cabbie a generous tip, saying, "That's for bringing her to me in one piece."

"Thanks, buddy," the driver shouted, touching the bill of his oversized cap.

Opening the door, Daniel extended his hand and helped her out. Rebecca felt the power in his fingers as he pulled her to his body. Her arms went around his waist and she froze when her fingers grazed the holstered off-duty revolver strapped to his waist. She had dated Daniel for seven months, and still had not gotten used to the fact that he was required to carry a firearm.

Daniel felt her slight hesitation, but ignored it. He knew she disliked guns and tried to conceal his from her whenever possible.

He looped one arm around her waist over her heavy coat. It was only November thirtieth, yet the temperatures were more in keeping with January or February. The meteorologists were predicting a colder than normal winter.

"Happy birthday, Love." Lowering his head, he brushed a light kiss over her lips.

Closing her eyes, she savored the sweetness of his mouth. "Thank you."

"Do you want your gift now or when we come back?"

Her eyes sparkled like stars under the glow of the streetlight. She paused, her mouth curving with a mysterious smile. Wrinkling her nose, she said, "It's up to you."

"I'd rather give it to you now." Tightening his hold on her waist, Daniel turned and led her up the stairs to the brownstone building. "How was your day?" he asked, smiling down at her.

"Wonderful." She gave him a sidelong glance, her gaze taking in his wide shoulders under a waist-length supple black leather jacket and his slim hips in a pair of black jeans as she followed his lead up to his third-floor apartment.

What she was feeling, had felt for a long time, surfaced, threatening to overwhelm her at that moment. Desire flamed uncontrollably as she bit down hard on her lower lip. She wanted Daniel the way a woman wanted a man. She wanted him to be her lover.

He unlocked the door and pulled her into a warm, sparsely furnished, neat, one-bedroom apartment. Without warning, she was in his arms, her mouth burning with the fire of his possession.

His fingers caught in the wealth of curling hair flowing over her coat collar and down her back. It was the first time he had seen her hair in a style other than a single plait. Cradling her face between his palms, he pulled back slightly and stared down at her.

She looked so young, so innocent and trusting. And he wanted her with a hunger that made it difficult for him to breathe. He couldn't count the number of times he wanted to make love to her, but hadn't because he knew she had never lain with a man. What he wanted to do was wait for her to come to him.

"Happy, happy birthday, sweet nineteen," he crooned, placing soft, nibbling kisses on her velvety face. His lips found hers and the kiss changed, becoming more demanding as she opened her mouth to him. His tongue eased into her mouth, curling around her tongue and eliciting a need that rose quickly in both of them.

Winding her arms around his slim waist, Rebecca pressed closer. Something alien, unknown communicated itself and she wanted Daniel to absorb her; she wanted to be with him and he inside her.

Her rising need lit a fire in Daniel and a slow, smoldering flame flared, scorching and sweeping over him and creating a maelstrom of desire that threatened to destroy him if she didn't extinguish it.

Pulling back slightly, he stared down at her flushed face. Desire had darkened her eyes so that they looked black in the muted light coming from a lamp on a small, round table. Unbuttoning her coat, he searched for a breast under her cashmere sweater, its fullness swelling against his fingers. "I can't take you out," he whispered hoarsely, his chest rising and falling heavily. "Not now."

Her large eyes widened as she became completely still. "Why? What is it you want to do?"

Daniel did not move or blink, but what his lips did not say his eyes did. It had taken them seven months to become attuned to each other, seven months for her to know what he wanted without him verbalizing his need.

She lowered her gaze, staring at the middle of his chest. Her heart pounded so hard and loudly that she was certain Daniel could hear it. She knew what he wanted, yet she needed to hear him say it. "You're going to have to tell me what you want, darling."

Her husky had dropped an octave, sending a chill up his spine. She'd asked the question. She knew, knew what he wanted. "I want you to spend the night with me." Tilting her chin, she met his gaze with a wide, trusting one of her own. Their gazes held for several seconds, she the first one to look away. Daniel saw her lower lip tremble slightly and the erratic beating of a pulse in her throat.

"I want to make love to you," he continued softly, his deep, rumbling voice floating around her like a cloaking fog, pulling her in and not permitting her escape him.

A shudder swept through her body as her knees buckled with the dizzying currents of desire making her feel and want something she'd never experienced. Her fingers caught the soft wool of his sweater as she tried supporting her quaking knees.

"Yes, Daniel!" she moaned, her need and desperation answered as he swept her up in his arms and cradled her against his chest. Burying her face against his hot throat, she tightened her grip on his neck. "I want you," she whispered in his ear. "I do want you to make love to me. I want so much to spend the night with you."

"Are you sure, Becky?" he questioned, his lips moving against her fragrant hair.

"Yes, Daniel. I'm sure. Very, very sure."

His dark gaze burned her with its intensity. "This will change the both of us. We will never be the same people."

Pulling back slightly, she stared up at him. "I stopped being the same person the day I met you, Daniel Clinton. I changed again when I fell in love with you. And after we make love I'll change once again."

Tightening his hold under her knees, he smiled at her. "I know you've never heard me say it, even though I've felt it for a long time. I love you, Becky," he stated simply, softly.

Rebecca closed her eyes, still hearing his profession of love echoing in her mind. She had waited so long, paused in anticipation each time she thought he was going to reveal his innermost feelings. His eyes, kisses, and hands told her wordlessly how he felt about her, but what she wanted were words, words that she could reach out to, grasp, and hold to her heart for an eternity.

Pressing her mouth to his ear, she ran her tongue around its distinctive shape, her hot breath filtering into the canal. Daniel jumped as if she had touched him with an electric rod. Gasping audibly and fighting for control, he carried her into his bedroom. She repeated the gesture and he nearly dropped her as he pressed her down to the large bed, his body following.

"Becky, no!" he gasped, trying valiantly to keep from spilling his passion before making love to her. "Please don't do that again, or you'll have to wait…"

"Wait for what?" she interrupted, her hands going to his shoulders to remove his jacket.

Rather than explain that she had nearly caused him to climax, he took her mouth instead. Unwittingly she had located his most erogenous zone.

A small lamp, with a soft pink bulb, on a bedside table provided enough light for Daniel to see how to undress Rebecca. Its glow slanted across the bed, leaving the rest of the room in shadows.

Removing her coat, he crossed the room and hung it in a closet. He took his time undressing her. He had all night to make their coming together special, because he had been waiting from the first time he tasted her mouth to make love to her. They'd waited seven months, and hours, minutes, seconds no longer mattered; before the sun rose again in the heavens to signal the birth of a new day Rebecca McDonald would be his; they would belong to each other.

Once she was undressed and lay naked on his bed, Daniel removed his own clothes, his gaze fixed on her face. She'd closed her eyes once he took off her sweater, her breathing deepening with the anticipation of lying naked under his hungry gaze. A slight smile softened his mouth with her display of modesty as his own passions increased with his ravenous need to take her while branding her with his love. He removed a small plastic packet from the drawer in a bedside table and placed it where he could reach it.

His clothes lay over hers on an armchair, then he moved to the bed and lay down beside her. Reaching for her hand, he threaded his fingers through her slender ones. He noted their trembling and tightened his grip.

"There is nothing to fear, Love. I'll try not to hurt you."

Rebecca's full breasts shuddered above her narrow rib cage as she drew in a deep breath. The possibility of pain did not frighten her, but would she enjoy it? Would the waiting, her saving herself for a man she loved, be worth it? She also wondered if she could satisfy Daniel. There was no doubt that he was much more sexually experienced than she, but would he want her again after tonight?

Shifting slightly, he withdrew his hand and pulled the pillows from under her head. He propped the pillows against the massive, carved mahogany headboard. His large hands spanned her waist and he eased her gently until she sat, her back pressed against the pillows.

Reaching around her neck, he removed the silvered barrette from her hair and placed it on one of the matching bedside tables. The curling strands floated out around her shoulders and down her back like wisps of Spanish moss. A slight smile curved his mouth as he stared at the desire in Rebecca's eyes. She was not afraid, and he knew that she had been waiting for the moment for as long as he had.

He had spent months wanting to make love to her, yet hadn't. He'd taken her out twice when she confessed that she had not slept with a man. Hearing her confession overwhelmed him. She was untouched, pure. But there were times when he doubted whether he could control his desire for her, but he had. Something told him that Rebecca McDonald was different, very special.

The last time she'd come to his apartment she almost wound up in his bed and he inside of her. It had been his day off and they had planned to spend the time together preparing dinner and watching the World Series. Rebecca had been in a teasing mood. When he least expected it she pressed her body to his, running her hands over his chest and back under his shirt. The moment her mouth replaced her hand on his breast almost proved his undoing. He'd swept her up in his arms and carried her to bedroom. Lowering her hot body to the massive antique bed, his mouth charted a greedy exploration from her mouth to her flat belly. It was only when his fingers searched beneath the layers of her jeans and panties to find her hot, wet, and pulsing did the sensual fog clear. A warning bell sounded when he'd moved away from the bed to retrieve the plastic covered latex in the drawer of the bedside table. Instead of following through, he walked out of the bedroom to the bathroom. He emerged a quarter of an hour later, finding Rebecca in the living room staring out the window.

He walked over to her and cradled her gently against his body. She turned in his embrace and raised her face for his kiss. The kiss was gentle, healing. They both knew that they'd crossed the line so that it was only a matter of time until they would share the other's body.

This was *that* time. This was the first time that they had bared their bodies to the other, the first time that they would tell the other wordlessly of their love.

Sitting and facing Rebecca, Daniel settled her legs over his thighs. Cradling her face between his palms, he kissed her mouth, his tongue outlining the shape of her lips and lingering at the corners. He alternated between deep kisses and soft openmouthed light, playful licks.

Her hands went to his lean cheeks, her sensitive fingers savoring the feel of his shaven jaw. The tip of her tongue traced the flesh covering the elegant ridge of his high cheekbones, while her fingers began their own erotic exploration of the thick, lateral neck muscles that ran from the base of his skull to his wide shoulders.

Daniel cradled her breasts and lowered his head. A gasp from her parted lips became a low keening when he suckled her mercilessly. His hands moved to her shoulders, easing her back to the pillows, his rapacious mouth inching down her body. After that the outside world ceased to exist for Rebecca. There was only the two of them as she gave into the desire that took her beyond herself.

His tongue was everywhere—under her arms, over her rib cage, navel, behind her knees and inner thighs. The nerve endings along her thighs tingled, and she felt a rush of moisture from the hidden place that throbbed erotically for his possession.

Gasping loudly, she arched when a finger searched between the wet folds. The pulsing flesh closed around his finger, and she arched again, a second finger joining the first. All she could think of was the size of Daniel's hand and the length of his fingers. She felt her tender virgin flesh stretch to accommodate his manual exploration. The slight discomfort disappeared as he withdrew.

Leaning over and reaching for the packet, Daniel withdrew the latex sheath. Seconds later, he moved over her again, this time his hardened sex replacing his fingers, his mouth covering hers and swallowing her gasps as he pushed gently into her resisting flesh.

Rebecca felt the burning and tried escaping, but couldn't move. Daniel's weight was overpowering as she tore her mouth away from his.

"No, *please*."

He heard her plea through the sensual fog and pulled out. Cradling her face in his hands, he kissed her mouth tenderly. Not only was she a virgin, but she was also very small. He'd hurt her and that was the last thing he'd wanted to do. He wanted her first time to be a wonderful, satisfying experience, not one of pain and fright.

Placing gentle kisses across her lips, he whispered softly, "It's all right, Becky. I won't touch you."

"I don't want you to stop," she whispered against the column of his strong neck.

Raising his head, he stared down at her, a slight frown creasing his forehead. "But, you asked me to stop. I don't want to you hurt you."

She flashed a shy smile. time. "It should only hurt the first time."

He arched an eyebrow. "You want me to continue?" Curving her arms around his neck, she nodded. "I want you to relax," he crooned. "Deep breaths, in and out. That's it," he continued as her chest rose and fell in a slow, deep motion.

He kissed her mouth, throat, moving down to her breasts and still further. Rising to his knees, he lowered his head and pressed his face to the hot, moist curls between her thighs. She jerked only once when his mouth supplanted his fingers and hardness had been, a slow writhing taking over her mind and body. He paid reverent homage to her pure body, taking both of them to another level of carnality.

Rebecca recovered from the shock of Daniel lying with his face between her legs, giving into the waves of ecstasy sending her spiraling beyond herself. Glimpses of desire paled in comparison to the shocks electrifying her body. What she could not do was stop the moans coming from her parted lips or her fingers from clutching the sheet while her thighs trembled uncontrollably. The waves washed over her, each one higher than the one preceding it as she was tossed about on a sea that threatened to drown her in unbridled passion.

Daniel moved fluidly up Rebecca's trembling body and fitted himself at her opening. He waited for her next spasm of undulating ecstasy, then with a powerful thrust of his hips entered her. A weak gasp of pain merged with the release of her dormant sexuality, and together they rode the turbulent passion sweeping them to a place of free-fall and weightlessness.

For Rebecca the pain and burning faded as she felt the strong, driving thrust of Daniel's flesh melding with hers. She registered his hot breath in her ear and his low moans of pleasure as he moved with a slow, heavy, rolling thrusting of his powerful hips. She had just floated back to reality when his passion rose to an awesome summit of complete fulfillment. His groans, beginning deep in his chest, exploded with a growl of surrender as he was stripped bare, leaving him open for any and everything.

Collapsing heavily on her slender body, he pressed his face to her scented hair spread out over the pillow like a delicate curtain. The breath was sucked from his lungs as he struggled to relieve the burning in his chest. He didn't know where he found the strength, but he managed to roll off her body. Rebecca had taken everything from him, leaving him vulnerable. He loved her; loved her more than any woman he had ever known.

Throwing a muscular arm over his face, he reveled in the aftermath of amazing completeness. Once his respiration slowed and his pulse returned to its normal rhythm, he turned and pulled Rebecca against his body. Kissing her forehead before moving to her moist, lush mouth, the smell of her heated flesh lingered sensuously in his nostrils.

The gentle, nibbling kisses soothed her as she pressed her breasts to his hair-matted chest, the motion sending electric shocks through her distended nipples and arousing her again.

Her small hand explored his naked body, tentatively at first before becoming bolder. Daniel smiled, savoring the feel of her fingers touching him. He wanted her again, but knew it could not happen. She was too newly opened.

Curving a finger under her chin, he lowered his head and kissed her until she moaned under the gentle assault. Pulling back he smiled at her. "Thank you for the precious gift."

Vertical fines appeared between her large eyes. "What gift?"

Leaning closer, he whispered, "Your body." Rebecca blushed, lowering her chin and glancing away. "It's your birthday and I'm taking a gift from you instead of giving." He kissed her hard, then sat up. "Don't go away. I want to get your present."

Closing her eyes, she smiled. She couldn't have moved if her life depended on it. All she wanted to do was sleep.

Daniel returned to the bedroom with a small, gaily-wrapped package. He stood at the bed, staring down at a sleeping Rebecca. The sight of her was imprinted on his brain forever. She slept on her right side, her left leg crossed over her right. Her hands were clasped under her cheek as her hair flowed over the pillow. He covered her with a sheet, placed her gift on the table and got into bed beside her. Pulling her gently against his body he joined her in sleep.

Rebecca woke up the following morning, disoriented. She wasn't in her bedroom in her parents' house in the Riverdale section of the Bronx, but in Daniel's bed. Stretching languidly like a cat, she rolled over. His side of the bed was empty. Sitting up, she saw him sitting on a chair watching her. Pushing her hair off her forehead, she shook it until the curls floated down her bare back.

Daniel didn't move, preferring to watch Rebecca awaken. She reminded him of a sinuous cat with her dark red hair, flawless tawny skin, and gray eyes. Bright red marks marred her upper body. The reminder of his passion was stamped on her neck and breasts like a brand. She *was* his!

"Good morning, Love. I've run water for your bath."

Holding a sheet to her naked breasts, Rebecca stared at him. He had shaved, showered and put on a pair of jeans with a stark white T-shirt. She could smell the lingering scent of his aftershave. "I prefer taking a shower to a bath."

Rising from the chair, Daniel moved over to the bed. "A bath will help ease the soreness."

Rebecca lowered the sheet and swung her legs over the side of the bed. The motion caused her to wince. Muscles she hadn't known she had ached. Taking the hand Daniel extended, she stood up and made her way gingerly to the bathroom.

Her entire body ached, but it was a good ache. It was a vibrant reminder of what she and Daniel had shared the night before. She did not protest when he twisted her unbound hair atop her head, picked her up and lowered her into the lukewarm water, then washed her gently. He drew a cloth between her legs, his gaze locked with hers. Color rose swiftly under her skin as she breathed heavily between parted lips. Both remembered the love and the passion that had fused them into one.

Closing her eyes against his intense stare, she savored the feel of his hands moving over her breasts, under her arms and down her back as he bathed her, opening them only when he eased her from the tub to dry her wet body.

Staring over his shoulder, she savored his touch, finding it hard to believe that she could love a man as much as she loved Daniel. In that instant she took a silent oath that she would spend the rest of her life with him.

Daniel covered her with thick black terry cloth robe that he wrapped twice around her willowy body. It wasn't until he'd awakened and stared down at her slender body that he'd actually realized how small she was. She was tall, but incredibly lean. If it had not been for her breasts, she would have been a slim as a young boy.

Sweeping her up in his arms, he carried her into the kitchen. The aroma of brewing coffee and broiling bacon filled the spacious eat-in kitchen.

He seated her on a chair in front of a place setting with a small, gaily-wrapped gift next to the plate. Pressing a kiss to her temple, he said softly, "It's a little late, but I found myself somewhat occupied last night with this beautiful woman who took me to heaven and back."

A sensual smile curved her full lips. "Do I know this woman?"

He arched a thick, black silky eyebrow. "I think you do."

Picking up the gift, Rebecca unwrapped it and flipped open a midnight blue velvet box. Her eyes filled with shimmering tears. She stared down at the antique filigree brooch she'd admired in a Madison Avenue jewelry shop window. The charming pin flecked with sparkling diamonds claimed a center of a flawless sapphire set in platinum.

Her hand trembled as she covered her quivering mouth. "Daniel." His name came out in a breathless whisper. "How can I thank you?"

Going to his knees beside her chair, he kissed the corner of her mouth. "You did." Their gazes met, her dark gray and his dark brown. "No gift will ever equal what you offered me last night. I will treasure it forever."

Curving her arms around his neck, Rebecca prayed they would be together—forever. She refused to think of the day when she would not have Daniel Clinton to call her own.

Rebecca had no idea how long she lay on the carpeted floor, recalling her first time with Daniel, but loathed getting up. What she did not want to go back to the bed where she had slept with her husband *and* her former lover. But she did get up and it was to pull out the sofa bed. She made up the bed then sat up watching television until she fell asleep. Fortunately there was no nightmare to remind her that she was alone.

CHAPTER FIVE

It was early April and Rebecca had been widowed exactly one month when spring made an early appearance in the northeast, even though the calendar had announced the new season March twenty-second. Daytime temperatures climbed to the sixties, while trees, shrubs and spring flowers bloomed in kaleidoscopic profusion. She left a city awakening from a long winter sleep behind when she boarded her flight a week later for Florida, along with what appeared to be thousands of college students on their way to the southern climates for Spring Break.

She had spent the past two days on her parents' patio, dozing in the hot Florida sun. Not even the raucous screams of her five-year-old niece and seven-year-old nephew bothered her. Rolling over on her back, she slipped on a pair of sunglasses and dozed off again.

Linda McDonald made her way out to the patio, her elder daughter Cynthia three steps behind her; both women carried platters filled with luncheon appetizers.

"Is it time to eat, Grandma?" asked seven-year-old Jarrett Franklin.

Linda smiled at her grandson. "Yes, it is. Take your sister into the house and help her wash up."

Cynthia gave her son a warning look. "I'm going to check the floor and walls when you and Brenna finish, and I'd better not see water anywhere except in the sink."

Jarrett took his sister's hand. "Yes, Mama," the two children chorused, flashing mischievous grins as they raced toward the sprawling Spanish-style structure.

Linda glanced over at Rebecca. Her swimsuit-clad body lay exposed to the hot sun, her skin tanned a deep, gold-brown. A slight frown appeared between Linda's large dark eyes. "I'm worried about Rebecca," she announced softly.

Cynthia, who looked enough like her mother to be her twin sister, stared at Linda. "She seems okay to me. She's not crying or moping around like I'd expected her to be. I know it's going to take her a while to get over Michael's death, but from what I've observed she's handling it quite well."

"I'm not talking about her grieving," Linda countered. "She just seems so listless. And we both know that she's not one to sleep a lot, but that's all she's done since she arrived."

A slight frown furrowed Cynthia's forehead. "You're right." She put her platter down on a large table under a bright yellow umbrella. "She's lost some weight, and I suspect she hasn't been eating on a regular basis."

"She's never weighed a lot," Linda insisted.

"But she's been heavier than she is now. Mom, why don't you have a talk with her. Find out what's bothering her."

"I think I'll leave that to your father. James has always been able to get through to her better than I have."

Cynthia glanced down at her watch. "When is Daddy coming home?"

Linda mumbled an oath under her breath. "He said he would be home in time for lunch. But when he gets caught up with those other golfing fools only time will tell. It's a good thing they haven't put lights on the course or I'd never get to see *your father*."

Cynthia smiled. Whenever her mother was annoyed with James McDonald she referred to him as "*your father*" instead of her husband. "I'll wake up Rebecca."

Rebecca heard the soft, feminine voice, but couldn't open her eyes. She was tired, more tired than she'd ever been in her life, and no matter how much sleep she got it was never enough.

"Rebecca, wake up!" Cynthia tugged at her arm, removed her sunglasses, then shook her shoulder. Large, dark gray eyes opened slowly, fluttered wildly, then closed again. "Rebecca!"

Her eyes opened and she pushed herself up into a sitting position. Recognizing her sister's face, she frowned. "Why are you shouting?" Her low, velvety voice was heavy with sleep.

"I wouldn't have to shout if you'd heard me the first time." Going to her knees beside the chaise lounge, she placed a hand on Rebecca's forehead, then pulled it back. "You're burning up."

Rebecca swung her legs slowly over the side of the lounge. "You would be too if you were lying in the sun."

"It's not the sun," Cynthia retorted, refusing to relent. "You have a fever." Rising to her feet, she turned to her mother. "Mom, come quick!"

Linda halted arranging cutlery on the cloth-covered table and walked over to her daughters. "What is it?"

"Rebecca has a fever," Cynthia stated, hands on hips and daring her younger sister to refute her.

"Mother," Rebecca sputtered as her mother placed the back of her hand against her throat.

"Don't you mother me, Rebecca McDonald Williams. Cyn's right. You do seem warm. Don't move. I'll be right back with a thermometer."

Cynthia leaned down and anchored a hand under her sister's arm and pulled her to her feet. "Come out of the sun."

Placing one foot in front of the other, Rebecca allowed Cynthia to lead her to the table where the umbrella shaded the area. She did not want to admit it, but she felt light-headed, and wondered if perhaps she had gotten too much sun.

By the time Linda had returned to the patio, Rebecca sat with her forehead resting on the table. "I think I'm going to be sick," she moaned weakly.

Linda watched the natural color drain from her child's face, then sprang into action. "Cyn, call the doctor. His number is on the refrigerator. Then start up my car."

Everything whirled in a haze for Rebecca. She did not know whether she wanted to faint or throw up. She heard her mother's calm voice, telling her that she was going to be all right. Then came the childish voices of her niece and nephew wanting to know what was wrong with Aunt Rebecca. The sound of a car pulling into the driveway and the sound of James McDonald's voice diverted the children's attention.

"Grandpa, Aunt Rebecca's sick," Jarrett shouted excitedly.

James sprinted to the patio and swept Rebecca up in his arms at the same time Cynthia raced from the house. "The doctor said to bring her right in."

"I'm coming, James," Linda announced, removing her apron and following her husband to his car.

Cynthia stood with her arms around her son and daughter, watching her parents as they sped away with her younger sister. The last time she and her parents were together it was at Michael's funeral, and she prayed silently that nothing was wrong with Rebecca.

Rebecca lay on the table in an examining room in the doctor's office, staring up at the ceiling. Her fatigue and extreme sleepiness were the result of her pregnancy. She was going to have a baby!

"I'll send your parents in," the doctor said, smiling at her stunned expression. He patted her shoulder, then walked out.

Linda rushed in as Rebecca rose to a sitting position and adjusted the cloth gown the nurse had given her once she'd removed her swimsuit. "You're going to be okay?"

She smiled at her mother, holding out her arms. Hugging Linda tightly, she whispered in her ear, "I'm pregnant."

Pulling back, her large dark eyes widening, Linda mouthed a soft, "No."

Rebecca stared at Linda, noting several tiny lines at the corners of her eyes for the first time. Her dark hair had silvered by the time she'd turned forty, but the rest of her was as striking at sixty as she had been at eighteen when she had all of Paris whispering about the tall, black American model who people came to see instead of the haute couture that hung so elegantly on her slim body.

Pulling her closer, Linda kissed her cheek. "Oh, baby girl, I'm so happy for you. You've waited a long time for this."

"Yes," she breathed out. "And so had Michael."

Rebecca closed her eyes, blinking back tears. Sadness descended, temporarily extinguishing and sweeping away her joy. Michael hadn't lived to see the child he had placed in her womb.

"Had you suspected you were pregnant?"

Rebecca shook her head. "With everything that happened this past month I forgot that I hadn't gotten my period. And it's not the first time I've been late." There was comfortable silence as the two women held each other. "He's still alive, Mom. A part of Michael will live on with this baby."

Linda smiled, feeling her child's heart beating against her own. "That he will, sweetheart." She pressed a kiss to Rebecca's curling hair. "I'll let you get dressed, then your father and I will take you home where we're going to have a blowout of a celebration."

The nurse knocked on the door before walking into the room. She gave Linda a warm smile. "I'll help her get dressed, Mrs. McDonald." Linda returned the nurse's smile and walked out, closing the door behind her.

Rebecca slipped back into her swimsuit, and used the examining gown as a coverup. The nurse gave her a pair of rubber-soled terry cloth slippers for her bare feet.

"Dr. Elkins would like to see you before you leave, Mrs. Williams."

She followed the nurse to a large office with diplomas, citations and certificates covering two of the four walls. Dr. Elkins rose to his feet, pointing to a chair beside his desk.

"Please, have a seat, Mrs. Williams." He reclaimed his own chair, smiling at her. "How are you feeling?"

"A little overwhelmed with the news." She ran a hand through her curling hair, pushing it off her forehead.

The elderly doctor shifted a white eyebrow. "You weren't expecting this?"

"Yes and no. My husband and I were trying to have a baby for the past five years, then we just gave up. We had talked about adopting."

"Now you don't have to adopt."

Rebecca nodded, still trying to accept the fact that she was pregnant.

"I recommend that you see your doctor as soon as you return to New York. But, don't hesitate to call me if you find that you need anything before you leave."

Rising to her feet, she gave him a tired smile and extended her hand. "Thank you."

Dr. Elkins grasped her proffered hand. "Congratulations and good luck."

Rebecca made her way out to the reception area where her parents waited for her. James McDonald stood up, his bright blue eyes racing frantically over her face. She felt a warm glow flow through her as she stared at the two people who were responsible for giving her life, nurturing her and loving her unconditionally.

And because of them she could repeat the process with her own child.

Seeing Linda and James together, arms around the other, made her aware of how dramatically attractive they were. Both were tall, silver-haired and lean. Her father's shockingly bright red hair had thinned so that he'd affected a close-cut style that flattered his well-shaped head. His bright blue eyes had not dimmed, and they sparkled like brilliant topaz in his perpetually tanned face. And her mother was stunning! Tall, slender, her dark brown skin smooth and flawless, her exotic features mesmerizing, Linda McDonald still turned heads whenever she entered a room, and there were times when James was unable to conceal his passionate possessiveness for the woman who had been his wife for forty of his own sixty-four years.

A smile softened Rebecca's lush mouth as she walked into the outstretched arms of her parents. Accepting James's kiss, she smiled up at him. "Let's go home and tell Cynthia that she's going to be an aunt."

Cynthia Franklin sat on the bed in her sister's room, holding her hand. "I can't believe it," she gushed, her eyes sparkling. "My little sister is going to have a baby."

Rebecca leaned back against the mound of pillows cradling her shoulders, smiling. "Your little sister is all of thirty-six, and is somewhat overdue for starting a family."

"Nonsense. How many teachers do you work with who are having babies or their first baby at forty?"

She nodded. "A lot. In fact, I went to two showers last year for one who was forty-two and the other thirty-nine. It was the first time for both of them."

Cynthia waved her hands. "See. So, you're right on time."

Rebecca closed her eyes and bit down on her lower lip. What she wanted to say was that both of these women had their husbands with them to share their joy, while she didn't. She opened her eyes and stared at her sister, a slow smile crinkling her eyes. She had her family, a family who was loving and supportive, and she also had friends—people she taught with and those she saw socially.

A knowing light brightened her eyes when she thought of Daniel, twice a lover and once a friend. He had made a promise to be godfather to her child, and she wondered if he would still keep the promise.

Cynthia leaned over and pressed a kiss to Rebecca's cheek. "Can I call Bill and give him the good news?"

"Of course. When you talk to him tell him not to work too hard."

"Oh, please." Cynthia managed to look insulted. "The hardest work William Franklin ever did was getting me to marry him, because scoring baskets in the NBA was like a walk in the park for him."

"Don't knock the brother, because it worked, Sister Girl."

Cynthia made an attractive move. "Tell me about it." She kissed Rebecca again, then stood up and walked out of the bedroom.

Sliding down on the pillows, Rebecca closed her eyes, smiling. Her sister had been introduced to William Franklin by a mutual friend when she was just twenty-two. She'd dated him for six years before accepting his proposal of marriage. She waited until he retired from professional basketball, because she said she did not want to become a basketball widow to a husband who cheated on her with groupies in every city he played. William, who was ten years older than Cynthia, moved his wife to a small town in New Jersey, then opened an upscale gourmet shop in a quaint historic village.

The Franklins' *Ye Fancy Feast Shoppe* had earned the reputation of carrying the finest caviar, wines and baked goods in the state.

Closing her eyes, Rebecca forgot about everything as she slipped back into the comforting arms of a dreamless sleep.

The soft buzzing sound of the radio alarm shattered the stillness of the bedroom, waking Daniel. Reaching over, he groped for the radio and slapped it. The buzzing stopped.

He counted to ten, then rolled over and sat up. The glowing numbers on the clock indicated four fifty-five. A sliver of light shone through the blinds he had neglected to close before he fell onto the bed the night before. He, like millions of others, had waited for the beginning of Daylight Savings Time. Even though he jogged at five in the morning, he preferred light to darkness.

Pushing to his feet, he stood up, then eased himself weakly back down to the bed. Lowering his head, he waited until the dizziness stopped. It was apparent whatever he'd eaten the night before still plagued him. The cramps, nausea and sweats had begun soon after he'd eaten dinner. But what he could not understand was that he'd never had a reaction to the chicken dish he'd prepared at least once a month.

"Maybe it's the flu," he whispered aloud.

A cramp seized him and he stood up quickly, bolting to the bathroom. Ten minutes elapsed before he emerged, face drawn, chest heaving, and his mouth tasting of bile from a vicious bout of retching. Making his way to his bed on shaking knees, he fell across it, closed his eyes and slept.

It was another two hours before he woke again, called Faith and told her that he would not be coming into the office. She reassured him that she had everything under control, and in the event of an emergency she would call him.

The telephone rang hours later, and Daniel thought that he'd been asleep for several hours, but was shocked when he saw the numbers on the clock radio. It was three-thirty. He had slept away the morning and half of the afternoon.

He picked up the receiver before his answering machine switched on. "Hello."

"Daniel? Are you all right?"

He recognized the low, husky voice immediately. "Becky, what's wrong?"

"That's what I should be asking you, Daniel Clinton? I called your office and Faith told me that you were sick."

Closing his eyes, he listened for the sound of her soft breathing. His head hurt, his stomach churned, and he felt as weak as a newborn, yet his pulse quickened with rising desire. What was the matter with him, other than a probable stomach virus, that made him react with such passion for Rebecca? He'd turned forty April first, yet with Becky his body responded as if he were twenty-three again.

The last time they'd slept together had ruined him for a physical relationship with a woman. His latest period of celibacy was not voluntary—it was just that his body refused to follow the dictates of his brain whenever he dated other women.

"I must have picked up a stomach virus," he admitted as another cramp tightened his middle.

"Have you eaten or drank anything today?"

"No. I…" He felt his empty stomach heaving and he hung up. Making his second trip to the bathroom, this episode resulted in a wretched bout of dry heaves. As he lay on the cool tiles of the bathroom floor, listening to the constant ringing of the telephone, Daniel waited until he felt strong enough to make it to the shower stall; he turned on the cold water, sat down on the floor, then let the water wash away the moisture coating his body, reviving him.

He had no idea how long it took for him to dry his body, brush his teeth and run a brush over his hair, but once he pressed his face close to the mirror over the bathroom sink he felt better than he had in hours. Now all he needed was to get something into his stomach. The question was what?

Walking back to the bedroom, he pulled on underwear and a pair of sweat pants, leaving his chest and feet bare. He made his way across the large bedroom, stopping when he saw the blinking red dial on his answering machine. He remembered. He'd hung up on Rebecca.

Pressing a button, he listened to her voice, registering the fear as she repeated his name over and over and asking what had happened to him. There was a noticeable pause before she hung up. He picked up the receiver and dialed her number. What he wanted to do was allay her fear; that he was all right, that he was going to survive.

Her call, before his second bout of retching, was the first time they'd spoken to each other since the day following Michael's funeral and burial. It wasn't that he hadn't thought of her, but he just could not bring himself to call or see her after their passionate encounter. He still had not been able to rid himself of guilt that attacked him whenever he thought or dreamt of Rebecca. Perhaps if he'd slept with her after she had been widowed for more than a week the feelings of guilt would not be as acute.

The ringing stopped and he heard her answering machine. Not bothering to leave a message, he replaced the receiver in its cradle, shrugged his bare shoulders, then made his way to the kitchen to find something to put into his sensitive stomach.

Daniel managed to drink a cup of warm tea with lemon and two slices of unbuttered toast, waiting with trepidation to see whether his stomach would reject its latest contents. He sat quietly at the table in the dining alcove, watching a cable news channel on the small under-the-counter television in a corner of the kitchen.

A wry smile softened his mouth under his mustache. Other than the usual skirmishes between warring factions in several countries, the world was safe enough to survive another day.

The peace and silence was shattered by the distinctive sound of the intercom. Pushing slowly to his feet, he walked on bare feet across the carpeted living room to the front door.

He pressed a button on the wall near the door. "Yes?"

"Daniel, it's Rebecca. Let me in."

"Becky?" Why had she left Long Island for Westchester County? What had happened to her?

"Let me in, Daniel."

He pressed the button, disengaging the lock to the door in the lobby, a frown creasing his forehead. He had less than two minutes to discover why she had come to him.

He opened the door and waited for her to step off the elevator. His eyes widened, his pulse quickened, and he felt the faint, familiar stirring of desire in his groin when he saw her racing toward him.

Her face was deeply tanned, making her eyes appear lighter, more luminous. She had blown out her curling hair and streaks of gold were visible in the dark coppery strands. Everything about her—her face, appeared lush and ripe. She was more than beautiful—she was magnificent!

Opening the door wider and stepping aside he watched as she walked into his living room. "What's the matter?" he asked her.

Spinning around, her soft hair moving sensuously around the nape of her neck, a look of concern settled into Rebecca's features. She had exceeded the legal speed limit driving from Long Island to New Rochelle, and she suspected she also set a record of making the trip under her normal fifty-five minutes, door-to-door, and he had the nerve to ask her 'what was the matter?'

Her annoyance waned and her concern intensified when she saw the shadows under Daniel's large, deep-set eyes. He did not look well.

"What's the matter with you?"

He shrugged a muscular bare shoulder. "Nothing."

Running a hand through her hair, she moved closer to him, tilting her chin. "You hang up on me, leaving me to believe that you either passed out or died and you tell me nothing." Throwing up both hands, she paced in front of him, chewing on her lower lip.

Daniel moved closer to her, capturing her arm and stopping all movement. "I'm alive and I did not pass out."

"Why did you hang up on me? Why are you home? Why did Faith say that you weren't feeling well? Why do you look like a truck hit you?"

A slow smile parted his lips. The flush of color darkening her tanned face was similar to the passion he'd seen whenever they made love. "Which question do you want me to answer first?"

Her hands tightening into fists, she rested them against his bare chest. Leaning forward, she pressed her forehead to his shoulder. "Don't do this to me, Daniel."

"Don't do what?" He lowered his head and buried his face in her hair.

It was as if they had never parted. The soft crush of her slender body, the distinctive fragrance of her skin and hair transported him back a world made of up with only the two of them. No one and nothing else had mattered.

"Make me worry about you," she breathed against his warm flesh.

"There's no need to worry about me, Becky. I must have picked up a stomach virus or ate something that didn't agree with me."

Pulling back, she stared up at him. "Have you seen a doctor?" He shook his head. "How do you know it's not salmonella poisoning?"

He smiled down at her, arching a thick, silky eyebrow. "I haven't barfed in more than an hour, and I've managed to keep down a cup of tea and a couple slices of toast, so I think I'll survive." Tilting his head at an angle, his smile vanished. There was something about Rebecca that was different. What it was he was unable to discern. "Why did you call me?" It had been almost six weeks since they'd last spoken to each other.

Her flush deepened as she thought of the tiny life growing within her womb, a warm glow warming all of her. "I wanted to know if you intended to follow through on your promise to be godfather to my child."

His hands dropped and he stared at her, his eyes widening in surprise. It was apparent that she had gone ahead with the adoption process even though she was widowed. He could understand the need for her to continue with her plans despite the fact that Michael was no longer alive. She'd grieved, healed, and moved ahead while he'd agonized over sleeping with her again, reliving their last encounter over and over. Every woman's face became her face and every voice hers.

"I always keep my promises," he replied solemnly. "When do you expect to get the child?"

"My approximate due date is anytime between November twenty- third and December eighth."

"Due date?" He said the words tentatively, wondering if he had heard her correctly.

Rebecca watched Daniel with smug delight. There was no doubt that he was as shocked as she'd been when the doctor told her that she was expecting a baby.

Nodding slowly, she flashed a satisfied grin. "I'm pregnant. I still have a part of Michael."

He opened his mouth, but nothing came out. *She couldn't be*, he thought. *Not now!*

"Aren't you going to congratulate me?"

Daniel broke his stunned silence and held out his arms. "Oh, Becky. I'm so happy for you." What he wanted to say, but didn't, was why did Michael have to die? Why couldn't he have lived long enough to see his child born?

Cradling her gently to his body, he he'd her, rocking her fromside to side. "You did it, Love. You're going to have *your* baby." Pressing his mouth to her fragrant hair, he kissed her forehead. "Let's share a glass of milk and raise them in a toast to motherhood."

CHAPTER SIX

Daniel admired the feminine softness of Rebecca's body outlined in a pair of tailored charcoal-gray wool gabardine slacks she had combined with a pair of low-heeled black leather and suede loafers and a soft pearl-gray cashmere sweater set. From the time that he first met her he'd only known her to wear sweaters made of that fiber.

"Make yourself comfortable while I put on a shirt."

"I like what you've done with your entertainment corner," she said as he turned in the direction of his bedroom. He'd purchased a massive armoire that concealed a large screen television and the components to his exquisite audio system.

It had been more than four months since she had come to New Rochelle and Daniel's condominium apartment. He had invited her and Michael for a tree trimming party celebration. A towering blue spruce had sat in a corner of the living room, the smell of its pungent pine needles blending with the many mouth-watering dishes Daniel had ordered from a local caterer. The thirteen invited guests had spent three hours eating and drinking before taking another two to trim the magnificent tree. The overall effect was stunned silence once one thousand minuscule lights strung over the eight-foot tree were lighted. It appeared as if stars had fallen from the heavens and settled onto the massive branches.

Rebecca had watched Daniel's date as she pressed her body close to his and smiled up into his dramatic dark eyes. There was no doubt that the woman was in love with him.

She had also watched his reaction to her, but failed to see the same emotion on his handsome face. It was at that moment that she wondered if Daniel Clinton would ever find the right woman to share his life with. She could not understand why he hadn't wanted to marry or have children.

His apartment, like her own, contained one bedroom, but it was twice as large. His had a full eat-in kitchen and a separate dining room. The ten-foot ceilings and sunken living room added to the overall spaciousness of the apartment in the pre-World War II building.

Daniel returned from his bedroom, wearing a white T-shirt and a pair of well-worn leather moccasins. "Where are the glasses and the milk?"

Rebecca smiled at him. "Should I get a tablecloth?"

"But of course."

Opening a narrow closet in the kitchen, she withdrew a laundered damask table cloth and matching napkins, and spread it out over a butcher block table positioned in a corner of the kitchen, while Daniel retrieved two crystal goblets from an overhead cabinet.

"Do you want your straight or mixed?" he questioned, opening the refrigerator.

"I'll take mine straight, thank you." Rebecca smiled at his teasing. Daniel always had a voracious appetite for milk. There were times when he drank a quart during a single meal. His only allowance was that it had to be icy cold and bottled.

He filled the goblets with the milk and carried them to the table. He flicked on the overhead Tiffany light and pulled out a chair for her. He seated her, then sat down opposite her.

Raising his goblet, he waited for her to do the same. "To Rebecca and motherhood." His lips parted in a wide grin. "May you be blessed with every happiness that you so rightly deserve. And I want you to know that I'll always be here for you and your child. God bless both of you."

Her hand shook and she blinked back tears as she took a sip of her milk. She did not know why but she had wanted things to be different. She did not want to be thirty-six having a child without a husband. Why couldn't she have gotten pregnant five years before, or even seventeen years before when she was still seeing Daniel? Why couldn't the father of the child nestled in her womb still be alive?

Daniel drained his glass, staring over the rim at Rebecca. He'd known something was special, different about her the moment she stepped off the elevator. He'd assumed her tan had come from spending the spring recess with her family in Florida, but it hadn't been just the added color to her face that had enhanced her beauty. When she'd told him about the baby she carried, he'd realized the added lushness was the result of her impending motherhood.

The thought of her gaining weight, her body slowing, and the inevitable labor elicited a shiver of uneasiness that visibly shook his body. What if her pregnancy wasn't uneventful? Who would take care of her? And it wasn't for the first time that he silently cursed Michael Williams for volunteering for an assignment that put him at even more risk. And he'd heard rumors circulation through the invisible NYPD underground that Michael's unit had failed to back him up once his cover was blown.

Putting down his glass, he wiped his mouth with a damask napkin. "How are you feeling?"

Rebecca stared at Daniel's unshaven jaw, unable to remember when she'd seen him looking so blatantly male. The white T-shirt stretched across his wide chest seemed almost too small for his broad shoulders. She glanced at his large, well groomed hands, remembering the feel of his magical, hypnotic fingers tracing the dips and curves of her body. Her gaze moved slowly up to his mouth. She could still remember the powerful possession of his mustached mouth on hers as he chased away her fears and soothed her pain.

She had spent the past month reliving his lovemaking in her dreams, awaking to shame and guilt. But she had shed the guilt with the news that she was carrying her late-husband's baby. A part of Michael was alive. She was alive, and Daniel was alive.

"Aside from feeling tired all of the time, I feel wonderful."

"When do you see the doctor again?"

"The middle of next month."

"If you need anything let me know."

"What could I possibly need, Daniel?"

He wanted to say a husband. She needed someone to protect her in the coming months. "A friend," he said instead.

A gentle light softened her delicate features. "I have that," she said in a low, quiet voice. "I have you."

"What about a husband?"" he questioned just as quietly, the word slipping out of its own volition.

Her eyes crinkled in a smile. "You think I need a husband? He nodded slowly. "Why?"

Propping his elbow on the table, Daniel rested his forehead against his fist. He clenched his teeth in frustration. Why had he brought up the subject? Why couldn't he just let it go? Why couldn't he let Rebecca go? *Because you love her*, a silent voice reverberated in his head. Because he had never stopped loving her.

"You're alone and you're going to have a child."

"I won't be the first woman to have a child and not be with the child's father."

His head came up slowly and he glared at her. "You teach young children, Rebecca. Do I have to remind you of the differences between children who are raised in a one-parent home and the ones raised with both parents present? Or do you need to hear how my life and my mother's was changed forever when my father waited until I'd turned ten then walked out? His rationale was that I didn't need him anymore. What he did not want to admit was that he didn't want the day-to-day responsibility of taking care of a wife and child. It wasn't that he didn't send money for our support, but we didn't need the money as much as we needed his presence and protection.

"Who's going to be there to protect you and your child? Who's going to take care of you when you don't feel well? When you don't feel like getting up in the morning because the baby kept you up all night? How are you going to manage a career and motherhood when you're still recovering from the fact that your husband was *murdered*?" He watched her eyes widen as he'd said the word. It was the first time that he'd said that Michael had been murdered instead of losing his life in the line of duty.

Rebecca stared at Daniel as if he were a stranger. It was the first time that he'd mentioned his relationship with his father. In the past he'd said that his parents were divorced and that there were times when he did not see or hear from his father for months at a time. And it was the first time that he had alluded to Michael being murdered, not killed.

Her mind was a jumble of confusion. He was coming at her too quickly, with too many questions. "Do you have someone in mind?"

Her voice was no more than a whisper. He nodded again, his gaze locked with hers. His chest rose and fell heavily as he counted the measured beats of his runaway pulse resounding in his ears.

"Who, Daniel?" She didn't know why she asked the question when she knew the answer. Closing her eyes against his intense stare, she waited.

"Me. I want you to marry me, Becky."

Her lids fluttered wildly before opening. They were words she wanted to hear when she was twenty; she was now hearing at thirty-six. She had waited eighteen years— eighteen years. It had taken him eighteen years from the first time she was introduced to him for Daniel Albert Clinton to ask her to be his wife. Now when she carried another man's child in her womb. Now when she had someone who would keep her from ever being alone again.

Now even though she still loved him, but did not need him.

Shaking her head, she glanced away. "No, Daniel. I can't."

His jaw tightened as did his fists. "Why not?"

She swallowed painfully, her shallow breath shuddering in her chest. "How can I marry you, become your wife and sleep with you, while another man's child kicks in my womb? Haven't I sinned enough by sleeping with you…"

"What we did was not a sin!" he interrupted, the words exploding from his mouth. "You were not married. Michael was dead." Daniel buried his face in his hands. "I'm not proud of what I did that night. I will carry the guilt to my grave, but if I had it to do all over again, I probably wouldn't change what I did." He lowered his hands. "I'd do it because I love you, Rebecca. I've never stopped loving you. I told myself that I didn't love you anymore once you married Michael, but that was a lie."

Rebecca stood up and her chair fell back to the floor with a resounding clatter. Daniel rose, but made no attempt to move to pick it up. "Why now, Daniel? I wanted you when I had no memories of any man except for you."

"You know why."

"I know nothing!" she countered. "All I know is that you gave me some lame excuse about not marrying as long as you were a cop. You haven't been a cop for five years, and I've seen you with women who loved you enough to marry you if you'd asked them."

"I didn't want to marry them."

"Why not?"

He pushed back his chair and circled the table, reminding her of a large, stalking cat. "Why not, Becky?" His deep voice rumbled in his chest like a purring growl. "Because they weren't *you*. Once I left the force I realized that I still wanted you, but that was out of the question because you'd become another man's wife. A man who was my best friend. A man who had become the brother I never had. I couldn't allow myself never to think of you other than that of his wife. I never lusted for you, not even in my head, as long as Michael was alive."

She tilted her head back as he stood over her, tall and powerful. "And now?"

"I want you and *only* you. But I give you my promise that if we marry I won't touch you until after you deliver the child. I will not defile you or the child in your womb."

Biting down on her lower lip, Rebecca tried bringing her tumultuous thoughts into some semblance of order. Daniel was offering her what she had wanted for years—the chance to be Mrs. Daniel Clinton.

"I don't know."

He cupped her face between his hands. "You don't have to give me an answer right away. Think about it."

She shook her head. "I should never have come here."

"You not coming here won't stop me from coming after you, Becky. You can't escape me or your feelings," he said confidently. "No more than I can continue to lie to myself."

Rebecca pulled away from him and walked into the living room to retrieve her handbag. She had to get away from him before she blurted out that she still loved him, that she wanted to be his wife.

Making her way to the door, she stared straight ahead. She felt the heat from his body as he followed her. "Feel better, Daniel."

Reaching around her, he unlocked the door, his hot breath sweeping over the back of her neck. He opened the door, then braced an arm over it. "I'll give you some time to think about my proposal before I call you."

Rebecca nodded, and it was only then that he dropped his arm. She walked the length of the hall, waited for the elevator, making certain not to turn around to see if he was watching her. It wasn't until she was safely in the elevator and on the way down to the building lobby that she let out her breath. Daniel Clinton had just offered her what she'd been waiting for all of her adult life, and she did not know why but she wanted to cry instead of rejoicing. What he'd offered had come too late. She loved him, but now she didn't need him.

Rebecca maneuvered out of the faculty parking lot after classes Wednesday afternoon, making a left turn instead of her usual right. An unseeing invisible force pulled her in the direction of the parkway rather than the local road leading to her apartment building, and the minute she entered the parkway she knew she had to *talk* to Michael.

She did not know why she had varied her normal routine of visiting her late husband's grave every Sunday morning, but after her third trip she finally concluded that it was the only day of the week that they'd had each other for the entire day. Their usual routine began with attending the early worship service at the local Presbyterian church, then brunch at their favorite diner followed by a leisurely walk where they'd catch up on what had occurred in their lives during the week. The morning concluded with perusing the morning newspaper.

Sunday afternoons varied from Sunday to Sunday. There were times when she prepared dinner at home or they ate out. Then there were the Sundays when they drove to New Jersey to visit her sister, brother-in-law and their children. But most times it was a day devoted solely to each other. Now her Sundays were spent with Michael—at his gravesite.

Rebecca did not know why she had broken the pattern until she stood at the place where a new headstone marked the position where Michael Harrison Williams' body lay under the cool, dark earth. Wrapping her jacket around her in a protective gesture, she stared down at the marble slab. Lengthening afternoon shadows filtered through massive trees that wore a summer dress of lush green, even though it was early May. The warm weather had not abated. Eyes closed, head bowed, she stood silent, motionless while a soft smile played about her lips.

"I suppose you're wondering why I'm here today," she began in a soothing monologue. "I need your help, Michael. I'm so confused and I wanted to talk to you before I make a decision that I know could change me and my life forever.

"Daniel asked me to marry him? He says that he promised you that he would take care of me if anything ever happened to you, and he's taking the promise literally. He also claims the baby needs a mother *and* a father.

"I know he's right, but what's bothering me is that he says he loves me, that he never stopped loving me. If he'd offered marriage because of his promise or for the baby I could accept it a lot more easily than his declaration of love. I'm confused, Michael. I don't know if he wants to marry me for the baby, or because he still loves me."

Why would you consider marrying him, a silent voice whispered in her head. A voice that sounded so much like her dead husband's. "Because a part of me loves Daniel," she said aloud in answer to the question. "A part of me has always loved Daniel Clinton."

Opening her eyes, she stared across the large expertly maintained cemetery, watching an elderly woman walk slowly along a path until she located the grave she sought. The woman placed a bouquet of flowers on a gravestone, waited a few minutes, then turned and retraced her steps to a car waiting outside the massive gates surrounding the property.

Marry him, the voice whispered. *Let him make you happy. You need to laugh again. You need a father for the child in your womb, a child I know you'll love unconditionally. And because you have so much love to give, I want you to give it to Daniel. Let him fulfill the promise he made to me.*

Rebecca nodded. She didn't know whether she imagined the voice because she needed so badly to hear it or if it were really Michael's spirit calling out to her. The first time she'd dreamt about her dead husband she'd awakened disoriented and frightened. His image had been so real that she'd been certain all she had to do was reach out and touch him. But when she attempted it she encountered nothingness. The next time he appeared in her dreams he'd warned her not to touch him and urged her to listen to him. And she had. He'd spoken of all of the wonderful times they'd shared and of how much he'd loved her and he'd promised to love her. And then he apologized for leaving her, and she'd awakened sobbing.

Anger followed the bout of crying. Like the first time Michael told her he was contemplating going undercover. They had argued so vehemently about the risks. In the end he ignored her protests and her verbal fears, accepted the assignment and lost his life. He had done to her what Daniel refused to do—marry and leave her widowed.

Turning her face skyward, she closed her eyes. Daniel—the man who introduced her to love and passion and the man who offered to love and protect her. A man who would become a father for the child another man had placed in her womb. A man she knew she would love forever.

Opening her eyes, she stared up at the clear blue cloudless sky as a feeling of peace pervaded her being. She had made her decision. She would marry Daniel Clinton.

CHAPTER SEVEN

Rebecca sat at a small, round table with Selma Jackson, sipping from a plastic cup of chilled water with a slice of lemon. She and her best friend shared what they had come to call their regular Wednesday night fish fry. The tiny restaurant along Seaport's waterfront area boasted some of the best fish dishes on Long Island's south shore. The only trade-off was the establishment's bare-to-the-bone ambience. Drinks were served in paper or plastic cups, dinner on paper plates with straw holders, and serving utensils were always plastic forks, spoons and knives. Many of the patrons came prepared with their own flatware and specialty forks to extract the succulent meat from lobster and crab claws.

Selma shifted a professional waxed eyebrow at Rebecca. "This is the second week you've decided to pass on your usual beer and drink water instead. What's up?"

Rebecca lowered her glass, smiling. Selma reminded her of a tiny, fragile doll. Her smooth, heart-shaped face was the color of highly polished teak. Her large, round, dark eyes, short, pug nose, and full, tiny mouth afforded her the look of someone in perpetual astonishment. She had recently cut her shoulder-length hair, adding gamine sophistication to her diminutive stature. Selma taught mathematics and science at the same middle school where Rebecca taught language arts.

"I'm off alcoholic beverages for at least the next year and a half," she informed her best friend.

Selma took a sip of her own frothy beer, licking the foam off her upper lip. "Why?"

Rebecca hesitated, then said, "Because I'm pregnant."

Selma put down her cup, at the same time she jumped to her feet, spilling a portion of the foaming brew on the table. "You're what?"

Placing several napkins over the widening spot, Rebecca frowned at Selma. "Sit down," she hissed.

Complying, Selma shook her head in confusion. "When? How?"

Rebecca waited until the waitress placed a napkin-covered basket filled with several varieties of broiled and fried fish on the table and walked away before she responded to Selma's queries, explaining how she had gotten sick during their spring recess.

Selma's mouth formed a perfectly rounded "0" before she pursed it, displaying a set of deep dimples in her smooth cheeks. "I'm so happy for you, but on the other hand I can't believe Michael won't be here to see his son or daughter."

Taking another sip of water, Rebecca nodded, recalling Daniel's offer of marriage. "Daniel Clinton asked me to marry him," she whispered.

If possible, Selma's rounded eyes appeared bigger. "Not the tall, gorgeous brother with the fabulous body?"

Rebecca laughed, the velvet, sensual sound causing several men to glance in their direction. Daniel had come to one of their school's Career Week fairs several years before and Selma took one look at him and swooned when Rebecca introduced the two.

"He's the one."

Selma sobered, a slight frown creasing her smooth forehead. "I know you told me that you and Daniel were a couple years ago, but I thought that was over."

"It was and it isn't."

"Come again."

"Michael made Daniel promise that he would take care of me if anything happened to him."

"Taking care of one doesn't have to include getting married," Selma argued.

"I don't think marriage would be an issue if I wasn't pregnant."

Selma's gaze narrowed. "It is about Daniel's promise to Michael, Michael's baby, or is it about you and Daniel still carrying a torch for each other?"

Leaning back against her chair, Rebecca let out her breath slowly. "I won't lie and say that I don't have feelings for him. He was my first love, Selma, and even though I married Michael there was a tiny part of me that I never gave my husband because Daniel had claimed that."

"Are you saying that you love Daniel more than you loved Michael?"

She shook her head. "I'm not saying that at all. I loved Michael, otherwise I never would've married him. But that love was different from the one I shared with Daniel. It was as if I was born to love Daniel. That our destinies were entwined from the moment we were conceived."

"Damn, Rebecca. That's heavy."

"It's eerie. I met Daniel at eighteen, slept with him for the first time on my nineteenth birthday, and I proposed to him when I turned twenty. He turned me down and years later I married his partner. Now we've come full circle because it's his turn to propose to me."

"Have you accepted?"

"Not yet."

"When?"

"When he contacts me."

Selma's smile was dazzling. "Good for you. No matter how liberated or independent we like to think we are, no woman should have to go through having a baby alone."

"That was Daniel's argument for proposing."

"He's right. I think I'm going to like the brother. By the way," she continued conspiratorially, "does he have a brother or cousin lying around somewhere waiting for someone to scoop them up?"

Rebecca laughed again. "No. He's an only child. But what's with you and Robb? I thought the two of you were going to tie the knot before the end of the year."

"The only knot I'm going to tie is my panty hose around that man's neck. I want out, Rebecca."

She often wondered how long Selma could stay in a situation that had gotten progressively worse. Whenever Selma talked about leaving her live-in boyfriend he offered marriage.

"It's that bad?"

Selma nodded, frowning. "Very bad. I'm waiting until the end of June, then I'm out. I'm going to need a place to live first. So if you hear of anything, let me know."

Reaching across the table, Rebecca held her friend and colleague's hand. "Anything I can do to help let me know. I'm going to ask a favor of you."

Her expression brightening, Selma said, "Ask away."

"Will you be my matron of honor if I decide to have a small ceremony?"

Selma's eyes filled. "Of course, Rebecca. Anything for you."

Rebecca blinked back her own tears. "Thank you, friend."

Daniel stood in front of the eight young boys and two girls, struggling against the rising nausea in his throat. What he thought had been a reaction to something he'd eaten or a twenty- four stomach virus proved unsubstantiated once he was forced to go to his doctor. Lab results showed that his intestinal tract was clear of any microorganism that would cause any gastrointestinal disorder. It had been one full week since the episodes of nausea began, and there was no indication of it subsiding. He had canceled the judo class the prior week and knew he couldn't cancel it for two consecutive weeks without disappointing his students. The only time classes were not held was during school recess, holidays, and summer break.

Inhaling deeply, he swallowed, momentarily settling his stomach. A slight smile curved his lips. Hands at his side he bowed slowly, gently from the waist, his charges imitating the gesture.

Straightening, he turned to where Derek Grady stood apart from the youngsters ranging in age from eight to twelve. The colors of the belts around their *gi* ranged from the novice white to an advanced purple.

"We have a new student in our class," Daniel began quietly, his deep voice carrying easily in the *dojo*. "His name is Derek, and he's what we call a novice." Some of the more experienced students wearing green and blue belts smiled at one another. "We're going to move a bit more slowly than usual so that Derek can become familiar with the Japanese terminology.

"What is the most important aspect of judo, Carla?"

"Courtesy and respect, *sensei*," replied a young girl of ten who wore her orange belt with obvious pride.

"Correct, Carla," Daniel replied, smiling. "That is why we bow. The *rei* indicates the physical courtesy and respect one has toward another student, his opponent or his *sensei*. We bow when we enter the *dojo*, mostly as a measure of respect for this place of learning. Most importantly, disciplined courtesy helps instill control of our emotions."

He studied each young face, seeing the determined eagerness coupled with a strong sense of disciplined control. Most of them had come to him exhibiting aggressive tendencies, but after two or three classes they had seemed to mature before his eyes.

"We'll begin with our warm up exercises. We'll stretch the back, hands, legs, and neck. Loosening and stretching these muscles is important, because it helps to prevent injuries when we fall."

Going very slowly for Derek's benefit, Daniel and the class went through a series of maneuvers of squatting, stretching and supporting the body by bending backwards, head on the mat, heels raised to stretch the neck muscles. After fifteen minutes of warming up, he patiently demonstrated *ukemi* or the practice of falling.

Sitting on the mat, knees bent, bare feet together, he propelled his body backwards. Just as his back was about to hit the mat, he slapped the mat hard with both forearms, his chin tucked in. He repeated it several times, then demonstrated it from a standing and squatting position.

The students were divided into three groups by level of experience and skill, and Daniel worked with each, perfecting throws from the easiest *osoto gari* to the more advanced *kouchi gari*. He and the twelve-year-old youth who had earned a purple belt demonstrated the *kouchi gari* for the class. With panther-like speed, he spun on his left foot and whipped his right foot around, slapping it against the youth's right heel. Using his arms, he upset the gangling adolescent's balance, and followed through with a powerful hip throw. Helping him to his feet, Daniel and the youth bowed to one another. The class concluded with ten minutes of a relaxing *T'ai Chi* workout.

"Next week we'll practice *seoi nage*," Daniel said once everyone opened their eyes after the last position. "It is a powerful weapon against a taller, heavier opponent because it provides a smaller person with enormous leverage." The students lined up and bowed from the waist as Daniel returned their bow. All of them turned and walked to the back of the *dojo* where they'd left their backpacks.

"Mr. C... *sensei*," Derek said hesitantly not following the others. "That was awesome."

"Change your clothes and I'll drop you off wherever you like. We'll talk in the car."

What Daniel wanted to do was give himself time to change his own clothes and splash cold water on his face. He'd been lucky he was able to get through the ninety minute class without embarrassing himself. Walking into the locker room he opened the door to a metal locker. He slipped out of his *gi*, pushing it and the accompanying black belt into a canvas bag, and quickly changed into a pair of jeans and a black pullover cotton sweater. Not bothering to put on his socks, he pushed his bare feet into a pair of running shoes and tied the laces.

It was another twenty minutes before he and Derek left the *dojo*; he had to wait for all of the students to be picked up by their parents or older brothers and sisters. He incurred the cost of renting space in the sports gym for ninety minute sessions once a week for the judo lessons, while charging the parents a nominal dollar a week for each child.

"Do you think you're going to continue coming?" he asked Derek as he pulled away from the curb and stopped at a red light.

Derek stared at Daniel as if he'd grown two heads. "Of course I'm going to come. Judo is better than pumping iron. With weight lifting you build up your body, but judo does something to the head. Just doing the *T'ai Chi* exercises made me feel like I was floating, flying."

Daniel smiled. "*T'ai Chi Chuan* is one of the greatest Chinese gifts to mankind. It helps you find your center so you can learn to relax your mind as well as your body."

"I think I'd like to study this Oriental stuff. *T'ai Chi*, judo, karate," Derek drawled. "Maybe even learn to speak the languages."

"You can begin with going to college. There are several local colleges that have programs devoted entirely to Asian Studies."

"Which ones?"

"Columbia."

"Columbia takes big bucks and brains."

"Brains you have, Derek. Wasn't it you that told me that you scored a fifteen hundred on the SAT?" Derek nodded. "If that's the case then apply and let your parents take care of the tuition."

"And I can always help out by saving some money from my pay check," Derek said, thinking aloud. "I think I'm going to look into it." It had taken a month for his father's threat that he was going to force him to leave home to change his thinking. He came to work and on time, and now he was giving serious thought about attending college.

"Where do you want me to drop you?" he asked the young man. He knew Derek had another four hours before he was to go on duty at a new office complex in the West Bronx.

Derek peered through the windshield. "Drop me off at the four-four. I think my Dad's working late tonight. I want to let him know that he's going to have to write a check for my tuition. I won't tell him that the payee will be Columbia until I hand him the application."

Daniel laughed, shaking his head. "You're a mean kid, Derek Grady." He drove up in front of the Forty-Fourth Precinct.

"I'm not so bad and you know it, Mr. C." He sobered, staring at his boss. "And you're not so bad either. It's too bad you don't have any kids, because you'd make a dynamite father." Derek opened the door to the Porsche, got out and closed the door behind him.

Daniel watched as Derek walked into the station house and disappeared from view. He didn't have any children because he'd wanted only one woman to have his children. His only experience with children had come from teaching the judo classes. He had joined the Bronx Business Alliance, committing a portion of his time and business proceeds to the betterment of the borough's youth. And over the past two years his time and money had not gone to waste.

He pulled away from the curb, thinking about Rebecca. It had been exactly one week since he last saw and spoke to her. And he'd told her that he would give her time to consider his proposal. A week was long enough for her to either accept or reject his offer.

Picking up the car phone, he pushed a button. The familiar sound of her number dialing reverberated in the hush of the auto's interior. He switched over to the speaker as he heard the low, husky sound of her hello.

"Becky, this is Daniel."

There was a stunned silence before she spoke again. "Yes, Daniel?"

"I'd like to come see you."

"The answer is yes, Daniel."

His fingers gripped the steering wheel in a deathlike grip as his pulse accelerated at the same time his chest rose and fell heavily under his sweater.

"I'll be there in half an hour." He pushed a button, ending the connection. "She said yes," he whispered as a wide grin split his face. "She's going to marry me," he shouted, ignoring the curious looks from several passengers in the cars alongside his.

He took the next corner on two wheels as he headed for the bridge that would take him out of the Bronx, through Queens and out to Long Island.

Rebecca opened the door and stared at Daniel as if she'd never seen him before. He'd lost weight—a lot of weight. He was thinner than when she first met him eighteen years before.

"What's wrong with you?" she whispered, staring at the sharp angles in his lean face. "You look like hell."

He smiled, thinking the same, but didn't say it. "Thank you for the compliment."

Opening the door to let him enter, she felt the heat in her face. "I didn't mean for it to come out like that. How much weight have you lost? Why aren't you taking care of yourself?" Daniel closed the door, then turned and leaned over to kiss her cheek. "I am taking care of myself. It's just that I can't keep any food down."

Rebecca took his hand and led him to the living room. "I'm the one who's pregnant, not you. All I have to do is smell something and I'm barfing."

"I wish it was that simple for me. I went to the doctor, but he couldn't find anything."

She sat down on the sofa, and he sank down beside her. "How do you feel?"

His dark gaze searched her smoky-gray one, lingering on her lush mouth. Faint blue shadows marred the flesh below her eyes, making them appear deeper-set, darker. "I should be the one asking how you feel."

"I'm making it. I haven't missed any days from school."

"Are you still tired?"

She nodded. "I can't get enough sleep. I've taken to setting my alarm in order to get up in the morning. The moment I get home I take a nap. I only get up because of hunger pangs."

He squeezed her fingers gently. "Do your students know?"

This time she shook her head. "No. I've told the principal and the AP and one of the teachers. I'm trying to make it through the next two months without a big fanfare."

Daniel released her fingers and put an arm around her shoulders, pulling her closer to his side. "Are you taking a leave of absence?" She nodded. "How long?"

"I'm going to take a three-year sabbatical. I'll return to teaching after the baby enters nursery school." What she did not say was that her savings and the monies she'd received after Michael's death would permit her financial independence for years.

Daniel smiled, inhaling the scent of her perfume. It was different from the one she normally wore. It was a lighter fragrance. It had only been a week since he last saw her, but seemed so much longer. How had he been able to exist without her? How had he actively put her out of his mind for eight years while she was married to another man?

"When do you want us to marry, Becky?"

She stiffened noticeably before she tilted her chin and stared up at him. She saw his gaze move slowly over her face as if committing each feature to his memory.

"I don't know. How about the end of the month?"

He nodded slowly. "That's okay with me. That should give me enough time to close on the house."

"Close on what house?"

"There's a house in Locust Valley that I said I'd buy if I ever married. It's less than a quarter of a mile from Long Island Sound. It's like having our own private beach."

"Wait a minute, Daniel Clinton." Rebecca pulled away from him, shaking her head. "You want to buy a house and expect me to live in it without seeing it or giving my approval? How do you know I want to live on the north shore. What if I want to stay here in..."

"Becky, darling," he interrupted, placing a finger over her lips. "We'll go look at it on Saturday morning. If you don't like it, then we'll look for another place. But something tells me you won't be able to resist it."

"How did you find this house?"

"I met the developer last fall when I wired his summer residence with the most sophisticated electronic system available because someone had burglarized it three times the prior winter. He put up several new homes along the north shore, and most of them were sold while they were still in the construction stages. I saw the plans for the one in Locust Valley and told him to save it for me. He called me last week to say that the landscaping was finished and I can finalize the sale and move in at any time."

Her eyes widened. "Is that why you proposed marriage? Because you wanted me to share your dream house with you?"

A swift shadow of barely controlled anger swept across his face. "If that were the case, then I could have any woman share the house with me. A woman that I would not have to marry. I would get all of the benefits of marriage without having any of the responsibility that goes along with it."

His anger fled quickly as his gaze softened when he saw the pain in her eyes. "I love you, Becky. You're the only woman I've ever said those words to."

Turning toward him, Rebecca pressed her breasts to his chest while curving her arms around his neck. "I'm sorry," she apologized. Her warm breath swept over his ear at the same time his fingers tightened on her slim waist. She felt the strong pumping of his heart against her sensitive breasts and pulled back.

She did not trust herself to remain in Daniel's arms. Wordlessly, silently he made her want him. It did not matter that she carried another man's child beneath her breasts.

All she knew was that something within Daniel Clinton called out to her to bare her body and her heart to him.

He had promised her that he would not make love to her until after the baby was born, and she knew the only way she would be able to keep her part of the bargain was if they did not share a bed.

"I'll go with you Saturday to see the house."

Daniel nodded, pressing a kiss to her forehead. What he wanted to do was kiss her mouth until she begged him to make love to her. He wanted to kiss her—all over. He wanted to be inside her where she would take both of them to heaven before they tumbled back to earth and reality. But it was not to be because he'd promised her that he wouldn't touch her until after the baby was born. They would have to wait. *He* would have to wait until the beginning of the following year to become her husband in the biblical sense. He only prayed that he would be able to hold out that long.

"Have you eaten?" he asked her quietly.

She arched a delicate eyebrow. "I was just going to ask you the same thing."

"Get a jacket, Love. I'm taking you out to eat."

The steady downpour that began late Friday night continued into Saturday morning, and when Daniel came to Rebecca's apartment she greeted him with a smile and breakfast. It was apparent she was feeling better because the dark shadows under her eyes had disappeared.

They sat in the dining area, eating sliced fresh fruit and Shredded Wheat while drinking several glasses of chilled milk. Daniel stared intently at Rebecca, unaware of what he was putting into his mouth.

She put down her spoon and returned his rapt gaze. "What's the matter?"

Lowering his head, he smiled. "You," he replied in a soft voice. "You look beautiful this morning."

"Why thank you, Daniel. Is this what I have to look forward to whenever we share breakfast?"

"That all depends on you," he teased with a sensual smile.

"It doesn't take much to please you, does it?" She hadn't worn any makeup and had brushed her hair off her forehead, securing it at the top of her head with an elastic band.

He sobered, his eyes widening. "That's where you're wrong, Becky. It takes a lot to please me. And you please me in and out of bed."

She stared at the man whom she had pledged to marry and spend the rest of her life with. The man who'd promised to protect her and her child, and her heart turned over at the sight of his large dark eyes under the slightly drooping lids; eyes that spoke volumes and eyes that seduced her. Her gaze moved lower to his mouth. It had been a long time since she'd seen the upper lip he now concealed under a black silken mustache. The lower one she knew from memory. It was full, petulant and sensual. Its fullness denoted Daniel's voluptuous sensuality. Sighing audibly, her lips parted as she recalled the last time she and Daniel had made love. It was a scene she'd replayed over and over in her dreams since she'd been widowed.

Daniel saw Rebecca's expression and he knew what she was feeling because he felt the same, only he could hide it better than she could. Her eyes darkened, a flush darkened her cheeks, while she struggled to control her labored breathing.

Standing quickly, he began removing the dishes from the table. "We'd better get going if we're planning to make it to Locust Valley by ten-thirty."

She needed no further prompting as Daniel circled the table and pulled back her chair. "I have to get a jacket," she mumbled under her breath.

He watched her retreat to the bedroom, unaware that his hands were shaking. How was he going to make it through the next six months without making love to her?

Rebecca watched the landscape change as Daniel turned onto a narrow road lined on both sides with towering trees. Wherein the south shore of Long Island was flat, its north shore was made up of hills. Some steep enough to require a four-wheel drive vehicle when snow covered its surface.

A steady rain forced Daniel to slow the sports car as he made his way up a private road. Sprawling structures were set on several acres, each one bearing a name to identify it from the next one. She read a "Black Acre," and a "Willow Creek," before a towering pale gray, white trimmed modern structure rose in front of them like a castle in the clouds.

Daniel downshifted, watching Rebecca's reaction to what she'd called his dream house. Her eyes widened until they resembled silver dollars.

"This is it," he said softly.

She stared at the structure with floor-to-ceiling windows, sloping roofs and skylights. It sat on a sea of manicured grass with a massive weeping willow tree and several towering blue spruce pine trees.

"It's beautiful," she whispered, unable to pull her gaze away.

Daniel pulled into the circular driveway behind a late model Lexus and shut off the ignition. The developer's representative had already arrived. He stepped from the car and came around to help Rebecca out. Holding an umbrella over her head, he lead her to the front door.

The door opened and a petite, porcelain-skinned, dark-haired woman flashed a warm smile. "Even though it's not a good morning with the rain I'll say it anyway. Good morning, Mr. Clinton."

"I beg to differ with you, but it is a very good morning for my fiancée and me. Mrs. Hertz, this is Rebecca."

"My pleasure, Rebecca. Please call me Jill."

Rebecca noted the woman's raw silk pants suit and Ferragamo footwear. It was apparent that the rainy weather did not inhibit her choice of attire. "Jill it is."

The older woman extended her hand. "Come, let me show you around. I'm certain you'll like what you see."

Glancing over her shoulder, she stared at Daniel who hadn't moved. Leaning against the door, arms crossed over his chest, he flashed her a warm smile. "I'm going to look around outside."

Shrugging her shoulders under her lightweight nylon jacket, Rebecca followed Jill across a highly polished wood floor in the entry to a sunken living room with a sloping ceiling that rose more than thirty feet above the parquet floor. A curving stairway, with iron railings, floated up to the second level. Other than the staircase, the focal point of the room was a massive hand-carved Mexican stone mantel above a huge fireplace and the floor-to-ceiling windows that looked out on a vista of wooded acres beyond the house.

Rebecca followed Jill Hertz from room to room, nodding her approval. The second floor contained four bedrooms, each with its own bath, and the two larger ones with adjoining sitting rooms. The first level claimed a formal dining room, full kitchen with a pantry and breakfast nook, family and laundry rooms, a space large enough to be used as a utility or storage room and another full size bathroom.

She was surrounded by white walls, parquet wood floors, and glass and light. Even with the cloudy, rainy weather the house was filled with light. After seeing the house for herself she knew why Daniel wanted to buy it. She looked forward to decorating it.

She found Daniel leaning against his car, a knowing smile curving his mouth. The rain had stopped and the emerging rays of the sun struggled to pierce the cover of watery clouds. Straightening when he saw her, he extended his arms and she did not disappoint him as she walked into his embrace. Rising on tiptoe, Rebecca fastened her mouth to his, wordlessly giving her approval.

"I take that to mean that you like it?" he asked against her lips.

Placing her cheek against his chest, she inhaled his cologne and the scent of his laundered shirt. Everything about Daniel was so male, so compellingly self-confident, and for the first time she realized that Daniel Clinton was in complete control of himself and his life. He knew what he wanted and did not want, and waited for the right time to execute his decisions. He loved her enough to marry her, but only on his terms. He'd waited eighteen years and he had won.

A warm feeling of victory surged through her. She was also a winner. It had taken eighteen years, and her wish had been granted. She would become Mrs. Daniel Clinton.

"I love it, Daniel. I want to live here, raise children here, and grow old with you in your dream house."

He tightened his hold on her slender body. "It's our house, Love."

Pulling back, Rebecca smiled up at him. "I want to give you money toward the purchase." He stiffened as if she had struck him. He was still, so still that if it hadn't been for the pounding of his heart against her breasts she'd question whether he was still breathing. A slight frown creased her smooth brow. "What's wrong?"

He blinked once. "I can't believe a woman of your intelligence would ask me what's wrong."

Something in his manner and tone irritated her. It was the first time she remembered him ever being condescending toward her. "And why not?" she shot back.

"I wouldn't have asked you to marry me if I couldn't take care of you. In other words, I don't need your money, *Rebecca*."

Her temper flared, along with the rising heat in her face. "It's not about my money, is it, Daniel? I think it's more about Michael than it is about me or *us*. I know Michael told you that we were going to move into a house once I became pregnant, and because that time is now you want nothing to remind you of Michael."

His hands fell away, as he stared at her as if she'd taken leave of her senses. "This has nothing to do with Michael."

"Then why won't you take my money?"

"Because I don't need it. Save it, put it away for *Michael's son or daughter's* education, or go into business for yourself once you retire from teaching." He ran a large hand over his face. "I really don't give a damn what you do with it, Rebecca. You can donate it to the charity of your choice or burn it. Just remember that whatever you decide to do with it is your business."

Michael's son or daughter. The four words cut her to the quick and she bled without bleeding. He had just unwittingly established their future together. She would become Mrs. Daniel Clinton, live under *his* roof, her child would carry *his* name, but the child would be her *son* or *daughter*. *Hers and Michael's.*

Jill Hertz locked the front door, then turned and walked toward Daniel and Rebecca. She had met Daniel more than a half dozen times and was always taken with his sensually attractive masculinity. She'd tried imagining what type of woman would get him to commit and give up his bachelor status, and failed. She never would've guessed that the tall, slender woman with dark red hair, cool gray eyes and palomino-gold brown skin would be the *one*.

Jill smiled at the attractive couple. "When's the big day?"

Daniel glanced down at Rebecca, smiling. As far as he was concerned there would be several *big* days: their wedding, moving into the house, the birth of the baby, and his making her his wife in the most intimate way possible.

"We've decided on Memorial Day weekend," Rebecca responded, speaking for both her and Daniel.

Jill pressed her manicured hands together, her dark eyes sparkling. "Excellent timing. You'll be able to close on the house at least a week before your wedding." She extended her hand. "Good luck and congratulations."

Rebecca and Daniel took turns shaking the proffered hand, then waited for her to get into her car. The shiny, dark blue Lexus eased forward in the circular driveway before moving down the private road and out of sight.

Turning back to Daniel, Rebecca stared at the solemn expression on his arresting face. He'd assumed his customary stance of crossing his arms over his chest. "I want to get married here."

His arms came down slowly. "Here?"

"Yes. Indoors or outside. It depends on the weather."

Their former tension forgotten, Daniel dropped an arm around her shoulders and pulled her to his chest. A satisfied smile softened the harsh angles along his jawline. He was going to get everything he'd ever wanted: woman, house and child.

Pulling out of his embrace, she took several steps. "I want to take a look around the back of the house."

Nodding, Daniel reached for her hand, holding it protectively in his as he lead her across the driveway and along the slate path to the rear of the house.

A rising wind had blown away the clouds and swatches of blue sky pierced the gray sky. Rebecca held her breath as she viewed the breathtaking panorama of the sloping hill leading to a narrow strip of beach and the dark, foam-flecked waters of Long Island Sound.

"Wind Watch," she said softly.

Daniel stared at the hair that had escaped the elastic band atop her head, admiring the soft curls lifting gently in the breeze. "What?"

"I've come up with a name for the house."

Moving behind her, he wrapped his arms around her middle. Her stomach was still flat despite the fact that she was nearly two months into her term.

"What is it?" he asked against her ear.

"Wind Watch." She pointed toward the sky. "See the wind chase the clouds."

"Yes, Love," he replied in a quiet voice. What he wanted to do was sit on the bluff and watch her. He still hadn't gotten used to the fact that everything he'd ever yearned for was about to become a reality.

CHAPTER EIGHT

The newly laid sod cushioned Rebecca's footsteps like a rubberized mat or the deep pile of a lush carpet. She made her way slowly over the luxuriately manicured lawn, putting one foot firmly in front of the other.

Everywhere she looked there was green and open space. Her fingers tightened within Daniel's when she saw it, and she stopped abruptly. Like the house, it rose before them, and gleamed a brilliant white in the emerging sun. A large, elaborately carved wrought-iron gazebo sat on a mound of grass, resembling a six-tiered wedding cake on a green tablecloth. She could feel the heat of Daniel's gaze on her face as she stared at the magical structure.

"Daniel." Her breath came out in a breathless whisper.

He released her hand and curved an arm around her waist. "I know, darling. It is beautiful." He smiled at her awe-struck expression. "It's the perfect place for a wedding."

A slow smile parted her lips. "I believe you're right, Mr. Clinton."

"Do you want something big?" he questioned, still staring at her enchanting profile.

Turning, she glanced up at his impassive expression. "I'm going to leave that decision to you. You have to remember I've done this before."

A frown creased his forehead. "Are you saying that marrying for the second time is not as significant as the first?"

"I'm not saying that at all. I've had the white dress, veil, attendants, and the red carpet. It's just that my marrying

Michael was a grand spectacle I don't want to repeat—not now." Her eyes darkened with emotion. "I'm older, different. And my reason for marrying you is not the same as when I consented to marry Michael." What she did not, could not, say was that she now realized why she'd become Mrs. Rebecca Williams. She loved Michael, but even more significant was that she hadn't wanted to be alone.

Her decision to marry Daniel was entirely different. She had always wanted to marry him since that moment when she had fallen in love with him on sight. It had nothing to do with her carrying a child or that she needed a father for the child in her womb.

Daniel studied her face, his dark gaze as soft as a lingering caress. A rising breeze stirred the curls falling down the nape of her neck and he resisted the urge to push them up into the elastic band atop her head. What he wanted to do at that moment was touch her—all over. He wanted to make love to her on the bed of grass with only the blue of the sky above them for a canopy. The day he'd watched the completion of the outer shell of the house he knew he wanted to live in it with the woman who would become his wife. What he hadn't consciously admitted to himself was that he wanted that woman to be Rebecca.

"Why are you really marrying me, Becky?" His voice was low, soft, and coaxing.

A gentle smile softened her lush mouth as she moved closer to him, her breasts brushing against his chest. Static electricity jolted her with the pressure of his warm body against her sensitive nipples. "I'm surprised you have to ask why, Daniel."

He also smiled. "It's not that obvious to me, Love."

"It should be." She arched an eyebrow as her smile widened.

Not moving, he lowered his head until his mouth was only inches from hers. "It's not to me. Why don't you tell me."

Rebecca found Daniel's nearness disturbing and exciting, but as she stared up at him she felt a surge of confidence. There was no need to play head games or hide her feelings. This man had introduced her to passion, an all consuming passion that had been lying dormant until he stoked the fires to make her fully aware of why she had been born female.

"Because I love you, Daniel Clinton," she admitted in a husky whisper. "I've always loved you."

His breathing quickened as his large hands took her face and held it gently. "And I you," he confessed seconds before his mouth covered hers, his tongue easing between her parted lips.

His kiss was gentle, healing. It masked the turbulent desire sweeping throughout his body. It was silent, yet it screamed out his love for her, his need to protect her.

Daniel's tongue tasted hers, moved slowly over the ridge of her teeth before tracing the outline of her full, lush mouth. He savored her mouth the way one would enjoy an exotic dessert. It was delicious, but eaten slowly for ultimate satisfaction and supreme delight.

"I want a small gathering," he mumbled between soft nibbling kisses. "Just family and close friends."

"Thank you," Rebecca breathed heavily against his moist mouth. She doubted whether she had the energy to go through the rigors of a large wedding celebration. Grasping Daniel's hand, she urged him forward. "As soon as I get home I'm going to call a friend of mine who is a wedding planner. She'll do everything from invitations to ordering the food and flowers. You'll have to give me the names and addresses of the people you want to attend."

Curving an arm around her waist, he pulled her closer. "That means we'll have to go back to my place before I take you home."

She nodded. "Right now I need to eat or…"

"Why didn't you say something before," Daniel interrupted. "Let's go." Swinging her up in his arms, he retraced their steps, walking back to where he'd parked the car, Rebecca protesting that she could walk.

"Allow me play the hero, Becky. Just this one time."

Staring up at him, she flashed a sensual smile. "You've always been my hero."

Daniel arched his sweeping eyebrows. "Always?"

"Forever." She tightened her arms around his neck. "And there will be no other man after you."

You're right about that, he thought. *The same way there will be no other woman after you.*

Opening the door to the sports car, he settled her on the seat and waited until she'd secured her seat belt before he circled the Porsche and slipped behind the wheel.

Glancing at his watch, he asked, "Brunch or lunch?"

Rebecca felt the gnawing hunger attacking her with a fierceness that left her lightheaded. "It doesn't matter."

Daniel drove quickly along the private road before he turned off to a main thoroughfare. Making two quick left turns, he maneuvered into a parking lot behind a row of stores in a shopping area that evoked memories of a bygone era. All of the elegant little shops claimed Tudor facades, reminiscent of the style of her sister and brother-in-law's gourmet establishment.

"Do we have time to look around after we eat?" she asked Daniel as he assisted her from the car.

Grasping her hand, he smiled down at her. "I have nothing but time today."

And neither did Rebecca. She wanted to take a leisurely tour of the little hamlet she would call home. Everything was happening so quickly, but then she had to tell herself that it actually wasn't that quickly. She had waited eighteen years to become Mrs. Daniel Clinton.

The small coffee shop was set up much like an indoor Parisian café with bistro tables and chairs, striped tablecloths, and tiny votive candles flickering on each table. A hostess greeted them warmly and within minutes they were seated and given menus.

"Someone will be with you shortly," she announced, smiling.

Daniel wafted until the young woman walked away, then asked, "Are you all right?"

She gave him a pained smile. "I will be as soon as I put something into my stomach."

"You're not going to be sick, are you?"

Shaking her head, she prayed she wouldn't be. She closed her eyes and leaned back against the cushioned wrought-iron chair. She'd managed to curb the nausea, but doubted whether she would be successful for much longer. The gnawing hunger warred with the rising nausea.

Daniel sat across from Rebecca, watching the natural color drain from her face. A coating of moisture gave it a sickly appearance and he knew she wasn't feeling well. Rising to his feet, he walked over to a waitress taking orders from an elderly couple at a nearby table.

"Excuse me, Miss, can I get something to eat for my wife. She's pregnant and I'm afraid she's going to be sick if she doesn't get something into her..."

"Right away, Sir," the young woman interrupted. Mumbling an apology to the older couple, she raced over to the counter and grabbed a handful of packaged crackers. She shoved them at Daniel as she took a furtive glance at Rebecca. "I'll be right with you after I take their orders." She gestured with a toss of her head at the other table.

Daniel gave her a wide smile. "Thank you very much."

He walked over to his table, opening a package and handing Rebecca a cracker. She bit into it, chewing slowly and nodding her own thanks. She followed with another as the natural color flooded her face once again.

"That was close," she whispered, smiling at Daniel.

He returned her smile, letting out his breath. The slight tightness in his chest indicated that he had been holding his breath. One thing he did not want to see was Rebecca sick. He refused to think of her sick and alone. She had been alone, but, in another three weeks that would be over. He would be with her.

He'd referred to her as his wife. The word had slipped out of its own volition, and he realized that he had begun to think of her as that. They would share a house, sleep under the same roof, and he would always be there to protect and care for her.

"Feeling better?"

"Yes, thank you, darling." She blew him a kiss. "Now, what do I want to eat."

Turning her attention to the menu, Rebecca perused the selections. The menu definitely had a French flavor. Hearty lentil soup was *La Soupe Aux Lentilles Bonne Femme*, and grilled pork chops were *Les Cotes De Porc*.

She decided on a grilled chicken breast with accompanying side dishes of steamed spinach and carrots, while Daniel selected grilled salmon, scalloped potatoes and steamed zucchini.

Taking a sip of water, she stared over the rim of the goblet at the man she had promised to marry. "How much weight have you lost?" she asked after putting down her water goblet.

He shrugged his broad shoulders. "I don't know. It can't be more than ten pounds." Leaning over the table, he shifted an eyebrow. "How much weight have you gained?"

"I don't know. I've decided not to weigh myself, but wait until I go to the doctor."

"When is your next appointment?"

"The twelfth."

"At what time?"

"Five-thirty."

Daniel mentally recorded the date and time. "I'll come with you."

Her eyes widened. "You don't have to come."

"I want to." There was a noticeable finality in the three words. "If we're going to be married, I'm going to be responsible for you. And if I'm going to be a father for this baby, I have a right to be involved in every phase of your pregnancy."

You may think of this baby as yours, but it's my body, she wanted to shout at him. Just because she'd consented to marry him it did not mean she was ready to surrender her entire life.

"I don't *want* you to come, Daniel."

He went completely still, only the rising and falling of his chest indicating that he was breathing. "Why not, Rebecca?" Daniel's lips thinned in frustration, flattening against the ridge of his upper teeth.

Closing her eyes, Rebecca bit down hard on her lower lip. What she wanted for an instant was not to be carrying a child and have Daniel want her and only her. That their planning a future together was not predicated on her being widowed and pregnant.

"I don't want you to smother me," she said softly and managing a slight smile. "I'm not that helpless."

Daniel's gaze, fixed on her face, softened. He nodded. "I've never been a husband before. You're going to have to let me know when I come on too strong. It might take some time before I have it down as well as Michael did."

Reaching across the table, she took his hands, holding them tightly. "This is not a competition, sweetheart. I would never compare you to Michael."

"Then why do I feel as if I am competing with him?"

"I don't know. I gave you what I should've saved for him. You were the first man in my life, Daniel. No one will or can ever take that away from you."

Pulling his hands from under hers, he reversed the position so that he cradled her slender fingers possessively within his. "I've known you and I knew Michael. Men talk, Becky. Michael and I used to sit in a cruiser for hours, baring our souls to each other. We talked about women we've loved and made love to. There were times when our discussions were raw, intimate, and after he married you the talks stopped. It wasn't that I wanted or needed to know what went on between you and Michael, but you becoming his wife changed our relationship somewhat. We remained friends, but the easy-going openness was over."

A slight frown furrowed her smooth forehead. "Are you saying Michael felt guilty about marrying me? That he felt as if he'd betrayed you?"

Daniel shook his head. "I really don't know what it was. Maybe it was me. I have to admit that I was shocked when he told me he was seeing you and maybe he sensed that."

"How long were we dating before he told you?"

"Six months."

What Rebecca could not tell Daniel was that it had taken her six months before she allowed herself to sleep with Michael. Each time he made an overture she came up with an excuse. She had dated Daniel for more than a year and a half, then waited almost six years before she took her clothes off to lie with another man. For six years she had remained celibate and faithful to the memory of the man who had claimed her virginity.

"Michael once admitted that he felt as if he lived in your shadow when it came to me. Please, Daniel, don't make that same mistake. I loved Michael. I love you, too. I always have. I would be dishonest if I said otherwise. But I've never confused you with him. The two of you are as different as night and day, and yet I've loved you both and you both have made me happy."

Tightening his grip on her delicate hand, Daniel stared at her with a hunger that robbed her of her breath. "I have a lot to make up for, Love. I feel as if I've wasted so much time."

"All we have is time, time to rediscover our love and to fall more in love with each other."

"I want to make you happy, Becky. I want to be a good father to the baby."

"Then the first thing you have to do is start to think of this child as *ours* and not Michael's or mine. If I'm going to marry you and share a house with you, then everything I have yours."

He nodded slowly. "You're right. Our son. Our daughter." He grinned, attractive lines fanning from at the corners of his eyes. "I like the sound of that."

"Wait until he calls you Da-da before he learns to say Mama."

"That's okay as long as you don't spoil him rotten."

"Me!" she exclaimed, trying to appear insulted. "I don't spoil children."

"That's not what I heard. I've been told that you get more gifts from your students than any other teacher at the school."

Blushing, Rebecca glanced over his head. "That's because I want learning to be fun. And speaking of learning, I have one more slot open for our Career Week Fair. Would you mind becoming a guest on a mock talk show about people who own their own businesses?"

He released her hands, leaning back in his chair and shaking his head. "No, Rebecca. I still haven't recovered from the last encounter with the barracudas you call students."

"That's because you were a police officer at that time. Some kids are very opinionated about certain professions. This year our focus is on the entrepreneur. I want them to know the alternatives to working for someone else, and you are a perfect example of that."

"Do you dislike me so much that you'd expose me to a group of fifth graders…"

"Sixth graders this year," she said, cutting him off. "The panelists will be sixth graders, while the audience will be made up of both fifth and sixth."

As the lead teacher in the Language Arts department of the middle school, Rebecca had come up with the Career Week and Book Week Fairs several years before, and both were popular events with students, teachers and parents.

Daniel affected a sorrowful expression. "I thought you loved me, Becky."

"I do," she replied quickly.

His eyebrows lowered in a frown. "Then why do you want to throw me back into shark, piranha, and barracuda infested waters? The last time it was fresh-face ten-year-olds, and now you're adding the wise-ass eleven-year-olds."

Rebecca laughed, the husky, haunting sound sending shivers up his spine. It was very much like the first time he noticed her. They were sitting in a restaurant when he heard her laugh, the sound drawing him to her like a moth to a flame.

"It should be a wonderful experience for you. Interacting with them will prepare you for impending fatherhood. It can't hurt to get a head start."

"I have enough with my judo class."

"Your judo students worship and respect you, Daniel. The classroom is a very different venue from a *dojo*."

"How right you are, Becky. If a kid gets out of line with me in the *dojo* I can always toss him or her just a little bit harder than necessary to solicit respect. I can't use the same technique in your classroom setting when they smart mouth me because I wouldn't answer what had been classified department information."

"It will different this time, darling."

Cocking his head at an angle, he glared at Rebecca. "Are you trying to get over on me?"

Running the tip of her tongue over her lips, she nodded slowly. "Of course, Daniel Clinton."

He went completely still, his dark gaze fixed on the erotic gesture as he felt the slow arousal between his thighs.

Did she know what she was doing to him? Had she any idea how much he wanted her?

Forcibly tearing his gaze away from her mouth, he nodded. "Okay. You win. I'll do it."

Her face brightened in an adoring smile. "They'll love you, Daniel."

"Yeah, yeah," he intoned. "They'll verbally abuse me, as well as insult me, but they'll love me."

She reached for his left hand, squeezing it gently. "As long as I love you that's all that matters."

He stared at her, a slow smile parting his masculine lips. "You're right about that, Love."

They finished lunch, both refusing dessert, then left the charming little eating establishment to tour the shopping area. Daniel disappeared in a bookstore, while Rebecca lingered in a florist's shop. Moments later she left the shop with her arms filled with a massive bouquet of wildflowers. Sweet pea, camellia, delphinium, foxglove, anemone, iris, heather, phlox, and baby's breath were nestled in clear plastic and secured with a trail of curling pale blue, lavender, pink, and violet-hued ribbons.

She spied Daniel standing in front of the bookstore, glancing up and down the street for her. He saw her and waved. She waited until for him to approach her before extending her arms. He grasped the bouquet, giving her a questioning look.

"I think congratulations are in order," she said mysteriously.

"What's the occasion?"

Leaning forward, Rebecca kissed his smooth jaw. "A new house, our upcoming wedding, and your impending fatherhood."

A foreign emotion swept through Daniel as he struggled for control. Never had *any* woman given him flowers. It had always been the reverse. But then he had to remind himself that Rebecca was not any woman. She was to become his wife and the mother of his children. And she was the only woman he had ever loved.

"Thank you, Becky." There was more than a hint of hoarseness in his voice.

"What did you buy?" She pointed to the small bag in his left hand.

"A how-to book."

"On what?"

He gave her a lingering look, then said, "Fatherhood."

Rebecca curved her arms around his waist. "Oh, Daniel, you'll be a wonderful father."

"I pray I will."

And he had prayed that he would be. After he offered to marry Rebecca, Daniel wondered if he could be a good father. Would he turn out like his own father, walking away from his responsibility when he felt overwhelmed, or trapped? He was forty years old and he never had to be responsible for anyone but himself.

Staring down at Rebecca's upturned face, his apprehension vanished quickly. No, he was nothing like his father. He would never leave the woman he married or his children. He had loved Rebecca and wanted her for so long that he could not remember any of the women that had come before or after her.

"Are you ready to leave?" he asked, pressing his mustached mouth against her ear.

"Yes."

Shifting the bouquet of flowers and the bag containing the book to his other hand, Daniel curved his free arm around Rebecca's waist and led her back to the parking lot behind the row of stores set up in an horseshoe pattern.

As she walked Rebecca catalogued all of the shops in the shopping area. There was the little café, along with the florist, a card and gift shop, bakery, jewelry store, hair salon, bookstore, leather and luggage establishment, and ice cream parlor. There was one vacant storefront, displaying an elegantly hand-painted sign in the window with a telephone number. Stopping abruptly, Rebecca stared at the sign, immediately memorizing the number.

"What's the matter, Becky?"

She hesitated, pulling her lower lip between her teeth. Forming her words carefully, she said, "I think I know what I want to do when I retire from teaching."

Daniel's eyebrows shifted. "What?"

Turning, she smiled up at him. "Something you said when I offered to give you money for the purchase of the house made me think about an alternative career."

"What's that?"

"You suggested that I could go into business for myself."

"Once you retired from teaching," he reminded her.

"I'm going to take a leave of absence."

"That's not retirement."

"I know," she conceded, her gaze swinging back to the sign. "But remember I am going to be home for three years. I don't want to go stir crazy in between my outings to the circus, ice capades, museums and puppet shows."

"You're taking off to nurture a child," Daniel retorted.

"A child who will not require that I interact with him or her twenty-four hours a day. A child who will probably sleep most of the time the first two or three months. What am I going to do with myself when the baby's asleep? I don't want to start watching the daytime soaps or talk shows to entertain myself."

His gaze watched her animated expression, seeing the shimmer of excitement lighting up her beautiful gray eyes. A slight flush darkened her gold-brown face, making her suddenly look riper, more lush.

"What kind of a business, Rebecca?" His voice was low, coaxing.

"I'd like to open a crafts shop. I'd offer supplies for all of the needle crafts, as well as instructional classes for knitting, crocheting, needlepoint, and quilting."

Daniel nodded, remembering the quilt she'd helped her students make one year. The school's theme had been "Love Around the World," and Rebecca had assisted her fifth and sixth grade students as they designed and sewed a quilt in which each square was embroidered with the word "Love" in more than sixty languages and dialects. The quilt was presented at an assembly program and was hung in the lobby of the middle school as a part of a permanent exhibit.

He thought of the sweater she had knitted as a gift for him for their first Christmas together. She had wrapped it in a large box with decorative ribbon, saying that she hoped it fit. Not only had it fit, but the intricate pattern and workmanship was the highest quality of any knitted garment he had ever worn. She confessed that her maternal grandmother had taught her to knit, crochet and sew.

"Okay, so when do want to open up shop?"

"Just after Labor Day."

He nodded. That would give her almost four months. "You're not going to try to run it by yourself, are you?"

"Of course not. I'll advertise for part-time help. It will be perfect, because once the baby comes I'll be able to bring him with me to the shop. I'll probably open three days a week, and maybe expand to four if business picks up."

"I'll help you anyway I can, Becky. But if running your own business endangers your health, then I'm going to put a stop to it." His hooded gaze lingered on her mouth, flashing a gentle but firm warning.

Her back stiffened noticeably as she took a step backwards. "If I need your help I'll ask for it. But I want you to remember, Daniel, that this business will be set up with my money, and I will decide what is or is not good for me. I want this baby, and there is no way I would do anything that will endanger my life or this child's." Her gaze locked with his. "Do I make myself clear?"

Daniel stared at her as if she'd suddenly grown another eye in the center of her forehead. There was just enough of an edge to her warning to let him know that the question was not spoken glibly. Rebecca McDonald-Williams had just challenged him.

His jaw hardened as he inclined his head. "Absolutely clear."

Those were the last two words they exchanged as they returned to where Daniel had parked the car. He helped into her into it, slamming the door. The solid thud echoed his own rising temper. Rebecca Williams was not the Rebecca he had fallen in love with eighteen years ago. She had changed over the years and he suddenly wondered how much he, too, had changed. And after they married, would they change again?

CHAPTER NINE

Daniel took the parkway west, heading toward New York City. He took surreptitious glances at Rebecca after she'd closed her eyes and pressed her head against the headrest. His gaze swept over the soft fullness of her breasts swelling against the cotton fabric of her blouse. Even though her stomach was still flat there was no doubt that she was carrying a child, because the increased fullness in her breasts was apparent.

He tried imagining what she would look like full term, her abdomen swollen, her breasts heavy with milk. *Like a Da Vinci madonna*, he thought. She would be as or more beautiful than she is now. The image made him chuckle audibly.

"What's so funny?" Rebecca asked. The soft dulcet sound of her husky voice feathered over him and his smile widened.

He gave her a quick glance. "I was just imagining you nine months pregnant," he replied, deciding to be truthful.

She winced. "Bite your tongue, Daniel Albert Clinton. I'll either look like a beached whale or a cow who needs milking."

"Bite *your* tongue, Rebecca McDonald-Williams, soon-to-be Clinton. You're going to be more beautiful than you are now."

"I'm not even two months and I'm spilling out of my bras."

"I don't see where that should be a problem, Love."

Rebecca stared at his strong profile. "You should see *me*."

"If you want I'll pull over and you can show me," he teased, giving her a lecherous grin.

"Daniel," she groaned as heat flooded her face. "This is serious"

He'd heard the slight tremor in her voice and knew she wasn't comfortable with the changes in her body. "What I see is a beautiful woman who is becoming even more beautiful. I knew there was something different about you the day you came to my place to tell me you were pregnant. Your face had a glow that radiated from within. You are lush, Becky. Ardently ripe."

Leaning to her left, she rested her head against his shoulder. "You are so good for me, Daniel. So good."

Signaling, he maneuvered over to the shoulder and put the car in park. Unsnapping his seat belt, he reached over and unhooked hers. He pulled her across his lap as far as the steering wheel would permit and cradled her to his chest.

"I'll always try to be good to you," he whispered in her hair, "because I love you."

Fighting back tears, Rebecca buried her face against his warm throat. She did not know what it was that had made her snap at him. Maybe it had something to do with the hormonal changes in her body, or the changes going on in her life because within a span of three weeks she would marry and move into a new house. And in less than a month and a half she would put her teaching career on hold and look back on fifteen years of classroom instruction, while within another seven months she would look forward to bringing a tiny human being into the world.

She had informed her family that she and Daniel would marry, and no one seemed surprised with her announcement. Her parents and sister said they would be available if she and Daniel decided on a ceremony. She hadn't wanted a ceremony, but decided to let Daniel make that decision, and he wanted a small gathering of family and close friends at Wind Watch.

Reveling in his warmth, her arm tightened around his neck. "And I love you," she whispered tearfully. "I don't like fighting with you, Daniel."

"Shh-hh, Love. We're not fighting. We can't agree on everything."

Pulling back, her eyes glistening with unshed tears, Rebecca smiled up at him. "We used to." What she did not say was that the only thing they did not agree on at that time was getting married.

"We were young and idealistic. I believe there were times when we tried too hard to please each other, Becky."

"It worked."

He nodded slowly. "Yes, it did." Reaching up, he removed the elastic band from her hair. A riot of curls spilled over her forehead and down around her neck. "It's different now because we're both older. I'm not the same and neither are you. But the one thing that has remained constant is our love. That will keep us together."

A warm glow settled in her middle and suddenly without warning she wanted Daniel. She wanted him to make love to her. His nearness made her burn with a rising desire that threatened to consume her whole. Reluctantly she eased out of his embrace. She knew they would not share the other's body until after the baby was born.

She combed her fingers through her hair, pushing the errant curls off her forehead. "I feel as if I'm not in control. I have to move, decorate a new house, prepare for a wedding, and hopefully set up a business all within the next three months."

Cradling her chin in his hand, Daniel raised her face to his. "Will you let me help you?"

"How?"

"You have your friend handle all of the wedding plans, while I take care of everything else. I'll contract with someone to pack up everything at your apartment. I'll also have my business agent see about renting the shop. If you decide to rent, then you'll have to let me know what you'll need to furnish it."

"We both have one bedroom apartments. That's hardly enough furniture to fill the rooms at Wind Watch," she argued softly.

He brushed a light kiss over her lips. "Before we start buying furniture I want to show you a few pieces. When my mother passed away I put everything in her house in storage. At the time I didn't know what I wanted to keep or give away. If there's anything you want, then you can put it in the house. What you don't like I'll give away."

Rebecca's gaze widened. "You kept her things all of this time?"

He flashed a mysterious smile. "After you see them you'll know why." He took a quick glance at his watch.

"The warehouse is in the Bronx. We'll go there first before we stop at my apartment."

"Speaking of apartments, what are you going to do with yours?"

Daniel leaned over and snapped her seat belt before repeating the motion with his own. He shifted into first gear, saying, "I have a buyer. What about yours?" He waited, then maneuvered back onto the parkway.

"I can always sublet until I sell it. One of the teachers just separated from her boyfriend, and has put the word out that she needs a place to rent."

"That takes care of one item on our lists."

Rebecca nodded, then settled back to relax. She listened to the gentle sound of her own breathing and within minutes she fell into a deep, dreamless sleep.

With one glance at the magnificently crafted furniture Rebecca knew why Daniel had elected not to sell or give away the pieces that had once graced the late Eunice Clinton's North Carolina home. She never met Daniel's mother, as the older woman had relocated to the state of her birth six months after her son was sworn in as an officer of the New York City Police Department.

Running her fingers over the smooth surface of a mahogany buffet server, she shook her head in wonderment. "Everything is so exquisite." Moving closer, she stared at the intricately carved design of the doors on the server. The design was familiar.

"Where have I seen this before?"

Arms crossed over his broad chest, Daniel leaned against a cloth-covered chest-on-chest. "The design is the same as on the armoire that I'm using for my T.V. and stereo equipment," he said cryptically.

Her head spun around as her mouth gaped slightly. "Who made these pieces?"

"My father. He was a master furniture maker."

Shaking her head in amazement, she said softly, "He is truly a genius. Why do you say was? Where is he? Who did he work for?"

Daniel always liked the fact that Rebecca was never content to ask one question, then have him answer it. There were always two or three strung together.

Pushing off his leaning position, he moved over to her. "You're right, he is a genius. He lives upstate in a little town near the Catskill Mountains. He's always worked for himself. He said he didn't have the temperament to work for someone else. Right now he's what I'd call semi-retired. He'll only accept a commission if it's what he says is worth his while."

"What would be *worth his while?*"

Daniel smiled. "I don't know. You'll have to ask him."

Rebecca looped an arm through his. "Are you inviting him to the wedding?"

He nodded. "Aside from you and *our* baby, an aunt and uncle, he's all the family I have left. Both of my parents were only children." He, too, had been an only child, but he was certain that he and Rebecca would have more than the child she was carrying. They would have at least one more.

"I'll want the furniture," she stated quietly. "Every piece." A corner in the one square city block warehouse was filled with head and foot boards, dressers, chest-on-chests, chairs and tables numbered and labeled with the name *CLINTON*. "They are truly family heirlooms."

Pulling her close to his body, Daniel rested his chin atop her tousled head. "Eunice will find a way to thank you."

"What I would've liked to do is thank her and your father for *you*."

He smiled. "My parents did not stay married very long, however, both always agreed that I was the best thing to have come from their relationship."

"Why did they divorce?"

"They married too young. They'd met in high school and got engaged in their senior year. My maternal grandfather had definite plans for his daughter. He wanted her to go away to college, while she balked because she had fallen in love with Albert Clinton. Albert had become an apprentice to one of the finest furniture makers in the country, so he had no intention of leaving North Carolina. In the end they eloped. She was seventeen and he had just turned eighteen. I was born a year later.

"My mother's plan to attend nursing school was put on hold as she stayed at home in the role as wife and mother. Their idyllic life fell apart after a couple of years. My father began coming home later and later, and there were times when he stayed away for days at a time, hanging out with his buddies. He claimed he felt trapped, that he'd missed so much because he'd married too young. The days became weeks, then months. After awhile I didn't look for him to come home at all."

"Was there another woman or women, Daniel?"

"He says there wasn't. He claimed he loved his wife, but he couldn't spend day after day with her. It all ended when I turned ten. My mother filed for a divorce and we moved to New York. She lived with an uncle and his wife in their house in Queens, enrolling in nursing school and graduating with honors. After securing a position with a major hospital, she moved out and purchased her own home. She completed her education and earned a graduate degree in public health. I was on the force six months when she made the decision to return South. She sold the house, gave me half the money, then relocated to North Carolina. Her parents were elderly and sickly, and she nursed them until both passed away within months of each other. What I didn't know was that my mother was terminally ill at the time. I didn't find out until after she'd passed away that she had moved back to North Carolina to die.

"My father came to the funeral and sobbed like an inconsolable child. Seeing him like that made me realize that he truly loved my mother. We spent some time together, becoming reacquainted. Last year he was diagnosed as a diabetic. He underwent a complete metamorphosis. He changed his diet, stopped drinking, sold his business, and moved from North Carolina to upstate New York where he spends his days fishing and relaxing."

"Have you seen him lately?"

"I drive up to see him every couple of months."

"What did he say when you told him that you were getting married?"

"He said, I can't wait to meet her.'"

Rebecca laughed softly, the sound low and seductive. "I
can't wait to meet him either."

Tightening his hold on her waist, Daniel steered her
toward the office in the enormous warehouse. "I'll arrange
for the delivery of the furniture after we close on the house.
I have an inventory of all the pieces, so you can decide on
which room you'll want each one to go."

She nodded. "That will certainly make it easier for me
when I make up a floor plan as to where I want everything
situated."

She still was not certain whether she would sublet her
apartment furnished or unfurnished. However, she was certain that if she left it furnished there would be certain
pieces of furniture or accessories she could not leave.

The drive from the warehouse to Daniel's apartment
was accomplished quickly. He gave her the names and
addresses of the people he wanted to invite to their upcoming nuptials.

Rebecca counted the names. He had listed eight people.
"It looks as if we'll have less than twenty, including the
bride and groom."

Daniel stared at her delicate profile. "It'll be perfect.
Small and intimate."

Turning her head, she stared at him staring back at her
as her gaze catalogued what had drawn her to Daniel
Clinton so many years before. She had been only eighteen,
yet she had been able to see the confidence and self-assur-

ance that he wore like a badge of honor, and the control that was so evident in everything he said or did. She fluttered like a moth around an open flame, while he stood still, assessing and reassessing everything around him. Only in the classroom was she in complete charge of herself and her environment. She had become a teacher of teachers, opening the minds of her colleagues and her students to the world around them through reading, spelling, literature and composition. Her primary aim was to develop a student's comprehension and capacity through the use of written and oral language. This she was able to do better than most of the other teachers in her district.

Her marriage to Michael had been solid and fulfilling. She had wanted children, but had resigned herself to adoption as an alternative. Now, however, her life was taking another turn. Within two months of being widowed she was expecting a baby, planning a marriage, moving to another community, and contemplating starting up her own business. Her life was taking on the components of Daniel's lovemaking intense and electrifying.

They discussed the details of their wedding, agreeing on what foods they would serve their guests as Daniel prepared a fresh fruit salad. Her eyelids were drooping again before she finished the salad and Daniel suggested she take a nap before he drove her back to Long Island. She did not need much urging as she made her way to his bedroom and lay on the same bed where she'd given him her body for the first time, and slept.

It was dusk when she awoke to find Daniel sitting on a chair watching her. Stretching, she held out her arms to him and she was not disappointed when he joined her on the bed.

"How do you feel?" he questioned, burying his face in her fragrant hair.

"Wonderful," she sighed, shifting for a more comfortable position. Throwing an arm over his chest, she rested her head on his shoulder.

"Hungry?"

Rebecca laughed softly. "No. If you keep feeding me I'm going to be huge by the time I'm ready to deliver."

"You'll be just right. How much weight does the doctor want you to gain?"

"He wants me to gain at least thirty pounds. He says I'm underweight."

Daniel silently agreed with the doctor. He suspected that Rebecca wasn't eating enough, but that would change once they were living together. He intended see to her every need. He wanted her healthy, and the baby healthy.

Tightening his grip on her slender body, he closed his eyes while his thoughts filtered back to the day he saw her for the first time. There were so many years between them, so many memories. But the best memories and years lay ahead of them.

Rebecca stood in the middle of her new bedroom in the house in Locust Valley, staring at her reflection staring back at her from the Cheval mirror. It was her wedding day. For the second time in her life she would exchange vows with a man.

She looked more like a virginal bride from one of Jane Austen's Regency period classic novels than one who was about to witness the arrival of a new millennium. Her hair had been styled in a profusion of curls that were swept atop her head and held in place with two jeweled hair clips and an iris-blue ribbon. The softly flowing pearl-gray Empire-styled dress with streamers of identical iris-blue ribbons falling from under her breasts was delicate and flattering to her ripening figure.

The past three weeks had passed quickly and smoothly. She had spent more than an hour with Daniel at the offices of the attorney who represented the developer, signing legal documents and making the property theirs.

Daniel's business agent secured an agreement where she would rent the vacant store in the mini-shopping mall for a year, with the option of extending the lease an additional year. His agent had also secured a guarantee from the land-lord that certain leasehold improvements would be com-pleted before she took possession of the shop September first.

All of the furniture in the Bronx warehouse belonging to Daniel's mother was moved into the house, along with the furniture in his apartment, the day after carpeting was laid in most of the rooms.

She had sublet her apartment, fully furnished, taking only her clothes, china, silver, and personal mementos. Selma Jackson was effusive in her thanks, while agreeing to stand-in as matron of honor for the small, private wedding ceremony.

Rebecca saw the reflection of two men move into view of the mirror; she turned slowly, a sensual smile softening her lips as she extended her manicured hands to Daniel. There was no doubt the man standing beside him was his father.

Daniel returned her smile and quickly closed the distance between them. "Dad wanted to meet you before the ceremony." He captured her fingers and led her to Albert Clinton. "Dad, this is Rebecca. Becky, my father."

Daniel released her hands and moments later, Rebecca found herself pressed against Albert's slim frame. Daniel had inherited his father's height and coloring.

"Welcome to my family, daughter," Albert said softly.

Pressing a light kiss to his smooth cheek, she whispered, "Thank you, Dad."

Albert released her, then stepped back to survey the young woman who was to become his daughter-in-law. His son had excellent taste. He winked at her. "I'll see you downstairs."

She nodded, smiling, then watched him walk away. Her gaze shifted to Daniel, admiring his neatly barbered hair and mustache, and moving down to the silk tie in the same iris blue shade as the ribbons on her dress and in her hair. He wore a crisply laundered white shirt and single pleated slacks that fell with precise tailoring from his trim waist to the tops of his Italian-made black shoes.

There was no mistaking the flicker of desire in his dark eyes as he closed the distance between them. They had moved into Wind Watch two days before, but had not shared a bedroom. She slept in the master bedroom in the bed that once graced Daniel's bedroom, while he had elected to sleep in the bed that had been his mother's in one of the other bedrooms.

Rebecca was glad that she had projected opening her shop in September, because it afforded her enough time to order stock, as well as select accessories for her own home. The school term would end in another month, giving her a full month to establish a routine where she would balance running a household and a business enterprise.

Her health had also improved. She wasn't as fatigued as she had been during her first month, and the bouts of nausea also subsided to one or two a day. She had gained two pounds and Daniel put back on most of the weight he'd lost.

Daniel cradled her expertly made-up face between his large hands, smiling. "You are more beautiful than I could've ever imagined."

"Thank you," she whispered, pressing her body to his. "And so are you."

He laughed, the sound rumbling in his deep chest. "Why, thank you, Love." Lowering his head, he barely touched her mouth with his. "You have only fifteen minutes to change your mind."

Pulling back, she frowned up at him. "Don't start with me, Daniel, or I'll leave you standing at the altar."

His smile vanished quickly, replaced by a deep frown. "You wouldn't, would you?"

Rising on the toes of her blue satin pumps, she wound her arms around his strong neck and pressed her breasts to his chest. "Of course not, my darling. I've waited too long for this day to consider backing out now."

"Not as long as I've waited," he confessed.

There came a soft knock on the open door, followed by a teasing voice. "There will time for that after you two get married." Daniel and Rebecca sprang apart, smiling. Cynthia Franklin stood in the doorway, both hands folded on her hips. "I'm sorry to interrupt, but I had to check whether Rebecca is wearing something old, something new, something borrowed, and something blue."

Daniel shook his head in confusion. "Say what?"

Rebecca thread her fingers through his. "It's a good luck thing," she explained. "My dress is new, the ribbon is blue, the hair clips are Mom's, and my brooch is old." The fingers of her free hand caressed the platinum pin with the sapphire center Daniel had given her for her nineteenth birthday. She had pinned the delicate pin to the bodice of the dress at the last moment. The single piece of jewelry would hold a greater significance for her than the band Daniel had purchased for their marriage. It represented a time when she had become a woman in the fullest sense of the word, the night she had first belonged to Daniel Clinton—totally.

Dropping a kiss on the top of Rebecca's hair, Daniel withdrew his hand. "I'll be waiting for you downstairs." He winked at Cynthia as he walked out of the bedroom, leaving the sisters staring at his broad shouldered back.

Cynthia let out a drawn out sigh. "As the kids can say, the brother is da bomb.'" She smiled at Rebecca, who nodded her agreement.

Rebecca smiled, joy and contentment shining from her luminous eyes. "I can't believe it, Cyn. I can't believe I've waited all of these years to marry Daniel, and it's going to become a reality in less than a quarter of an hour."

Cynthia shifted a professional arched eyebrow. Her dark eyes, glowing like polished onyx in her rich sienna-brown face, matched her hair. Even though she resembled her mother in every physical characteristic she had not inherited her gene for graying prematurely.

"What's happening today should've occurred eight years ago. And before you go off on me I'm going to say it. You should've married Daniel first instead of Michael."

Rebecca's mouth dropped open, and she was too stunned to form a quick comeback. What she wanted to tell her sister was that she couldn't marry Daniel eight years before because he had been a police officer, that he would never marry as long as he was a cop.

"Michael was a good husband."

"I'm not saying he wasn't," Cynthia countered. "I liked him a lot, but what I'm saying is that he wasn't what I'd consider your soul-mate."

"That may be true, but how many women get a second chance to marry their first love? I get to have it all—the first man I'd ever loved and a child from the man I loved enough to marry."

"Am I interrupting?" came a softly modulated feminine voice with a Midwest inflection. Selma Jackson walked into the bedroom, her large eyes sparkling with excitement. Clusters of baby's breath were o the elaborate coils of braided hair she had pinned atop her well-shaped head. "I don't know about either of you, but I'm ready for a wedding." She handed Rebecca a bouquet of white roses, irises, and powder blue larkspur.

"And so should you, baby sister," Cynthia agreed.

Inhaling deeply, Rebecca nodded. "I'm ready. Do you have the ring?" she asked her matron-of-honor. Selma held up her thumb. A heavy gold band encircled the manicured digit. Turning, she headed for the door. "Let's go, ladies."

Cynthia and Selma exchanged a smile, then followed the bride down the staircase to where Daniel waited to make Rebecca his wife.

CHAPTER TEN

Rebecca made her way down the curving staircase and across the highly polished living room floor. Streams of golden sunlight poured in through floor-to-ceiling windows and walls of glass, illuminating her slender form like a spotlight on a nymph.

James McDonald stood in the open doorway, waiting to escort his daughter to the gazebo. A long time McDonald family friend had offered to perform the civil ceremony that would bind Rebecca and Daniel together as husband and wife.

She met her father's bright blue gaze, smiling broadly; she was certain that he registered her trembling as she looped her arm over the sleeve of his dark jacket. His right hand covered hers, squeezing gently.

"Are you ready, baby girl?"

Nodding once, her smile brightened. "Yes, Daddy. I'm ready."

Rebecca and her father waited until Cynthia and Selma raced across the lawn to join the other invited guests, then strolled leisurely toward the gazebo.

A warm breeze momentarily lifted the silk-lined chiffon dress draping her ripening body before the airy fabric was molded once again to her slender frame. Daniel stood in the cool shade of the towering wrought-iron white gazebo, staring at the ethereal vision of the woman seemingly floating toward him. He registered the slight intake of breath from his father. He had invited Albert Clinton to come down to Long Island the day before to meet Rebecca and join them for dinner with the other out-of-town guests he and Rebecca had hosted at a local restaurant, but the elder Clinton had refused. Albert Clinton said he wanted to meet his daughter-in-law for the first time as a bride.

"She's stunning," Albert whispered in awe.

Daniel nodded in agreement, his dark eyes mesmerized by the overt lushness of the woman he would finally claim as his wife. She was still slender, yet she reminded him of an overripe piece of fruit. He wanted to pluck it from the vine and sink his teeth into it, savoring the thick, sweet juice, but couldn't because of his longing to visually savor its beauty, waiting and catching it before it fell to the soft cover of the earth.

Even though she hadn't gained more than two pounds her face had filled out and the dark shadows under her large smokey gray eyes had faded. The brilliant late-spring sun glinted off her glossy auburn hair entwined in a mass of tiny silky curls where they resembled bright new pennies. Everything about her was fresh—as if she were nineteen again—and untouched.

A slight smile played about the corners of his mustached mouth, widening as James escorted her up the stairs to the gazebo. Streamers of ribbons fastened to the elaborate swirls of wrought iron, in Rebecca's hair, and on her bouquet in the wedding colors of white and iris-blue fluttered wildly in the warm air.

James McDonald placed Rebecca's hand in Daniel's. "Take good care of my baby," he said in a hushed whisper.

Daniel's head came up quickly and he stared at the man who was to become his father-in-law. The spoken challenge was issued and he accepted it. "It is my intention to do just that."

James nodded, stepped back, then retreated down the three stairs to stand beside his wife. Linda reached for his hand. Tilting her chin, she noticed that her husband's eyes were swimming with unshed tears. Tightening her grip on his fingers, she moved closer to his side. She had given birth to two children, and without anyone admitting it, she and James each had a favorite. Appealing to her own vanity because of their uncanny resemblance, Cynthia had become hers and Rebecca was James's.

The wedding claimed a fairy tale setting with the gazebo and a large white tent set up shading an oversize table. Each place setting claimed exquisite bone china, delicate crystal stemware and gleaming silver. The color scheme was repeated in the centerpiece of snow-white roses surrounded by irises and larkspur and on the striped cushions on each of the delicate folding chairs. The party planner had retreated to the kitchen with her staff, waiting for the ceremony to conclude before they could begin serving the bride, groom, and their invited guests.

Five-year-old Brenna Franklin stared at Rebecca and wiggled her lace-gloved fingers, unsuccessfully hiding a missing-tooth smile. Her customarily plaited hair was curled and swept up in a soft ponytail surrounded by a profusion of blue ribbons. Her white dress in organdy had a blue silk sash, while her older brother stood at her Aide in a pair of white linen slacks, shirt and a miniature blue bow tie. Both children had bragged incessantly to their friends that were going to be in a wedding, summoning a shouting match where Jarrett was branded a liar. Jarrett made Rebecca promise that she would give him a photograph to show his friends that he wasn't lying.

Judge Peter Hurston squared his shoulders under the jacket of his light gray suit, nodding at the bride and groom. The judge had been James McDonald's protégée before he retired, and Peter had risen quickly to the New York State Court of Appeals, making him the youngest African-American judge in the State's history to sit on that bench.

Daniel's gaze never strayed from Rebecca's delicate profile as he listened to Peter Hurston. He repeated his vows like a man in a trance, hearing his own voice even though he couldn't recognize it. He closed his eyes as Rebecca's low husky voice swept over him when she repeated her vows. He felt as if she was making love to him as she promised to honor him and forsake all others.

The soft haunting sound of her voice faded away like a lingering sigh on a breath of wind. He would love, honor, and cherish her for all of the days of his life.

Peter waited, then said, "Daniel, Rebecca, you may exchange rings."

Opening his eyes, Daniel turned to his father, seeing the stunned expression on the older man's face. He knew his father was reliving his own wedding ceremony. Albert reached into the pocket of his jacket and withdrew a circle of gold and handed it to his son. His hand was shaking uncontrollably, and Daniel reached out and held it firmly until the trembling subsided.

"Thank you, Dad," he whispered.

Turning back to Rebecca he slipped a ring with alternating marquise-shaped diamonds and round sapphires on the third finger of her left hand. She repeated the motion when she took the wide gold band from Selma's thumb and slipped it on his left hand.

Both shifted and stared at Judge Peter Hurston for the first time. It was over. They were married.

"By the power given me by the State of New York, I pronounce you husband and wife. Rebecca, you may kiss your husband. Daniel, your wife."

Not giving Rebecca the opportunity to catch her breath, Daniel swept her up against his body and ravished her mouth. She gasped once, giving him the advantage he needed when his tongue tasted all her mouth had to give him.

"Daniel," she whimpered, her face hot with embarrassment.

Pulling back, he grinned at her. "The judge said that I could kiss you."

Lowering her head, she pressed her nose to his chest. "Not like that," she admonished in a soft tone.

They turned and faced the small crowd who had come to witness their union, smiling. Hand-in-hand they walked down the stairs of the gazebo and were greeted warmly by Daniel's guests.

Standing in the receiving line was Faith and Leroy Robinson, Otis, Derek and Mildred Grady, and Howard Sanders and his wife Thelma.

Rebecca remembered Faith Robinson and her husband when Daniel's office manager had come to Michael's wake;

she was more than familiar with Otis Grady. Otis had risen to the rank of lieutenant in the police department, but he had also been the desk sergeant at the precinct where Michael and Daniel met and were assigned as partners.

Howard Sanders was Daniel's late-mother's uncle. Howard had taken Daniel and his mother in when she left husband and North Carolina. Cocking his head at an angle, Howard smiled at Rebecca. "My Eunice would have loved you. I'm certain she's smiling down on Danny right now."

Rebecca hugged the elderly man before pressing a kiss to his cheek. "I'm sure she knows that I love her *Danny* very much."

"I know you do, child. I can see it in your eyes."

Daniel accepted hugs and handshakes from his father-in-law and the other men present, while listening carefully to the women who cautioned him to take good care of Rebecca.

After receiving their guests, they posed for photographs at the same time a quartet made up of a drummer, guitarist, keyboard player and sax player set up under a smaller tent several feet from the larger one.

Rebecca watched the activity as she stood at Daniel's side, smiling. She posed with pictures with only the two of them, followed by many others with her parents, sister and brother-in-law, and her niece and nephew. It continued with shots of her, Daniel, Albert and Selma.

The photo shoot was interrupted when Daniel insisted that Rebecca stop long enough to nibble on a few crackers and drink some water. He'd noticed the unnatural sheen of moisture on her forehead. The afternoon temperatures had peaked in the mid-seventies, definitely not warm enough for her to feel bothered by the heat; he suspected that she was putting on a brave face when he knew she wanted to retreat to her bedroom where she could lie down.

Appetizers were made of smoked salmon on slices of flour tortillas topped with dill sprigs, chopped fresh chive, sour cream, plain yogurt and golden caviar, a warm chicken liver salad on crackers, endive with créme fraîche and golden caviar; there were stuffed grapes leaves, stuffed mushrooms, large boiled shrimp with a variety of accompanying sauces for dipping, and strips of fried chicken breasts with cumin cream served to the guests while the photo session ensued.

A smiling bartender concocted exotic drinks from Campari and soda to a hibiscus cooler. There were non-alcoholic beverages for nineteen-year-old Derek Grady and Jarrett and Brenna Franklin.

Rebecca did retreat to her bedroom to repair her make-up. She took a quick at her reflection in the mirror on the triple dresser, noting that her eyes appeared unusually large. She looked different, much different than she did after she'd married Michael. She *was* different because she was now thirty-six, not twenty-eight; she had been a widow and pregnant, but after exchanging vows Daniel Clinton had changed all of that. She was now Rebecca Clinton, wife and mother-to-be.

Her gaze fell on the card on the dresser, eliciting a smile. Mother's Day had passed and Daniel had taken her out to dinner where he'd given her a sheer silk dressing gown with a card honoring her as a mother-to-be. He accepted her passionate kiss, saying that he would be more than willing to have her model the gown for him later that evening. She did not model the revealing midnight-blue garment, but promised him she would wear it after the baby was born. Her statement reminded him of his promise he would not make love to her until she had given birth.

She did not know why, but his promise not to sleep with her saddened her because she craved him with a passion that she had never felt before—not with him nor with Michael. There were times when she feared that she would blurt out how much she wanted and needed him.

Dusting a light layer of loose powder over her nose and forehead, she saw Daniel's reflection in the mirror. He leaned against the door, hands in his trouser pockets, watching her. He reminded her of a large cat waiting for the heat of the day to subside so he could hunt.

Putting down the sable brush, she turned and stared back at him. He straightened, but did not push off the door. He was waiting, waiting for her to come to him. She did not disappoint him as she crossed the length of her bedroom and stood in front of him. He removed his hands from his pockets and curved his long fingers around her bare upper arms. A slight smile curled his lip.

"What are you smirking about?" she asked softly.

His grip tightened as he pulled her up close to his chest. His half-hooded lids lifted until she saw into the depths of his eyes, drowning in the fathomless dark pools.

"I'm quite pleased with myself, Rebecca Clinton."

"Why would you say that, Daniel Clinton?"

"Because I just married the woman I've always wanted for my wife."

She stared up at him from under her lashes. "Good things come to those who wait."

"Amen," he murmured seconds before he took her mouth in a soul searching, passionate kiss.

"Daniel," she moaned. "I just made up my face."

"What do you think our guests would say if we disappeared for an hour?" he mumbled against her moist lips.

"Doing what?"

"Crawling into bed together."

She went still and he released her. Why was he giving her double messages? He said he wouldn't make love to her until after the baby came. Did he plan to renege on his promise?

Moving back and away from him, she shook her head. "No. We can't." She would not allow him to send her on an emotional roller coaster.

Daniel felt as if something or someone had kicked him in his stomach. He had hoped beyond hope that Rebecca would change her mind about sharing a bed with him. He hadn't pressed her, but he wanted her. As her intended her needed her, but now as her husband he wanted her.

He had to continually remind himself that the child in her womb wasn't his, and that he would not dishonor the fruit of Michael's seed.

Forcing a smile, he said, "Of course we can't. I don't know about you, but I'm starved. Let's go down and eat." offering his arm, she took it and together they descended the stairs to join the people who had come to witness their union.

The afternoon wore on and the celebration continued. The elegant appetizers were followed by a sit-down menu of radicchio and artichoke hearts with a raspberry vinaigrette dressing, apple vichyssoise, baked brie with walnuts and apples, cranberry bread with whipped butter, filet mignon, thyme-marinated roast pork, roast turkey, wild rice, grilled portobello mushrooms, and sautéed spinach. Dessert was a two-tiered wedding cake, one tier filled with chocolate cranberry torte and the other fresh coconut with a raspberry puree. The smiling bartender topped off everyone's beverage as soon as the glasses were half-empty, prompting most of them to place their hands over their glasses when he ventured near their place settings.

Jarrett exclaimed loudly that he liked everything, but the soup was too cold. Cynthia leaned over and informed him quietly that vichyssoise is always served cold. He glanced at his father, his mouth forming a perfectly rounded 0 before he clamped a hand over it.

The band members, who had taken time out to eat, took their positions and began playing softly. Daniel rose to his feet, smiling down at Rebecca. He held out his hand and she took it as he pulled her up.

Leading her out of the tent, he swung her around until she was pressed against his chest. "Our first dance as Mr. and Mrs. Clinton," he whispered, smiling down at her upturned face.

It took Rebecca only a moment to recognize the song the band was playing. It was the classic Robert Flack and

Donnie Hathaway "The Closer I Get To You." Closing her eyes, she listened to Daniel singing the words softly in her ear. The rich timbre of his baritone voice seemed to come from his soul.

Pulling back she stared up at him, feeling what he was feeling, knowing that he loved her as much as she loved him. And at that moment she wished that her marriage could be a normal one, that she would go upstairs to her bedroom after everyone left and take off her clothes and bare her body to her husband. She wanted so much to give him the love swelling in heart. Her eyes filled with tears and she could not stop them as they overflowed and stained her cheeks.

Daniel felt her quaking as she struggled for control. "Becky," he crooned softly, withdrawing a handkerchief from his breast pocket and blotting her tears. "What's the matter, Love?"

Touching her face with her fingertips, she smiled through her tears. "You know that I cry when I'm happy."

He arched a questioning eyebrow. He did not believe her, but decided not to press her. It wasn't as if they were alone. Tightening his grip around her waist, he picked her up and swung her around until she begged him to stop. Both were laughing as the sky swirled above them in a dizzying kaleidoscope of blue and white puffy clouds.

Albert Clinton claimed the next dance, and Rebecca found herself in the arms of the man who was now her father-in-law. Albert was only fifty-nine. He appeared older than her own father who had recently celebrated his sixty-fourth birthday. Gripping his shoulder, she felt bone where she should have felt solid bulk. "When are you going to come down and spend some time with us, Dad?"

"I'm going to give you and Danny a chance to get used to being married before I start visiting."

Rebecca stared at the neatly barbered gray hair and the dark eyebrows over a pair of soft brown eyes. "Don't make me drive up to get you," she teased. "I want you to come before the summer is over."

"I'll come. But you must promise me that you'll come up with my son when you have a free weekend. Danny's told me about the baby, so if there are times when you're not feeling well I'll understand."

She nodded, glancing away. Daniel did not tell her that he'd told his father that she was pregnant. She wondered if he'd told Albert that the baby wasn't his, but her late-husband's. Albert swung her around in a smooth two-step. "I screwed up big time as a father. I'm just hoping that I'll make a better grandfather."

"I'm sure you'll be wonderful."

"What I can't understand," Albert continued as if she hadn't spoken, "is that Danny never condemned me. I pissed away so many good years of my life and he never said anything to me about leaving him and his mother. All he had to do was look at me and the guilt ate me up whole. There's one thing I'm certain of, and that is that my son will be a much better husband and father than his old man was."

James McDonald tapped Albert Clinton on the shoulder, ending the confession. Albert leaned down and kissed Rebecca's cheek before relinquishing her to her father. She snuggled against her father while smiling at Daniel who was now dancing with her mother. The band changed to an upbeat tempo and everyone was up and dancing with Peter Hurston sharing Selma with Derek Grady.

Rebecca noted that never-married Peter Hurston's gaze had followed Selma constantly, and there was a time when she saw the two standing under the sweeping branches of the weeping willow tree, engaged in an animated conversation.

There was a running joke at the school that if Selma Jackson had to choose between an angel and the devil she would select the devil. Rebecca always told her that she was too giving, too nice, and that the men she attracted always took advantage of her kindness.

After awhile Rebecca found herself in her husband's arms once again. He tightened his grip on her waist and she pressed her breasts to his hard chest. The pressure of her sensitive nipples against his body elicited a soft gasp of pleasure. She was certain Daniel heard her, but he did not miss a step.

"Tired, Love?"

"A little," she confessed.

Both had been up at dawn, and it was nearing five o'clock in the afternoon. She hadn't wanted to leave her guests, but she needed to lie down. Her lids were drooping and she doubted whether she could stay awake another hour.

"What do you say I chase everyone out of here?" he suggested.

"Daniel, no. They're having a good time."

"Then why don't you go upstairs and lie down for an hour. Everyone will understand."

She wanted to protest, but didn't. "Come and get me in half an hour."

"Better yet. I'll take you up and tuck you in."

Linda hurried over as she saw Daniel leading Rebecca toward the house. "Are you all right?" she asked her daughter.

"I'm fine, Mom. I'm just going to get off my feet for a while."

Linda's dark gaze swept from her daughter to Daniel. He nodded, and she turned and retraced her steps.

Minutes later Rebecca stood in the middle of her bedroom and presented Daniel with her back. "You're going to have to unbutton me."

Slowly and methodically he unbuttoned the many covered buttons on the delicate dress until the bodice fell away from her upper body. Rebecca turned and faced him, stepping out of the dress as he leaned down and swept it from the floor. Holding the dress in one fist, he reached out and deftly removed the straps from a matching slip, it too sliding down and pooling around her feet.

Heart pumping wildly in his chest, Daniel stared at the swell of her breasts rising above the lacy cups of her bra. He felt a sudden heaviness in his groin, but there was nothing he could do to prevent it; the swelling began as a slow arousal before becoming a surging ache. He wanted her! The woman standing before him was his wife, and he wanted to make love to her and couldn't.

Rebecca stepped out of her slip and handed it to Daniel. Her pantyhose followed, then she reached around her back and unhooked her bra; his eyes widened noticeably when he viewed her bared swelling breasts for the first time.

They rested above her narrow rib cage like ripened fruit, waiting to be picked. Swallowing painfully, he wondered how was he going to make it to November without breaking his promise not to make love to her.

Gritting his teeth, he closed his eyes, hoping to shut out the vision of her standing half-nude in front of him. "Get into bed, Rebecca!"

Resting both hands on her hips, Rebecca frowned at him. "Excuse me."

He opened his eyes, realizing he'd raised his voice. "I'm sorry. I didn't mean for it to come out like that. Get into bed, so I can tuck you in."

Turning, she made her way to the large bed. She pulled back the antique quilt that had belonged to her great-grandmother and slipped under the cool, crisp sheet.

Daniel laid her dress, slip and underwear on a chair before making his way over to the bed. He sat down on the side, hoping that Rebecca hadn't noticed his aroused state. Leaning over, he kissed her cheek. "I'll come and get you in half an hour."

She reached up and wound her arms around his neck, bringing him closer. "I love you, Daniel Albert Clinton." Her tongue outlined his lower lip, then swept over the thick silky brush of his mustache. She had come to enjoy the hair on his upper lip as much as the hair on his broad chest.

Inhaling deeply, she breathed in the scent of his haunting cologne.

Daniel pulled her arms from his neck, kissing her fingers. "Sleep, Love." She turned away from him, closing her eyes and falling into a deep slumber minutes after he'd walked out of the bedroom, closing the door behind him.

It had been a long time since he'd prayed, but he prayed now that he would make it through the next seven months without losing his control *and* his sanity.

CHAPTER ELEVEN

Daniel returned to the bedroom to check on Rebecca after an hour, and found her sleeping soundly. Standing at the bedside and staring down at her, he decided not to wake her. He would offer his regrets to their guests, explaining that his wife was exhausted. He knew instinctively that she would be angry with him for letting her sleep, but he was willing to face her wrath for the sake of her health.

In his spare time he had read everything he could get his hands on about pregnancy and childbirth. He still had reservations about Rebecca opening her own business while pregnant. It wasn't that he was opposed to her running her own business enterprise, he just preferred she begin after the baby was born. But then he thought of what she'd had said about not having anything to do when she wasn't teaching. If she had held a traditional nine-to-five, year-around position, then she would not have that dilemma. She only had another three weeks before the school term ended and there would be another five months before she would expect to deliver.

He'd promised to help her, and he would, supporting her throughout her successes and failures. He had taken a vow to love, honor, and protect her, and he would willing-ly forfeit up his own life to accomplish all of the three.

Rebecca woke up, totally disoriented, and for a moment she did not know where she was or what time it was. Raising her arms above her head, she stretched languidly while inhaling and exhaling deeply. Her nose detected the faint scent of a familiar man's cologne, and she knew she was not alone in the bedroom. Rolling to her left, she saw the reclining figure of Daniel on an armchair, his bare feet resting on a footstool in the darkened room.

"Is it good morning, afternoon, or evening?" Her husky voice floated across the space like a lingering fog.

"It's good morning. Very early good morning." Daniel's baritone voice rumbled deep in his chest as he lowered his feet, then pushed off the chair.

An erotic smile softened his mouth. He had continued the habit from years before of getting up before Rebecca, shaving and showering, then returning to the bedroom to watch her sleep. She had always reminded him of a tan and orange marmalade cat with smoky gray eyes stretching sensuously. He found it hard to believe that he had met her a month before his twenty-fourth birthday, and had waited sixteen years before he could claim her as his wife.

There had been times when he cursed himself for letting her go, for not marrying her sooner. Then there were the times when he realized he wasn't that much different than his father. Albert had run from his responsibility of being husband and father, while he had balked at becoming a husband. He had set up roadblocks in the attempt to find happiness with Rebecca, while a higher power deemed that he would not die in the line of duty. He had wasted sixteen precious years not claiming the woman he loved because of a feeble excuse that he did not want to leave her a widow with children. He had been injured, yet those injuries had not resulted in death. He had been given a second chance at life and with Rebecca, and she could have been with him through all of the changes in his life.

Sitting down on the side of the king-sized bed, he leaned over and brushed a light kiss over her soft mouth. "Good morning, Mrs. Clinton."

Clutching the sheet to her chest, Rebecca wound a slender arm around his strong neck and buried her face against his warm throat. "Good morning, Mr. Clinton. I thought you were suppose to wake me up in an hour."

"I wanted to, but your mother said that you needed your sleep. I came to look in on you after an hour and I agreed with her. You were snoring."

"I don't snore and you know it."

"You did last night."

She snuggled closer, pressing her breasts to his chest. It was unnatural that they had not shared a bed, that they woke up in separate bedrooms. "I'm sorry, Daniel."

Pulling back, he tried making out her delicate features in the diffused light coming in through the floor-to-ceiling vertical blinds. "For what?"

"For cheating you out of a wedding night."

His shook his head, a smile curving and lifting his upper lip. "Don't even go there, Love. You've given me many wedding nights, nights I'll never forget."

"But last night should've been different."

"How different? Our standing in front of a judge and repeating words doesn't change what we are, or our love for each other. Even though I could never admit it to myself, but the night of your nineteenth birthday I was joined with you. Joined in my heart, body, and my spirit. It was the first time I could openly admit what I'd been feeling since I first saw you. That I'd fallen in love with you." Closing his eyes, he drew in a deep breath. "And it is only now that I can admit that I never stopped loving you even though you had married another man. I did not want to openly acknowledge that I lusted for you, but I know I did. Michael claimed what I had rejected."

Rebecca felt a shiver of apprehension race up her spine. What she had one time imagined had just manifested itself. There were times when she was with Michael and she saw Daniel staring at her with the same expression he'd worn once they began sleeping together. Without saying a word, his eyes had betrayed his lust for her. And it had shocked her, because she was married. And she'd been frightened because she'd wanted him, too. She wanted the passion that Michael did not want, or was unable to give her.

Now, for the first time she could admit that she'd slept with Michael sometime fantasizing that her husband was Daniel. And that Michael was always taken aback by her insatiable lust. Afterwards she always prayed for forgiveness. In her heart she had committed adultery over and over, but maybe now she had redeemed herself, for the man she'd lusted for had become her husband before man and God.

"Michael's gone, Daniel, and we are here. We are now husband and wife. I don't think we'll ever forget Michael, but I can't allow the fact that I was once married to him come between us. And when I lie with you I don't want

Michael in the bed with us." *Not the way you were in the bed whenever I slept with Michael,* she continued to herself.

"You're right, Becky." He did not want to compete with her late husband. Not in or out of bed. "We only have three days for our honeymoon. What do you want to do?"

"I want to stay close to home."

Daniel nodded, smiling. He, too, wanted to stay home. "I'll set up the grill and we'll have a picnic brunch in the gazebo." He combed his long fingers through her curling hair. "After we eat breakfast, how would you like to go shopping? After all it is the Memorial Day weekend."

"What do you want to buy?"

"I want to go to a nursery and order a few things for the outside of the house and some potted trees for indoors. I'd also like to put in a flower garden."

Rebecca ignored the hunger pangs rumbling in her stomach. "Are you going to do the gardening yourself?"

"Yes, Love."

"That's going to be a back-breaking job. Where are you going to find the time to do all of the work?"

Daniel dropped a kiss on the top of her head. "The inside of the house is your domain, Rebecca Clinton, and the outside is mine. Don't worry yourself about my finding time, Love. Instead of lounging around watching television I'll work in the garden. If you feel up to it, I could always use an assistant," he teased.

"I don't work well in dirt."

Daniel had relinquished complete control when it came to the interior of the large house. She had decided which rooms the furniture belonging to Eunice Clinton would

grace, and she had also made a list of what other furnishings would be needed to complete decorating the house.

The butter-soft burnt orange leather sofa and love seat,
the armoire with his electronic components, and tables that
had once graced Daniel's living room were now in what
they referred to as the family room. His gleaming rosewood
dining room table and six chairs claimed a space in the
kitchen's breakfast nook.

A massive octagonal mahogany dining table with eight
matching chairs upholstered with burgundy and dark-green
striped silk seat cushions sat magnificently in the dining
room. Rebecca was once again awed by the exquisite crafts-
manship of the carvings on the doors of the china closet
and buffet server after the movers had positioned all of the
pieces according to her floor plan. Albert Clinton was to
furniture making what Michelangelo was to sculpture.

She and Daniel agreed to carpet all of the bedrooms, as
well as the family room and the large space they decided to
set up as their office-in-the home. They talked at length
about the parquet floors in the living and dining rooms,
then decided to purchase Persian rugs that would cover the
floor while not detracting from the elaborately herringbone
patterned wood.

The bed and matching furnishings from Daniel's New
Rochelle bedroom were now in the master bedroom, and
the bedroom furnishings belonging to Albert and Eunice
sat in the larger of the three remaining bedrooms. She slept
in Daniel's bed, while he claimed the one belonging to his
parents. They'd decided to put up floor- -to-ceiling fabric
vertical blinds in a cool sand-beige in all of the bedrooms

for absolute privacy, leaving the other windows bare. She had suggested utilizing towering potted plants instead of window dressings, which would play off the outside light and landscape. What they hadn't decided on was living room furnishings. She wanted modular pieces in a pale silk and chenille fabric, but hadn't had the time to order them. One of the features she loved most about the house were the tiny recessed lights in each room, all of which could be dimmed with a touch of switch.

"How would you like breakfast in bed?"

Pressing her nose to his sweet-smelling laundered T-shirt, Rebecca nodded. "Only if you'll join me."

"You've got yourself a deal."

Pulling away from him, she smiled. "Do I have time to shower?"

"I'll allot you fifteen minutes and no more. I don't want you fainting on me."

"Aye, aye, sir," she sputtered, saluting him smartly with her free hand. He kissed her cheek, then stood up and walked out of the bedroom. It was only then that she dropped the sheet covering her bare breasts and left the bed for the adjoining bath.

She was washed and dressed in a T-shirt and pair of shorts when Daniel reentered the bedroom carrying a wicker bed tray. The mouth-watering smell of freshly baked orange and cranberry muffins wafted throughout the space.

"Get into bed," Daniel ordered with a wide grin. "I have to go back downstairs to get my tray."

Settling herself on the bed, Rebecca stared at the tray Daniel had positioned across her lap. It contained a plate filled with steaming grits covered with fluffy scrambled eggs and sliced grilled beef sausage. Her vitamin supplements were placed in a tiny paper cup. The large tray also held a glass of orange juice, milk and a small dish with a large muffin filled with spicy cranberries and tart orange zest. He'd remembered. He knew she loved his orange-cranberry muffins.

"Thank you, darling." Her voice was filled with heavy emotion.

"You're quite welcome, darling," he returned, noting the appreciation shining from her gaze. "Start without me."

She wanted to wait for him, but couldn't. It was now six-thirty in the morning and more than twelve hours since she had put anything in her stomach, and she recognized the lightheaded feeling that she had come to detest as much as the nausea, which usually occurred without warning. Her doctor insisted that the nausea would subside and probably disappear completely by the time she began her second trimester. What she wanted was for it to go away—*now*!

Daniel joined her on the bed, his denim-covered leg pressing against her bare one. His tray held everything hers did with the exception of the vitamins and milk. He had elected to have coffee instead of milk.

She swallowed a mouthful of grits and eggs. "That smells good."

He arched an eyebrow at her. "What?"

"Your coffee."

He nodded. "It tastes good."

"Can I have a sip?"

"Nope. No coffee for you."

"Why not?"

"The caffeine will give you a rush of energy only to be followed by a low period. You don't need to add to your mood swings."

Her jaw dropped and she sputtered but couldn't get the words out. "Mood swings? Caffeine rush? How dare you, Daniel Clinton, fix your mouth to…"

"I don't intend to discuss it, Becky. No coffee for you."

"What would you know about a caffeine rush? You hardly ever drink coffee."

"That may be true, but I read that caffeine is not good for a pregnant woman."

She gave him a knowing sidelong glance. "Oh, I see. You've been reading."

He picked up a forkful of eggs and grits, nodding. "Pretty interesting stuff, if I have to say so myself. I've memorized exactly how much dairy, protein, vegetables, fruits and complex carbohydrates you'll need on a daily basis." He put the fork in his mouth, chewing slowly and watching her expressive face. "I also know that you're going to have to undergo a few tests in another month to screen for birth defects and genetic disorders. I let you talk me out of going to the doctor with you this month, but don't even think about trying that again. I'm your husband now and that changes a lot of things.

What he did not say was that he was nothing like his father. He would be with her from the beginning to the very end. He loved her and he was certain he would love the child in her womb.

Rebecca stared at him, her eyes narrowing. "Why are you trying to bully me?"

Shifting, Daniel placed his tray on a bedside table and turned to her. "I'm not bullying you, Becky. Why is it so difficult for you to let me take care of you? I love you, and all I want to do is protect you. And I can't do that if you push me away."

"I'm not pushing you away. I just don't want you to think that I'm helpless, darling. I'm not going to fall apart if you're not there to hold me together."

"I don't think of you as helpless." Their gazes met, the desire shining from his dark eyes. "Why can't you indulge me?" he crooned. "Let me spoil you, my darling. Only until the baby comes."

What she needed to do was fight her overwhelming response to him, her need to be close to him. And how could she do that if he would not permit her any space? What she did not want to do was beg him to break his promise that he would not make love to her until after delivered. She did not want Daniel wallowing in guilt because of *her* insatiable carnality. It was ironic that she constantly craved a man she'd married who had promised not to consummate their marriage.

"If you feel me smothering you, then let me know," Daniel offered as alternative.

She felt like a witch. She was punishing him when he only wanted what was best for her. He deserved better. She couldn't continue to hurt him. "Okay, Daniel. You can spoil me." Her eyes were shimmering with moisture as she leaned over and pressed a light kiss at the corner of his mouth.

Splaying a hand along her cheek, he held her jaw and deepened the kiss. Both of them were breathing heavily when Daniel finally released her and reached for his tray.

"Can the spoiling go both ways?" she asked softly.

"Of course," he said, smiling.

"Good," she replied smugly.

Rebecca and Daniel made it through their first day of marriage smoothly. He drove to a nursery that was situated over a full square block, and they spent more than two hours selecting potted trees and plants for the interiors, flats, flowering bushes for the exteriors, and a massive stone fountain that allowed flowing water to spill over from three levels. Daniel had decided he wanted all of flowering plants and bushes in varying shades of white and off-white.

She was fascinated by his knowledge of differing flowers and trees. She'd known of his interest in cooking, jazz, computers, and the martial arts, but hadn't been aware of this other hobby.

She had known Daniel Clinton for eighteen years, but truly did not know him at all. She had fallen in love with him, slept with him yet he was still a stranger to her.

Daniel paid for his purchases, then set up a time for everything to be delivered to the house. They returned home and he busied himself setting up a gas grill while Rebecca sat on the carpeted floor of the family room opening their wedding gifts.

Streams of bright sunlight pouring through the sliding French doors and glinting off the pale-yellow carpet and orange furniture gave the pale walls an orange-gold look. Rebecca had come to love this room, and from the first it had become the one which appeared most lived in.

The comfortable leather sofa and love seat, the heavy, dark tables and the massive mahogany armoire that concealed the large-screen television, stereo components and Daniel's extensive collection of long-playing vinyl records, cassettes and CDs was the focal point of the space. They had yet to unpack boxes of books stored in a corner of the three-car garage because they hadn't decided whether to buy bookcases or have them built into the walls.

Their wedding invitation had specifically read "no gifts please" yet all of their guests had ignored the disclaimer. Her parents had given them an exquisite fruit bowl in her favorite Waterford design. Cynthia and William Franklin's gift was a set of sterling silver frames in three different sizes. She smiled at her sister's handwritten note: *For your wedding picture, for the baby's picture, and for a family picture.*

Otis and Mildred Grady had given them a check, while their son Grady had penned a separate note to Daniel thanking him for believing in him. She had noticed the subtle affection between her husband and the teenage boy in his employ. It was evident that Grady was in awe of his boss, while Daniel's treatment of Grady was more like an older brother than an employer.

Daniel's aunt and uncle's gift was the deed to an ancestral home situated on Hatteras Island, North Carolina. Howard and his wife had never had any children and had come to regard Danny as their own. She placed the deed on the table with the other gifts, wondering how Daniel would react to the bequest from his elderly relatives.

Slipping the letter opener under the flap of another envelope, Rebecca saw Faith Robinson's handwriting. She'd liked Daniel's office manager from their first meeting at a Clinton Securities Christmas party. Faith and her husband had come to Michael's wake, and she had appreciated the other woman's sincerity and words of comfort. And there was no doubt about her loyalty to Daniel. The Robinsons had given them a gift certificate from Tiffany. Faith had written on an accompanying card: *"A little something for the bride, a little something for the groom, and a little something, something for the house."*

Selma's envelope contained a gift certificate to a store that catered to infant and children's clothes. Selma was one of two other teachers who knew she was pregnant.

Picking up the last envelope, she tapped it against her open palm. It was from Albert Clinton. She thought about waiting for Daniel before she opened it, but changed her mind. Sliding the letter opener under the flap of the envelope, she withdrew a square of parchment. Her gaze raced quickly over the bold script. *To Grandbaby Clinton: When you sleep in your bed, sit on your chair, or put your toys away in your chest, please remember me. Love, Grandpa.*

Clapping a hand over her mouth, Rebecca could not stop the tears from welling up in her eyes and overflowing. Pressing her head against the cushion of the sofa, she cried until she was spent.

Daniel walked into the family room and saw his wife sitting on the floor, her face streaked with tears, and it hit him that he would never get used to seeing her cry.

Dropping to the floor beside her, he pulled her across his lap and buried his face in her hair. "What's the matter, Love?"

Rebecca sniffled and pressed her nose to the solid hardness of his shoulder. "Read this." She handed Daniel his father's missive.

He read it once, twice, three times. Nodding, he closed his eyes and rocked Rebecca back and forth as a new wave of tears flowed. *Remember me.* Albert Clinton had acknowledged his own mortality. It was something Daniel refused to do—not now. Not when he had just begun to live out his greatest yearning.

He was forty, married for the first time, and looking forward to raising a child. He would not think of leaving Rebecca or his children.

"My Dad's probably getting up before the sun comes to begin working on his grandchild's pieces. I suppose this project will be worth his while.'"

"He just seemed so sad, Daniel."

"My Dad is healing, Becky. Give him time and you'll see the man my mother fell in love with. He happens to have a wicked sense of humor."

She waved a hand toward the table. "They brought gifts anyway."

"Did you really expect them not to?"

Sighing, she shook her head. "I suppose not."

Tilting her head at an angle, she stared up at Daniel. His masculinity was so overwhelming that she found it hard to breathe normally. His gray-flecked hair, dark penetrating eyes, sensual mouth, and his large hard body screamed boldly and silently at her own femininity. Didn't he know that she wanted him? Wanted him inside her? Wanted them joined as one in the most intimate way?

Dropping her gaze, she rested her cheek against his chest, counting the strong steady beats of his heart. Her arms curved around his neck as she melted against his strong body. She never knew when her eyes closed that she would fall asleep in her husband's embrace.

CHAPTER TWELVE

The Clintons settled into a comfortable routine befitting a married couple with the exception of not sharing a bed.

Daniel got up early every morning, and instead of jogging at the track at the New Rochelle High School he jogged along the stretch of beach bordering Long Island Sound.

By the time he returned to the house to shower and dress for the day Rebecca was up fixing breakfast. They ate in silence, watching the morning news on CNN. Daniel usually put away the remains of breakfast, rinsing dishes and stacking them in the dishwasher while Rebecca saw to preparing herself for classes. At exactly seven-fifteen they walked to their respective cars and bade each other goodbye, with a parting, "Have a wonderful day."

The longer ride to work gave Rebecca the time she needed to assess her marriage. There was no doubt that she loved Daniel and he her, but something unknown communicated that they could not continue to reside under the same roof while sleeping apart. She felt like a woman estranged from a husband who refused to vacate the premises.

Daniel was considerate and sensitive to her needs. He overindulged her to the point of making her want to scream for him to stop. She returned the favor whenever she baked homemade bread or picked up the latest CD of a jazz artist he liked.

When not preparing lesson plans, she spent her spare time pouring over catalogues of companies who sold yarn and needlecraft supplies. She needed to order enough inventory to stock her shop before her post-Labor Day grand opening.

She had been married exactly ten days when she reminded Daniel of his promise to attend her school Career Week Fair that morning. He groaned aloud, called Faith to tell her that he would be in late, then retreated to his bedroom to change out of the khaki Dockers and brown and white checkered shirt and into a pair of black slacks with a matching single-breasted jacket and an off-white banded collar silk shirt. He exchanged his brown loafers and socks for black imported slip-ons and socks.

Rebecca's eyes widened when he reentered the kitchen. Her smile mirrored her appreciation. "Very nice, darling."

"Too nice for the little predators."

Picking up her leather handbag and shopping bag tote, she wound her arm through his. "They are going to love you."

"Yeah, yeah," he intoned as he led her out of the house and to his car parked in the driveway. Waiting until she was seated and belted in, he closed the door and circled the shiny black sports car.

Whenever he got up to jog he pulled his car out of the garage, allowing Rebecca more maneuvering room when she backed her Honda out of the three-car garage.

Pressing a button on the dashboard of the Porsche, he remotely activated the electronic alarm system. Two days after he'd closed on Wind Watch he had had it wired with a sensitive system he could activate and deactivate with a manual remote. If anyone attempted to enter the premises without deactivating the circuits a signal went directly to the alarm company, who in turn contacted the police department. There was little or no traffic along the private roads, but burglars did not discriminate with regard to neighborhood or the economic status of the inhabitants.

Installing the alarm system had put his mind at ease whenever he came home late on Wednesday evenings, because he did not like the fact that Rebecca was alone in the large house with their nearest neighbor more than half an acre away. There would be another three classes of judo instruction before the term ended, then he would be able come home at the same time every night.

"I'm going to have to go shopping for clothes," Rebecca announced after Daniel accelerated onto the parkway.

He gave her a quick glance. "You don't look as if you've put on anymore weight."

Slipping on a pair of sunglasses, she turned her head toward the open window, letting the warm breeze sweep over her face. "My waist is getting bigger. Things I used to wear are now too tight."

"I'll pick you up at three and we'll go shopping."

Staring at him behind the dark lenses, she smiled. "Thank you."

Daniel smiled, concentrating on the taillights of the car in front of his. "You're welcome." Traffic slowed, then stopped completely. Raising the windows, he flipped the switch for the air-conditioning, then waited for traffic to move again.

Taking a furtive glance at Rebecca, he noted the subtle changes. Her face was fuller and tanned to a healthy-looking golden palomino-brown. The hot sun had lightened her hair until it appeared a red-gold, while bringing out a profusion of freckles across her short straight nose and high cheekbones. Her hair had grown rapidity, and heavy curls framed her oval face and touched her. shoulders. He found it hard to believe that she was thirty-six. She could easily pass for twenty-five.

Removing his hand from the gearshift, he laid his right hand over her left, his thumb caressing the diamond and sapphire ring on her third finger.

Closing her eyes, Rebecca breathed heavily through parted lips. *Daniel,* she groaned inwardly. *Don't!* Didn't he know what he was doing to her? Every time he touched her she dissolved into a heated mass of throbbing desire. A heated tremor swept down her chest and settled between her thighs.

Opening her eyes, she stared at him staring back at her, and before she could react he removed her sunglasses. His dark gaze swept over her face like a flash of lightning; he leaned over and fastened his mouth to hers, the fire between her thighs reversing direction and sweeping up to her mouth as her right arm curved around his neck, holding him fast.

Daniel moaned, struggling for a more comfortable position as his tongue slipped into her mouth. He had spent the past week tiptoeing around Rebecca in fear of breaking his vow that he would not make love to her. They shared breakfast, dinner and an hour or two watching television or listening to music before they went to bed. Most times Rebecca went to her sitting room after dinner, preferring to work on her lesson plans while reclining on the comfortable armchair with a matching foot stool.

When the weather wasn't too hot, they sometimes went for a walk along the beach. They'd walked side-by-side, not touching or speaking. Neither wanted to invade the other's privacy.

Sitting in the car with her was the closest he'd been since the weekend of their wedding. Knowing she sat less than two feet away and inhaling the sensual haunting fragrance on her warm body was his undoing.

What he wanted to do was unbutton every button on her blouse and bare her breasts where he'd visually feast on her ripening flesh. The urge to fasten his mouth to her breasts and taste her until she pleaded for him stop nearly drove him insane. He heard a cacophony of honking and pulled away. The car in front of his had sped off and he was holding up a lane of traffic.

Shifting quickly, he let out the clutch and the car shot forward. Biting down on his lower lip, he tasted the sweetness of Rebecca's mouth for a second time while she stared out the windshield, stunned.

She replaced her sunglasses and pretended interest in the drivers of the cars in the next lane. If she had glanced over at Daniel she would have recognized his expression of supreme satisfaction. An expression that faded the moment he drove into the faculty parking lot at the middle school.

Daniel stopped at the central office and secured his Visitor's pass, while Rebecca signed in. He was led to the auditorium by a six grade girl who gave him a "you don't look like much" once over.

Sitting at the back of the large room, he observed scores of ten and eleven year-olds racing up and down the aisles, calling out to one another while the public address system blared a message he couldn't understand. Minutes later the auditorium filled up with teachers leading their classes down the aisles. Several boys threw wads of rolled up paper at one girl, who displayed her maturity when she refused to acknowledge their antics.

Will my son or daughter act out like this? he wondered, shaking his head. The thought was barely out of his head when he felt the warmth of a body and a familiar fragrance.

Rebecca stood over him, smiling. "Mr. Clinton, you're supposed to sit down front," she said softly.

Rising to his feet, he stared down at her. She had brushed her hair and secured it up in a twist. The hairstyle, along with her tailored suit and conservative blouse transformed her appearance, and for the first time he saw her as the teacher she was trained to be.

He made his way to the first row and sat down beside another man who was busy studying a stack of index cards. There was no doubt that he was uneasy as evidenced by his continual tapping of the cards against an open palm.

Daniel watched the stage as two boys and two girls took their places behind a table. Several microphones sat on the table in front of the students. A sofa was positioned a few feet from the table, with two more standing mikes.

Inquisition. He didn't know why, but the word came to mind when he recalled his last appearance when he sat on another sofa on the very stage.

It was another five minutes before the auditorium was filled to capacity. There was occasional hushing by the various teachers standing and sitting around the large space.

The lights dimmed and a spotlight shone on Rebecca as she climbed the stairs to the stage. Daniel hadn't realized he was holding his breath as she adjusted the microphone to her suit her height.

"Good morning and welcome to Seaport Middle School's Career Week Fair." Her husky voice carried easily throughout the auditorium. He missed her opening statement as he stared at the slender figure in red and white highlighted in a flattering gold from an overhead spotlight.

"We're very fortunate to have two people who have taken time from their busy schedules to enlighten us about the advantages of owning their own businesses.

"I'd like to call to the stage someone whom I've known for a long time." Her gray eyes locked with his dark brown ones. "Mr. Daniel Clinton."

Rising slowly to his feet, Daniel made his way to the stage amid a spattering of applause. He took the hand Rebecca extended, shaking it gently. She led him over to the sofa and he sat down.

Rebecca retraced her steps and introduced the next guest. Keith Valdes-Martinez stood up and made his way up the stage and sat down beside Daniel.

Daniel smiled at the man. "Piece of cake," he whispered, hoping to put him at ease.

"Your kid out there?" Keith Martinez asked between clenched teeth. Daniel shook his head, but wanted to say that his wife was. "I've got two out there who begged me not to mess up in front of their friends."

"You'll do okay," he countered, praying for his own confidence. The last time he'd appeared on this very stage the middle school students had made mince meat out of him.

"Justin, you may begin," Rebecca announced. She walked off the stage, taking a seat in the front row. She stared at Daniel, giving him a wink and a thumbs-up sign.

Justin Gilmore's orange-red spiked hair, freckled face, and gold hoop and stud earrings in his left ear were a deceptive foil for a brilliant young mind. Clearing his voice, Justin said softly, "We'll begin our questioning with Mr. Clinton. What made you decide to start your own business?"

Leaning forward, Daniel pulled the microphone closer to where he sat. "Necessity. I was out of a job."

"I take that to mean that you were discharged from a prior employer."

Wise-ass kid is starting in already, Daniel fumed inwardly. "No, I was not discharged from a prior employer. I voluntarily retired from law enforcement because of an injury I had sustained in the line of duty."

"In other words, you were shot," stated a petite girl with a beautiful brown face framed by a cascade of braided extensions.

"That was not the case at all. I was not shot."

"Will you elaborate on your career-ending injury, Mr. Clinton?" the girl continued with her questioning.

"I'd rather not, Miss Shelton," he argued, reading the placard on the table identifying her as Nikki Shelton.

Justin glared at Daniel. "Since Mr. Clinton is exhibiting some resistance to answering our questions we'll move along. Mr. Clinton, what enterprise are you currently involved in?

Daniel stared down at Rebecca before redirecting his attention to the students on the panel. She would pay for setting him up again. Managing a warm smile, he said, "I own and operate my own security business. I contract with individuals and companies who require uniformed guards to protect their property and employees."

"How many do you employ?" asked another young boy on the panel.

"Last count was twenty."

"Are any of them armed?" It was Nikki Shelton, the young girl with the braids.

"None are armed." He wondered about her fixation with firearms. "Security can also mean equipment. I employ technicians who set up surveillance cameras and wire both businesses and residences with security systems."

"Are the cameras like the ones in a bank?" questioned the remaining girl at the table.

"Some are similar to the ones in a bank, while others aren't easily detectable. Here's an example. Suppose you have an office with a door that doesn't have a security eye or glass for you to identify who's on the other side. What I do is set up a monitor inside of the office and install a camera outside, but conceal it along the wall or in the ceiling. The person sitting at the monitor can see who is at the door or anyone else out in the hall.

"How do you bill for services?" Justin questioned.

"Some contracts are set up for clients to pay monthly, quarterly, semi-annually or annually."

Miss Braids smiled sweetly at him. "How is your company's revenue in relation to expenses?"

Leaning forward on the sofa, Daniel returned her smile, winking. "Excellent. In other words my company is solvent."

"Do you work long hours?" she continued.

"I did initially. I've hired an office manager who has proven to be invaluable. So much so that I was able to come here this morning."

"What are your regularly scheduled work hours?" Justin asked.

"I'm usually in the office by eight. Now that I have a family I try to leave by five."

"Do you have any other interests? In other words what do you do in your spare time?" This question came from someone in the audience.

Daniel peered out into the darkness, trying to access whether the question had come from a boy or a girl. "I jog and I teach a ninety-minute judo class once a week."

"Do you have any kids? And if you so, do you teach them any of your judo moves?"

"I don't have any children at the present time."

Rebecca met her husband's direct stare. He appeared relaxed as he answered the students' questions, refusing whenever they became too personal.

The attention shifted to Mr. Martinez, who operated an office cleaning enterprise. He answered all of the questions put to him by the panel and after a while also appeared to relax.

"I wanna know somethin', Mr. Martinez," shouted a girl from the front of the auditorium. "My mother said that the people who clean the offices in the building where she works use the same dirty water to mop all of the bathrooms. Why is that?"

"Yo, Makia, don't try to dis my Pop!"

Keith Martinez stiffened as if he had been slapped when he recognized his son's voice. He leaned forward, but Daniel clamped a strong hand on his arm. "Don't lose it, man. She's trying to bait you." His warning was low enough not to be picked up by the microphones.

Keith recovered quickly. Leaning over, he grasped the microphone. "If you give me the address of the building where your mother works I'll approach the building management to see whether they'd like to change maintenance companies."

"Tell her, Pop!" the younger Martinez shouted, applauding.

Daniel nodded. "Nice comeback."

"Thanks," Keith murmured.

Justin tapped his microphone with a forefinger. "There will be no further outbursts from the audience please."

The questioning continued, this time from the audience, and Daniel had to admit to himself that the queries were intelligent and well thought out.

"Mr. Clinton, what are advantages and disadvantages of owing your own company?" a teacher queried.

Resting his forehead on his fist, Daniel pondered the question. Raising his head, he stared out at the crowd. "The advantage is that you can't be fired." He waited for the laughter to subside. "The disadvantage is that you are always responsible for the company's payroll. There are times when someone has to be let go, and that is never a pleasant task. People who are self-employed usually work long hours, but if successful the rewards are worth it."

"Has it been worth it, Mr. Clinton?"

Daniel smiled down at Rebecca when he registered her dulcet voice. "It has been more than I'd ever expected it to be."

Justin nodded at her and she rose to her feet, making her way to the stage. "I'd like to thank Mr. Martinez and Mr. Clinton for sharing with us this morning." She waited until the thundering applause ended. "We'll take a five minute break before our next two guests take the stage."

She shook the hands of both Daniel and Keith as they rose to their feet. "Congratulations, gentlemen. You've survived the gauntlet. Thank you for coming."

Keith nodded, then made his way off the stage to greet his son and daughter who stood near the front waving to him.

Daniel escorted Rebecca off the stage, smiling down at her. "I'm going drop off my pass at the office. I'll be back to pick you up at three."

She returned his smile. "You were fabulous."

"We'll talk about it later." He walked out of the auditorium and turned in his Visitor's pass at the office. Minutes later he slipped behind the wheel of his car and headed for the Bronx.

Faith Robinson glanced at the clock on her desk when the door opened and Daniel stepped into the reception area. "Good morning, Boss Man."

He gave her a warm smile. "Good morning, Faith. Any messages?"

"I left one on your desk. Don't forget that you have to attend the bid opening in Manhattan tomorrow morning."

"Thanks for reminding me."

He walked into his office and closed the door. He had submitted a bid for a proposal to secure a fleet of cars to provide mobile security for two major shopping centers. Winning the bid would lead to potential employment for more than two dozen additional employees. His major focus was not larger profits but an increase in employment. He sought out the unemployed and the underemployed, providing them with a means to earn a living, while supporting their families.

Sitting down behind the desk, he picked up the telephone message. His father had called. Dialing Albert Clinton's number, he waited for the break in the connection.

"Hello."

"What's up, Dad?"

"Nothing much. I was just calling to say hello. How's married life?"

"Wonderful." What he could not say was that he wasn't sleeping with his wife. "How are you feeling?"

"Great. I'm inviting you and Rebecca to come up whenever you want a change of scenery."

Daniel knew that whenever his father invited him to visit it was because he was lonely. "Let me check with Becky and I'll let you know."

"How about the Fourth? You're welcome to spend the weekend."

The Fourth of July was a month away. "Thanks, Dad."

There was a noticeable pause before Albert continued. "I'll expect you and your lovely wife next month."

"I'll call you. Take care of yourself."

"Thanks, Son."

"Bye, Dad."

They hung up simultaneously. Daniel exhaled, staring down at the telephone receiver. His relationship with his father had improved, while the intimacy between he and wife was non-existent.

He'd thought about discussing it with Rebecca, but quickly changed his mind. What he did not want to do was have her think that he'd married her solely for sex.

Closing his eyes, he meditated, allowing his mind to drift beyond his body. The meditation and *T'ai Chi Chuan* had worked whenever he woke up, fully aroused. But he wondered if he could hold out until the end of the year.

CHAPTER THIRTEEN

Rebecca was never prepared for the end of a school year. The hugs and kisses from her students, along with a few stuffed animals, books and fancily wrapped bottles of cologne, always elicited a few tears from both her and the students.

This June had become even more poignant because of her decision to stay away from the classroom for the next three years. What she wanted to do was *be there* for own her child during the first three years before the onset of registration for day-care or nursery school.

Even if she hadn't married Daniel she would have been able to go through with her original plan to take a three-year sabbatical. She and Michael had earned good salaries and had invested well. The proceeds she had received from the insurance companies after Michael's death, coupled with their savings and investments, had provided her with financial independence for many years to come.

Sitting at her desk in the empty classroom, she listened to the raucous voices of the students as they raced across the playground to awaiting buses. It was over. The school year had ended and so had her teaching career for the next three years.

Classes were dismissed at eleven-thirty, which meant she had time to visit her bank where she would close out her safe deposit box. All of her other accounts had been transferred electronically to a Locust Valley branch.

Her body was changing rapidly, not outside as much as inside. Daniel had accompanied her to the obstetrician's office for the second-trimester tests. He was awed by the image of the tiny baby generated by the ultrasound, but quite shaken when the doctor began the procedure for an amniocentesis.

When he saw the needle he asked if the procedure was absolutely necessary. The doctor explained that it was because Rebecca was labeled as high-risk due to her age. The results from all the tests were within the normal range, while the amniocentesis had identified the sex of the fetus.

She and Daniel discussed at length whether they wanted to know whether they would be parents to a son or a daughter, then decided to ask.

They were going to have a daughter!

Daniel was delirious with the news, shocking Rebecca. She'd thought that he would prefer a son whom he would teach to tinker with tools and computer gadgets, or work out with at the *dojo*. But, he'd quickly explained that he would do the same things with a daughter.

Selma Jackson walked into her classroom at the exact moment she gathered her handbag and two shopping bags filled with the gifts from her students. "Well, this is it, Mrs. Clinton."

Rebecca gave her a sad smile. "It's not *it*, Ms. Jackson. I'm only going to be away for three years."

Selma shook her head, holding out her arms. "You're not coming back, Rebecca. Face up to it. You have it all: a perfect husband, home, and I'm certain you're going to have a perfect child."

Laughing, Rebecca hugged Selma. "A perfect child that will keep us up all night then sleep all day."

Selma hugged her back. "Bite your tongue." Pulling back, she looked Rebecca up and down. The loose-fitting cotton knit dress in a soft melon hue flattered her coloring and her figure. "You look wonderful."

"Thanks. Now that the morning, afternoon, nighttime sickness is over I have cravings. Wonderful cravings."

"Pickles? Potato chips?"

"No. Italian food. Exotic pastas and sauces."

"Are you waking Daniel up in the middle of the night to pick up dishes from a take-out restaurant?"

"No," she replied, laughing. "He's doing the cooking. He bought several cookbooks and every night I have a different dish from a different region. The pantry and the refrigerator are filled with dried and fresh *capelli d'angelo*, vermicelli, fettuccine, linguine, perciatelli, fusilli, penne, and of course shells and ravioli."

Selma gave Rebecca a closer look. "How far along are you and have much weight have you gained?"

"I'm ending my fourth month and I've gained five pounds."

"You're good."

"I've taken to walking every night after dinner. If I didn't I probably wouldn't be able to get through the door."

"I repeat you look wonderful."

And she did. Her hair had grown and was full and lustrous. Her skin was clear and moist, her eyes bright. She had a lot more energy and no longer needed to take naps.

"Thanks, Selma."

"You're welcome. But before you go, I want to do is thank you again for letting me sublet your apartment."

"Anytime, Girlfriend. As soon as I settle into a routine I'd like for you and Judge Hurston to come out to Locust Valley for an intimate dinner party."

Selma's mouth formed a perfect 0. Rebecca smiled at her friend. When she first met Selma Jackson she reminded her of one of her favorite dolls when she was a young girl. Selma's round face was the color of powdered cocoa. Her large chocolate-brown eyes made her appear in a perpetual state of surprise. A pug nose and a small lush mouth completed her adorable baby-doll look.

"How did you know I was seeing him?" Her voice came out in a breathless whisper.

"He's a family friend," she reminded Selma. "He talks to my father at least once a week. It appears that he's quite taken with you."

A frown creased Selmal's smooth forehead. "That may be so, but I'm not going for it. I've had enough bad luck with men to last me two lifetimes."

"Peter is nothing like that last loser you hooked up with," Rebecca argued. "Tyrone was so controlling he made you give up your place and everything in it so you would have to depend on him. And the dependence was akin to bondage. Then when you rebelled he showed you the door."

Crossing her arms under her breasts, Selma shook her braided head. "I don't care. I have dinner with Peter, sometimes a movie, then I make him leave me at my door."

"That's okay. But if I invite Peter to come to my place, will you come with him?"

Selma shrugged her shoulders. "I suppose I can."

"Good. Look for an invitation in the mail."

"What are you and Daniel doing for the Fourth?"

"We're going upstate to visit his father. Why?"

"I thought about inviting myself out to your place."

Selma was a native Chicagoan who now claimed no family members east of the Rockies.

"Why?"

"Well, Peter asked me to go to his sister's house with him for a cookout. It's also supposed to double as a mini family reunion for all of the Northern Hurstons."

"Go with the man, Selma. You have nothing to lose."

"Nothing but my heart."

"You like him, don't you?"

Selma nodded. "What's not to like?"

"Hello."

"Why didn't you ever go after him, Rebecca?"

"I couldn't, Selma, because I was already in love with Daniel when we were introduced."

"It would've been hard for me to choose between the two."

Rebecca shook her head vehemently. "Not for me."

"I hear you," Selma crooned.

The two women walked slowly out of school and out to the parking lot to their respective cars. They hugged briefly, then got into their cars and drove away from the school, Rebecca for the last time for the next three years.

She spent less than ten minutes in the bank, emptying out her safe deposit box. Now there was no reason for her to return to Seaport where she had spent twelve of her fifteen years of teaching with the Seaport School District. She would miss the school, her students, and the picturesque fishing village.

Daniel pushed the button for the garage, waiting for the door to slide up smoothly. Rebecca's car was parked next to several cartons he knew contained knitting and crocheting yarn. She had begun purchasing supplies for her crafts shop. She had signed a lease for the space and the landlord was busy making the necessary renovations she requested. The renovations were projected to be completed by the first of August. Rebecca said she would need a month to complete sample pieces for display and to select and purchase enough inventory before her projected grand opening.

He was charmed by her enthusiasm and her general feeling of good health. Her nausea had disappeared, as well as her earlier fatigue. He enjoyed taking walks with her after dinner. There were times when they'd walk more than a mile before turning to retrace their steps.

She was surprised as well as pleased when he told of his father's request that they come up to visit him for the July Fourth weekend, and because the official celebrating would be on a Monday, she suggested they leave Long Island on Thursday and return on Sunday to avoid the traffic jams. He agreed with her and called Albert to confirm their arrival.

He heard the soft, muted tones of a Miles Davis piece playing the moment he walked into the living room. They had finally completed decorating the house. Contemporary modular pieces covered in a gray-beige silk and chenille fabric grouped on the highly polished parquet flooring set the stage for towering indoor trees, some rising more than twenty feet toward the towering cathedral ceiling. Six tall raffia palm trees by the windows afforded them the privacy they sought from the outside without compromising natural light or the splendor of the professionally manicured landscape.

Daniel had single-handedly planted flats of snow-white impatiens, climbing roses, azaleas, baby's breath, peonies, sweet pea, and chrysanthemums, even though he'd hired a landscaping crew to maintain the grounds. The sweet pea and baby's breath had flowered first, and the delicate flowers filled a large crystal vase on a table in the living room and another table in the family room.

He walked into the family room, searching for Rebecca. The room was empty despite the fact that she had filled the CD carousel with six discs. Making his way out of the room and up the curving staircase to the second floor, he walked into her bedroom. What he saw shocked him where he wasn't able to move or utter a sound for a full minute.

Rebecca stood in front of a Cheval mirror, naked. He could see from her reflection in the mirror that her eyes were closed as she cradled her belly.

His gaze lingered on her hips and thickening waist before moving down to her long, slender legs. He hadn't realized he was holding his breath until he felt the burning in his lungs.

Feeling the blood pooling in his groin, he walked silently across the carpeted floor and stood behind her. He wanted to touch her, but curled his hands into fists instead.

"Becky," he breathed close to her ear.

Not opening her eyes, Rebecca smiled and leaned back against his chest. She didn't know why, but she'd sensed his presence even though she hadn't opened her eyes.

"She moved, Daniel. The baby kicked me."

Placing his right hand over hers, he pulled it away and laid his outstretched fingers over the slight swell of her belly. He watched her face in the reflection, seeing the heightened color suffuse her cheeks. He had not seen her nude since the day of their wedding, and the roundness of her belly and the prominent blue veins in her heavy breasts made it difficult for him to breath normally.

Never had he seen Rebecca more beautiful. Her hair had grown out so that it caressed the smooth skin over her shoulders in a mass of sensual curls.

He felt it. The slight fluttering movement under his fingers. His mouth curved into a smile as he marveled at the miracle of creation.

Rebecca opened her eyes, a sweep of lashes setting off her silvery gaze. "Did you feel her?"

"Yes, Love, I felt her."

Turning slowly to face him, Rebecca smiled up at Daniel. "I thought I felt a kick earlier, but dismissed it. Then when I came upstairs to change my clothes she kicked again, and I knew for certain that she was moving."

Daniel's hands moved up her arms to her throat, then up to cradle her face. "She probably auditioning for the cheerleading team."

"She's going to be beautiful, Daniel."

"Just like her mother."

Her fingers curled around his strong wrists as she pressed her body close to his. "I've missed you, my darling. I've been your lover, but not your wife."

He frowned. "What are you talking about? You are my wife."

"Not in the biblical sense."

"What do you want, Becky?"

"I want to sleep with you. I want you to make love to me. I need you to consummate our marriage."

A tense silence enveloped the room as Daniel and Rebecca stared at each other. She had just verbalized what both of them had wanted for months; what both of them needed from the first time they'd shared a bed—each other.

Daniel felt his pulse quicken. "Are you sure?"

Rebecca nodded, smiling. "I'm sure," she said quietly.

Bending slightly, he swung her up into his arms and carried her to the bed. Holding her effortlessly against the length of his body with one arm, he pulled back the antique quilt on the large bed, then lowered her gently to the pale blue and yellow striped sheets.

She lay, staring up at him as he slowly and methodically removed his clothes, certain that Daniel could see her trembling as well as her hunger for him. Her heart hammered against her ribs while her fingers ached to reach up and help him undress. Closing her eyes briefly, she pulled her lower lip between her teeth. Her shallow breathing caused her breasts to tremble above her rib cage.

She felt the mattress give as Daniel placed a knee on the side of the bed, then the other and knelt beside her.

Opening her eyes, she saw his sex, swaying thick and heavily between his hard, muscled thighs.

"My precious, precious, Becky," he crooned, lying down beside her and pulling her up close to his chest. "I can't put into words how much I've missed you." Shifting to his side, he lowered his head and claimed her mouth.

Parting her lips, Rebecca's tongue moved sensuously over his lower lip, lingering leisurely over his mustache. She had missed his touch, his kisses, and his strong, unrestrained possession. Whenever she lay with Daniel she surrendered completely, because her desire for him had always overrode everything else.

She moaned aloud with rising pleasure when his hand cradled her breast. She did not recognize her own voice once his head moved down to her chest.

Daniel suckled his wife, praying it would give him time to bring his runaway passions under control. The last time he'd made love to her was early March, and since that time he had been celibate. He had managed to dam his desire for almost four months, but doubted whether he would be able to hold back any longer.

The silken feel of her skin, and the sensual fragrance of her naked body was hypnotic. He felt her trembling, her legs entwining against his.

Eyes closed, head thrown back, Rebecca shuddered as the flames of passion flared within the soft core of her body. She ached for him, her body crying out silently that he take her. His teeth fastened on her sensitive nipples and she could not control her cry of pleasure.

"Take me. Take me," she pleaded over and over, but he ignored her plea. *"Dan-i-e-l."* His name came out in a tortured moan.

He answered her by splaying a hand over the small mound of her belly, his fingers inching lower until they captured the heat of her femininity. The pad of his forefinger swept over the tight nodule of flesh hiding under the silky down at the apex of her thighs. She arched off the mattress and Daniel knew if he did not take her it would be over for the both of them.

Curving an arm around her waist, he shifted her body until her back was pressed against his chest. He cradled an arm under her shoulders, providing support for her head, while parting her thighs with his knee. Angling his lower body, it took one, swift, strong thrust for him to enter her from the rear.

Rebecca inhaled sharply, then let out her breath as Daniel cradled her hip, pushing and rolling his own hips when he drove into her hot, tight flesh with deep, powerful motions. Holding his chest away from her back permitted him deeper penetration. The blood rushed to his head and he felt as if he were poised on a precipice, unable to move, unable to breathe. He did not want to fall—not yet.

The pleasure Daniel gave Rebecca was pure and explosive. She was being swallowed up by wave after wave of fiery, throbbing delight. The feel and heat of her husband's body, the unyielding strength of his maleness sliding in and out of her pulsing flesh, and the warmth of his shuddering breath against the nape of her neck increased her desire.

Whimpers of pleasure blended with measured groans of rising passions. Rebecca and Daniel floated beyond themselves to a world populated only by the two of them. They soared, higher and higher, their bodies completely attuned to the other until it was impossible to distinguish where one began and the other ended.

It happened simultaneously. Their passions peaked, the floodgates opened, and their bodies vibrated with a showering of liquid fire that drowned both in a flood of whirling ecstasy.

Burying his face in his wife's sweet-smelling hair, Daniel struggled to catch his breath and slow down his runaway pulse.

"What are you doing to me, Mrs. Clinton?" he gasped.

Rebecca smiled. "I was just going to ask you the same thing, Mr. Clinton."

He kissed the nape of her neck. "Do you feel married now?"

She moaned sensuously. "Quite married, thank you." Turning her head, she kissed his arm cradling her shoulders. "I love you."

"Thank you, Love." Pulling his arm from under her shoulders, he moved over her. He was careful not to put too much weight on her body.

He studied her face, noticing the flush of fulfillment had darkened her face, eyes, and chest. He lowered his head and licked her erect nipples, arousing her again. Her eyelids fluttered, then closed.

"I can't, Daniel."

"Neither can I, darling," he whispered against her moist mouth. Pulling a sheet up over her naked body, he stared at his sleeping wife. He would let her rest while he showered. Then he would wake her to eat.

CHAPTER FOURTEEN

Rebecca and Daniel settled into a routine of making love early in the morning. Both lay silent, holding hands, while relishing in the aftermath of their sated passions. Then they showered together before walking along the beach and watching the sunrise.

They returned to the house where Daniel retreated to their bedroom to prepare for his commute into the city while she prepared breakfast.

Daniel had moved all of his clothes into their bedroom after the first time they'd made love, and after two nights she could not remember when he hadn't shared her bed.

With the end of the school term she established a routine of doing her housework after Daniel left for his office. She put up her wash, cleaned the kitchen, made the bed, and planned what she wanted to prepare for dinner.

She had become a very good cook, and she looked to surprising Daniel with some of the dishes she had prepared only a few times. She had to admit that her husband was an excellent chef, but he deferred to her when it came to baking. She knew he loved homemade bread, and she had begun the practice of putting up enough dough for several loaves every Saturday night. The aroma of baking bread Sunday morning had quickly become a tradition they looked forward to sharing for many years.

Rebecca went up her bedroom and opened the sliding door to the closet which covered an entire wall. Her gaze fell on the clothes she had purchased for her pregnancy. Oversized T-shirts, smock tops, leggings, and loose-fitting dresses in basic black with contrasting solids and prints coordinates would prove serviceable over the next five months. Her wardrobe also included practical everyday footwear, along with a pair of low-heeled black patent leather dress pumps.

Taking down enough clothes to sustain her for their weekend in upstate New York, she folded the garments and packed them in a leather and canvas bag. Walking to the opposite wall, she opened Daniel's side of the closet. Slacks, shirts, jackets, suits, ties, jeans, and T-shirts hung with meticulousness, according to color. Shrugging her shoulders, she slid the heavy door close. She would let him select and pack his own clothes.

Her light housework behind her, she retreated to the family room, settled herself on an overstuffed armchair with a matching footstool and picked up a knitted garment from a large wicker basket.

She always felt a ripple of excitement when she thought about opening her shop, envisioning the unique little touches she wanted to incorporate in what she knew would become an elegant space for the residents of the Long Island hamlet community.

It took her less than four hours to knit and complete an infant ensemble of a tiny hat, booties, and a sweater. She wove a narrow satin ribbon in a matching ice-green through the hat, the tops of the booties and along the neckline of the sweater. Placing the three garments on the tissue paper she had laid out on the coffee table, she admired her handiwork, smiling. She hadn't lost any of her skills.

After taking a break for a lunch of steamed broccoli, a small baked potato, and a broiled chicken breast, she went for a walk along the beach. She had swept her longer hair up in a ponytail as a warm wind off the water caressed her face and lifted the curls off her long neck.

The weather was partly clouded, the sun playing hide and seek behind low-hanging clouds. Rebecca felt a peace she had not thought possible. There were times when her thoughts strayed to Michael. It was odd how peaceful she felt and she thanked him for the gift he'd given her when he'd blessed her marriage to Daniel that day she last visited his grave. She hadn't returned since then, but a silent voice told her that there wasn't any need to return because she would always have him. The child she carried in her womb would be a constant reminder of her first husband.

Her eyes narrowed behind the lenses of her sunglasses when she noticed a figure coming towards her. Slowing her steps, she saw it was a man. One she had never seen before. She did not know too many of the people who lived in the area, but she recognized the faces of the ones who traversed the beach at the same time each day.

The man passed her, nodding. She returned the nod, quelling the impulse to turn around. He was a lot younger than the men who were usually out at midday. His body appeared to be in peak condition, with hard muscles flexing through his deeply tanned olive skin. She couldn't detect the color of his eyes because of the mirrored sunglasses, but something about him disturbed her. What it was she could not identify.

Continuing her stroll, she glanced over her shoulder. The man was nowhere to be seen. Perhaps he had turned off at one of the paths leading to the large houses situated at the top of the hill.

She passed the point that Daniel had calculated was a mile from their house, then turned and retraced her steps. Reaching the path leading up to the house, she pressed the remote in her pocket, deactivating the silent house alarm. The comfortable coolness of the central cooling system caressed her moist face when she opened the front door.

A feeling of fulfillment swept over her as she surveyed the spaciousness of her home. The image of a little girl sliding over the waxed floor elicited a smile. December twenty-fifth would be her first Christmas with Daniel, living under the same roof. This Christmas would also be special because they would share it with their daughter.

Walking into the downstairs bathroom, she rinsed the sand from her feet. She had just walked into the kitchen for a glass of milk when she heard a door slam and Daniel's voice as he called out her name. Her heart thudded in her chest. What was he doing home so early? She did not have long to wait for an answer.

He rushed into the kitchen, picked her up and swung her around until she begged him to stop. He set her down, supporting her swaying form.

"What's the matter with you, Daniel Clinton? Have you lost your mind?" Her gaze raced over his face. Attractive lines fanned out at the corners of his eyes and creased his lean cheeks.

His fingers tightened on her waist. "I got it, Becky. I won the bid!"

A frown marred her smooth forehead. "But you told me that you lost that bid. That you had come in too high."

"The first bid was disqualified. And because I had the next lowest I won by default."

She shrieked, rising on tiptoe and pressing her mouth to his. "Daniel. I can't believe it. Oh, darling," she crooned against his mustached mouth.

Lifting her off her feet, Daniel kissed her mouth, nose, eyelids, then returned to her soft, moist lips. What had begun as soft, nibbling kisses changed, becoming stronger and more possessive.

A slow, simmering fire flared, igniting their passion. Sweeping her up in his arms, Daniel took the stairs, two at a time. Everything blurred as he stalked into their bedroom and placed Rebecca on the bed. Without pulling his mouth away, he tore at the buttons on his shirt, scattering them over the carpet. He had to release her to take off his shoes, slacks, and to remove her leggings, T-shirt and underwear.

Moving over her, he pulled her hair loose from the elastic band and spread it out on the pillowcase. Seeing the curtain of curling hair spilling over the stark white pillow reminded him of the first time he had claimed her body when he'd released the waist length hair she had worn in a single plait.

Kneeling and supporting his greater weight on his extended arms, he lowered his body until his chest touched hers. Rebecca gasped aloud when the coarse hair on his hard chest grazed her distended nipples. She gasped again, this time when Daniel pushed into her pulsing flesh.

His excitement, his dreams and fantasies were communicated to her as they became one being with the other. Everything in his world was right, perfect. As perfect as the woman lay writhing beneath him, offering him all of herself.

He loved her and the child beating beneath her heart. Those were his last thoughts before he surrendered and gave himself up to the awesome, shuddering ecstasy shaking him from head to toe.

Gasping and trying to force air into his lungs, he went still, head lowered, eyes closed, savoring the pulsing aftermath of his explosive release.

Rebecca's head rolled back and forth as she tried assessing the magnitude of her own passion and her response to her husband. Making love with Daniel was never the same. Each time they came together was another adventure that was always awesome, always different, and always exciting.

A satisfied smile touched her thoroughly kissed mouth. "Congratulations on winning the bid, darling."

Daniel opened his eyes and returned her smile. "Thank you, Love."

Albert Clinton stood in the doorway to his house, waiting for the sleek black car. He had been waiting since he'd gotten up earlier that morning. He was not disappointed when he saw his son drive up, shut off the ignition, then alight to assist his now quite obviously pregnant wife. His dark eyes revealed no emotion when he saw the tenderness in Daniel's touch as his arm curved around Rebecca's waist.

Waiting for them to come closer, he held out his own arms. He embraced his son, then his daughter-in-law. "Thank you for coming."

Rebecca stared up Albert. "Thank you for having us." She noticed that Albert did not even look like the same man who had attended her wedding. He had put on weight, and his dark eyes were sparkling. "You look wonderful," she stated with a smile.

Albert inclined his silvered head. "So do you, dear daughter."

She felt her face heat up. "A little rotund."

"A lot beautiful," father and son chorused.

Rebecca's eyebrows shot up. "A duet."

"It's uncanny, but there are times with Dad and I are thinking the same thoughts," Daniel explained, smiling broadly.

She gave him a look which said she doubted whether Albert harbored the lavacisious notions that had occupied Daniel's, so that his sexual appetite was more in keeping with a man in his early twenties instead of his early forties.

Albert grasped Rebecca's hand. "Let me show you where you can freshen up, while Danny brings in your bags."

Albert Clinton's house was an A-frame dwelling with a loft claiming two bedrooms and another on the first level. Palladian windows, white walls and bleached pine floors gave the house a sense of airy spaciousness.

The bedroom he had selected for her and Daniel was charming. It was the largest bedroom in the house, with an adjoining bath.

"I sleep downstairs," Albert explained when she gave him a questioning look.

Walking over to the window, she stared at pine-covered mountains with discernible ski trails. "It's so peaceful."

"That is why I decided to move up here. I needed to be alone." Rebecca stared at the fifty-nine-year-old man with a full head of silvered hair. He was causally dressed in a pair jeans that caressed his tall, slim body better than men several decades younger, and a laundered plaid cotton shirt. His feet were covered in a pair of sturdy hiking boots.

"Are you lonely, Dad?"

Albert smiled, shaking his head. It pleased him that she'd called him *Dad*. "Never. I have my workshop and my wood. I go into town once a week to shop for groceries, and I manage to take in a movie every time the theater has a new one. I know most of the people who live around here. I don't visit much, so that way I don't have to contend with uninvited company. Danny comes up every two months, and I'm grateful that he does"

"When are you going to come down to visit with us?"

"I'll drive down when I finish the baby's furniture."

"It's going to be a girl."

Albert's smile was dazzling. "I'm glad to hear that. Men need daughters to humble them. Little girls tend to take the arrogance out of their hard heads."

Rebecca had thought Daniel was a lot of things during the years she'd known him, yet she had never thought of him as being arrogant.

Albert made his way to the door. "Take your time settling in. You can even take a nap if you want. Lunch will be ready in about an hour."

Waiting until Albert closed the door behind him, Rebecca walked around the large room. She knew without asking that Albert had made every piece of furniture. The four-poster bed with the elaborately carved designs was massive. Matching stools were positioned at both sides to assist one climbing onto mattresses which were at least three feet from the floor. The crocheted coverlet matched the sheers hanging from the floor-to-ceiling windows.

There was something about the bedroom that boasted of a woman's touch, and something told her that the reason Albert Clinton wasn't lonely was because he was seeing a woman.

Daniel opened the door and walked into the bedroom, carrying their bags, a frown set into his features. "What did you say to my father?"

Turning away from the window, Rebecca stared at him. "What are you talking about?"

"You had to have said *something* to make him threaten to *thrash* me. My father never raised a hand to me in his life, and now he's talking about *thrashing* his forty-year-old son."

She gestured, throwing up her hands. "You're not making any sense. What did he say?"

"He said that if I ever hurt you in any way he would thrash me."

"Hurt me how?"

"I don't know." He set the bags down near the door.

Rebecca crossed the room and stood in front of him. "Maybe he's thinking of what he did to your mother."

"I'd never leave you."

She took his hand in hers. "He doesn't know that."

Daniel's frown vanished as he pulled her against his body. "You're right. He's probably thinking that because I'm his son I might do the same thing he did."

I pray he's wrong, she mused. She had waited too long for Daniel Clinton to have him walk out on her.

Rebecca understood why Albert Clinton had elected to live in the mountains. Despite the summer heat, it was noticeably cooler in the higher elevation. His house was erected in a clearing surrounded by towering pine trees.

She noticed that Daniel had not inherited any of his father's facial features, yet their body language was similar. They held their heads at the same angle when listening to someone speaking, and their voices were the same. It was a rumbling baritone, that seemed to come deep from within their chests.

Daniel helped his father prepare lunch while she decided to take a walking tour of the surrounding area. The underbrush was alive with woodland creatures. Birds called out to one another, flitting from branch to branch in carefree abandon.

Sitting down on a large rock, she fanned her face with her hand. The fiery rays of the brilliant sun had penetrated the thick curtain of leaves, heating up the dark, cool earth. She unbuttoned several button on the shirt she had taken from Daniel's closet, hoping to cool down her moist flesh. Wearing his shirts had expanded her wardrobe considerably.

She heard the crackle of dry leaves and the snap of fallen twigs and branches. Turning to her left, she saw Daniel striding purposely toward her; she admired his powerful body in a pair of jeans with a matching denim shirt.

"You look like a wood nymph from *A Night's Dream*," he teased. Her smile was dazzling as she rose to her feet, offering him her hands. Grasping them in his, he brought them to his lips and kissed her fingers, his gaze locked with hers. "It's time to eat."

Rebecca took a step closer and pressed her body to his. Why was it that she wanted him so much? Why couldn't she get enough of his lovemaking?

Daniel felt the crush of her breasts against his chest and curved his arms around her middle. He couldn't remember when her stomach had actually expanded. One day it was almost flat, then it was significantly rounder. Most times her condition wasn't apparent because of her loose-fitting clothing, but whenever they went to bed together he was more than aware that a child kicked vigorously in her womb. She had taken to sleeping on her side with her abdomen pressed his back, and there were times when he felt strong movements of the baby.

"Dad fixed your favorite dish."

Pulling back, she stared up at him. "You told him, didn't you?"

Daniel shrugged a broad shoulder. "He asked me."

"But isn't roast chicken a little fancy for lunch?"

"We'll pretend it's seven in the evening." He leaned over and kissed the end of her nose. "Let's go back before he comes looking for us."

Lunch was served on a screened-in patio with a view of pinecovered mountains. The table was set with a snowy white tablet cloth, flatware with ivory handles, and antique blue depression glass goblets. The large chicken was roasted to perfection golden brown and gleaming, tender and juicy. It lay on a platter with golden browned roasted potatoes and cooked carrots. Another serving bowl was filled with steamed spinach with garlic and olive oil.

Daniel seated Rebecca, then took a chair opposite her place setting. He waited until his father sat down before taking his own seat. Albert bowed his head and said grace, following by a chorus of "amens."

Albert handed Daniel the carving utensils. "Will you please do the honors?"

Quickly and expertly Daniel carved the large bird, serving Rebecca first. She spooned a portion of potatoes, carrots and spinach onto her plate.

She bit into a slice of chicken. The tender, juicy meat, seasoned with a sprinkling of garlic and thyme, seemed to melt on her tongue. "How often do you prepare lunches like this?" she asked Albert.

"Not too often. Usually when I have very special company."

Daniel glanced up at his father, studying him intently. "You must be entertaining quite a bit of special company, because you've gained back some weight."

"I was too thin."

A knowing smile inched up the corners of Daniel's mouth. "Who are you entertaining, Dad?"

Albert stared down at the contents of his plate, chewing slowly and ignoring his son. He gave Rebecca a sidelong glance.

"How is everything, Rebecca?"

She gave him a bright smile. "Excellent."

"What's her name, Dad?" Daniel knew his father was deliberately evading him.

"Helen," Albert mumbled under his breath.

Rebecca met Daniel's gaze across the table and they shared a secret smile. She'd recognized the subtle feminine touch with some of the furnishings in Albert Clinton's mountaintop home.

Daniel's gaze shifted to his father, seeing the older man's uneasiness. Albert had told him there had been no other women while he was married, and had hinted that there were very few since his divorce.

"Is she worthy of my father?"

Albert put down his fork, a smile very much like Daniel's curving his mouth; a deep dimple winked in his left cheek. "The question should be whether or not I'm worthy of her."

Daniel nodded slowly. "Nice going, Dad."

"I'm only trying to catch up with you, Son. I'm kind of rusty, so perhaps you can give me a few pointers."

"No can do. Becky has me on lock down."

Her jaw dropped. "Daniel, no!"

Daniel winked at her. "Just kidding, Love."

The light banter continued throughout lunch, the three diners laughing more than eating. Albert shyly revealed that Helen, widowed several years ago, was away for the holiday, visiting with her adult children in Cleveland.

The weekend sped by too quickly for Rebecca. It afforded her and Daniel the opportunity to relax. They slept late, hiked in the woods, and toured the neighboring towns.

She had been transfixed by the enormous, one room workshop Albert set up at the rear of his house. Piles of wood in every variety were stacked against one wall, along with differing tools Albert used to plane and crave the intricate designs in his treasured creations. She saw a sketch of the pieces for her daughter, and was amazed by the intricate carvings on the posts for the bed, and the top of the toy chest.

She and Daniel reluctantly said their good-byes early Sunday morning, extracting a promise from Albert that he would come to visit Long Island before the birth of his grandchild.

CHAPTER FIFTEEN

The onset of Rebecca's third trimester coincided with the opening of The Golden Needle. Subdued excitement lit up her luminous eyes when she greeted the crowd of curious onlookers who had come to the pre-opening celebration.

Daniel stood in a corner of the shop watching the potential customers inspect the assortment of yarns in varying colors, textures and weight displayed in plexiglas cubicles. Spindle racks were filled with knitting and embroidery needles, crochet hooks, and ceramic buttons. A bookcase displayed books and magazines specializing in handicrafts with classic patterns for sweaters and many other wearable garments.

She had decorated the shop with a Country French desk, several small, round tables and more than a half dozen chairs. The dominant colors of navy blue and white were repeated in the striped seat cushions and area rugs.

He knew she had pushed herself to complete the samples displayed on wooden dowels and padded hangers around the shop. All of her waking hours during July and August had been spent knitting and crocheting. Smaller samples of quilted squares and novelty needlepoint canvas hung in antique frames for everyone to view.

A refreshment table, filled with wines, including champagne, herbal teas, gourmet coffee, sparkling water and miniature pastries had become the center of attraction for the milling crowd.

Daniel's admiring gaze lingered on Rebecca's delicate profile as she laughed at something her part-time assistant whispered close to her ear. *Eleven more weeks*, he mused. She had less than three months before she was due to deliver, but as the time approached he found himself becoming more and more apprehensive. He was aware that her legs were cramping, even though she had not said so. He found her automatically massaging her calves whenever she sat down and elevated her feet.

They had become a married couple in a way he had not thought possible. When they lay in bed together he found talking with her as pleasurable as sharing her body. Their lovemaking had tapered off to one or two times a week, for the advancing stages of her pregnancy placed additional stress on her back; she had taken to sleeping with two pillows under her head and another under her belly.

His dark gaze lingered on the large potted plants from the local chamber of commerce and other business owners in the mini-mall. Enormous vases cradled flowers with accompanying cards from her parents, sister and brother-in-law. The Golden Needle would not officially open for business until Tuesday, but he had no doubt of its success if the number of people signing up for instructional classes was an indicator.

The three hour gala wound down at five and, as soon as the last person walked out of the door, Rebecca flopped down on a rocker and raised her feet to an ottoman.

Closing her eyes, she did not see Daniel and the retired schoolteacher who had answered her ad for an assistant put everything in order. She was past exhaustion. All she wanted to do was go to sleep, not waking up until hunger forced her from the bed.

After she and Daniel returned from Albert's upstate home, she began her needlework projects. All of her household duties were taken over by the woman Daniel hired to come in three times a week, freeing her up to concentrate on knitting, crocheting, and quilting the samples she wanted to display for shoppers.

Catherine Cunningham had proven herself an invaluable assistant. She had been the first and only person to respond to the advertisement for a needlework instructor. Catherine retired from teaching junior high school social studies after thirty years, but discovered after a year that she was too young to retire completely. Now at fifty-six, she was ready to embark on another career even if it was part-time.

Catherine was an adequate knitter and crocheter, while excelling in embroidery, quilting and needlepoint. She had brought samples of her work to the interview, and Rebecca hired her on the spot.

Shifting uncomfortably on the rocker, she reacted to the strong kicking movements of the baby. Her overall weight gain had reached fourteen pounds, and she felt enormously clumsy. She had gained most of the weight over the past two months because of inactivity, and was well aware that she had to resume her exercise regimen of walking the beach.

Feeling the brush of hair against her face, she opened her eyes. Daniel, hunkering down beside the rocker, had pressed his mouth to her cheek. She had fallen asleep.

"Are you ready to go home, Love?"

"Yes," she sighed, permitting him to ease her gently from the chair.

The shadows lengthened, the days grew shorter and the nights longer and cooler with the passing of summer. Business at The Golden Needle was lively, the tiny bell over the door ringing constantly the three days it was in operation.

On her days off, Rebecca bundled up against the fall chill and strolled leisurely along the beach before retreating and spending time in the gazebo catching up on her reading.

This morning dark clouds and a rising wind stung her cheeks as she quickened her pace; she would have to forfeit her walk because of an earlier prediction of rain.

Hearing a pounding, grating sound, she glanced over her shoulder. A man was gaining rapidly on her as sand spewed in every direction under his running shoes. He was medium height, dressed in a black nylon jogging suit and a black baseball hat. Something about his physique was familiar, even though she did not recognize his face. He rushed past her, breathing heavily.

Rebecca watched his retreating figure until he left the beach and jogged onto one of the private roads. It was another ten minutes before she walked through the front door of Wind Watch, seconds ahead of fast-falling fat, wet drops.

Her gaze swept over the living room, noting that Daniel had filled the large brass pail next to the fireplace with wood before leaving the house earlier that morning. Nighttime temperatures dipped into the forties, and they had taken to lighting a fire in the fireplace in addition to switching on the heat.

The night before they'd turned off the lights and sat in front of the fire listening to music floating from the speakers Daniel had skillfully concealed throughout the downstairs. A switch on a wall regulated the speakers in each room.

The independent grouping of two facing love seats in a gray-white chenille and silk, with a large matching ottoman facing another love seat placed on an exquisite cream, blue and green Persian rug set the stage for dramatic living under the colorful glow of priceless Tiffany table lamps.

She had wanted to host a small, intimate dinner party, but decided to wait until after the birth of the baby when Daniel suggested they open their home for a Christmas gala.

Stopping to pour herself a glass of milk, Rebecca headed for the spacious alcove where she had set up an office-in-the-home workstation. The modular system held a large screen monitor, computer, printer, fax and answering machines, and separate telephone lines for her shop and Daniel's office.

She did all of her ordering from vendors directly through the computer. Daniel showed her how to set up her inventory on a program, linking it with her store's electronic cash register. It had taken him two weekends to scan very item of merchandise with a bar code, so when she or Catherine rang up an item it was automatically deducted from her inventory. At any given moment she knew what she had on hand and what needed to be ordered.

Switching on the computer, she waited for it to boot up, then selected the half dozen vendors she did business with, ordering what she needed to replenish her stock.

She had just completed the task when the doorbell chimed melodiously throughout the house. A slight frown creased her forehead when she glanced down at her watch. It was only eight-fifteen, and much too early for the woman who came to clean the house.

Making her away across the living room, she spied a dark colored late model car through the expansive glass wall. She peered through the security eye on the door, seeing a pair of green eyes staring back at her.

"Yes?"

"We're Officers Britt and Cuadrado from NYPD Internal Affairs, Mrs. Williams."

Mrs. Williams. She had stopped being Mrs. Williams when she married Daniel. Surely they should've known that.

"What do you want?" she questioned, not opening the door.

"I would like to talk to you," the man continued.

Her pulse quickened. If they wanted to talk to her it had to be about Michael. "What about?"

"I'd prefer if we didn't have to talk through the door."

She did not want to open the door, and she also did not want to talk to anyone from the New York City Police Department's Internal Affairs. Those were the two words every police officer dreaded most. They loathed their brethren investigating their own comrades.

"I can't open the door. I'm not feeling well," she lied smoothly. "Leave your card in the mailbox and I'll call you when I'm able to talk to you face-to-face." She needed time to talk to Daniel. More than that she needed Daniel present when the men returned.

"I'm sorry you're not feeling well, but we won't take up more than five minutes of your time."

"Leave your card," she insisted.

There was a noticeable pause. She heard two male voices, but could not make out what they were saying.

"Thank you, Mrs. Williams."

Rebecca moved from the door to the window, trying to make out their faces as they retreated to the car. She made out the license plate easily. She repeated the numbers to herself, then made her way to a table in the living room and picked up the telephone. She dialed Daniel's private line, relieved when he answered the call after the first ring.

"Clinton Securities."

"I had a visit from Internal Affairs." The words poured out like a rushing waterfall.

"Calm down, Becky, and tell me everything."

She did, leaving nothing out and giving him the license plate number of the dark blue Ford Crown Victoria.

"I'm glad you didn't open the door," Daniel said after she finished. "I'll call Otis and have him check this out. Hopefully he'll be able to give us a reason why IAB would send investigators to our home."

"Do you think Michael could've done something wrong?"

"I don't know, Love. If he did, there's nothing they can do to him now. Let me put in a call to Otis, then I'll get back to you."

"Daniel…"

"Do you have plans to go out today?" he questioned, interrupting her.

"No."

"Good. Stay in until I get home. Love you, Babe."

"Love you back." She heard the drone of a dial tone, then hung up.

Please, please don't let them have found something on Michael. She repeated her plea while the two words Internal Affairs attacked her relentlessly.

Daniel came home early. His expression was a mask of stone.

"What did you find out?" Rebecca asked as soon he walked through the door.

What he could not tell her was the truth. There were investigating allegations that Michael Williams was a dirty cop. That he had sold drugs, then stole them back, only to resell them again. That the Department had gotten word of his double dealing an hour before he was killed. What IAB wanted to know was if Rebecca had had any knowledge of her late-husband's criminal activities, and if other under-cover officers were also involved.

"Not much," he lied smoothly, staring at the expectant look on her face. "There was talk that Michael's backup team wasn't where they were supposed to be. IAB wants to know if Michael ever discussed his undercover activities with you. If he ever complained about not getting along with people who were suppose to watch his back."

She shook her head. "Never. We argued about him taking the assignment, but after that I told him that I never wanted to talk about it ever again. He promised he'd never bring it up, and he took that promise to his grave. Do they still want to talk to me?"

"Yes. But I'll make certain that they don't interview you unless I'm present."

Running a hand through her unbound hair, she nodded. "Thank you."

Daniel reached out and curved an arm around her burgeoning waist. He stared at her staring up at him, a wealth of dark red curls framing her face and spilling over her shoulders. Her eyes were luminous, trusting. She trusted him, while he'd lied to her. For the first time since meeting her, he had lied. He'd rationalized it was to protect her, but it still disturbed him. It was six weeks before she was due to deliver, and he wanted nothing to jeopardize her health—physically or emotionally.

He forced a smile. "How would you like to go out on a date?"

"With whom?" she teased, smiling for the first time since the doorbell rang six hours ago.

"With a guy in love with a gorgeous woman who's just a little thick in the waist at the moment."

Her delicate jaw dropped and her mouth opened, but no words came out. "How—how can you say that," she sputtered, after she found her voice. "Not when I look like this."

Curving both arms around her waist, he laced his fingers together at the small of her back; lowering his head, Daniel nuzzled an ear. "I can say it because I love your life, and never have you looked more beautiful than you do now. Whenever I see you without your clothes I think of how Adam must have felt when he saw Eve for the first time, her body heavy with child."

"How do you think he felt?"

"He must have fallen in love with her all over again."

Rising on tiptoe, Rebecca fastened her arms around his neck, bringing his head down. She pressed her mouth to his, placing soft nibbling kisses from one corner to the other.

"Where are we going?" she crooned softly, continuing her soft assault on his mouth.

"Out to dinner, then perhaps to take in a movie if you aren't too tired."

"I'd like that very much." Pulling out of his loose embrace, she turned and made her way slowly across the living room.

"Where are you going?"

She stopped, not turning around. "I'm going to shower before changing my clothes.

Daniel took a half dozen long strides and caught up with her. Grasping her hand, he led her up the staircase. "I'll join you. I happen to be the best back washer in the house."

She giggled like a little girl. "Right now you're the only back washer in the house."

They shared a leisurely shower, splashing each other like mischievous children. Daniel ended their playful encounter when he wrapped Rebecca in a bath sheet and carried her to into their bedroom where he dried her body before applying a specially blended lotion that had been marketed with a guarantee that it would prevent unsightly stretch marks.

His strong hands and fingers massaged the tense muscles in her upper arms and upper back, kneading out the knots. He then concentrated on her legs and calves. When he completed what had become his night ministration, Rebecca kissed him passionately. He helped her from the bed where she began the slow, measured ritual of getting dressed.

An hour and a half after Daniel had walked through the door, he and Rebecca left Wind Watch to enjoy dinner at one of their favorite restaurants. They would decide over dinner what film to see.

The officers from the Internal Affairs Bureau did not return, nor did Rebecca contact them. She had deliberately put the notion that Michael may have been engaged in criminal activities when he'd gone undercover out of her mind; however, a week later when she attended a retirement dinner for an officer that Daniel gone through the academy with, everything about the NYPD came rushing back.

Walking into a popular Long Island catering hall on Daniel's arm made her aware that everyone in the large ballroom was involved in some aspect of law enforcement. None of the guests were wearing uniforms, but there was something about their body language and the occasional glimpse of a bulge from a concealed firearm that made her apprehensive.

Daniel smiled, shook hands with people he hadn't seen in years, and proudly introduced Rebecca as his wife. He noticed a few startled glances from some who knew she had been married to Michael Williams, but most of the men stared numbly at the breathtaking vision she presented. She'd washed her hair, permitted it to air dry after applying a styling mousse, then pinned it up in a loose chignon, and allowed a few tendril to escape around her face and neck in sensual disarray. Her gunmetal gray satin long sleeve tunic and slacks were a perfect match for her radiant eyes.

"I lost count of how many faces hit the floor when you introduced me," she whispered to Daniel as he led her to their table.

"They're stunned by your beauty," he countered softly, pulling out a chair and seating her. He was smiling when he sat down beside her.

"They're stunned because I'm Mrs. Daniel Clinton and in the last stages of pregnancy when my late husband hasn't been dead a year."

"Stop that!" There was no mistaking his annoyance. "Our private life is just that. Private! I have not and will not explain why I married you. This baby you're carrying is our baby. And if anyone has anything to say about it, then they'd better say it to my face and not let me hear about it from someone else."

Rebecca placed a hand over his, her fingers feathering gently over his tightly clenched fist. "I'm sorry I mentioned it."

"So am I," he shot back. "I'm going to the bar for a drink. What do you want me to bring back for you?"

She managed a tight smile. "A cranberry juice, please."

There was no doubt that her assessment of the reaction to their marriage had upset him. But it wasn't him his former colleagues had stared at with open mouths. It was her! The widow of Michael Williams. The same Michael Williams their Internal Affairs was investigating. The very same Detective Michael Williams who had been given an inspector's funeral after he'd been killed in the line of duty.

Had Daniel also thought that Michael was dirty? Was that why he'd refused the money she offered when he bought their house? Did he suspect that the money Michael had left her had been derived illegally? That an investigation would result in them losing their home as a result of the RICO law?

She stared at her husband's broad shoulders under the tailored charcoal gray double-breasted jacket. The wool fabric draped his magnificent body like watered silk on a marble statue. All she saw was the fabric. Her husband was mouth-watering, heart-stopping, drop-dead gorgeous. The overhead lights glinted on the gray in his close-cut hair and the rich sienna-red undertones in his healthy-looking skin. As if sensing her gaze, he turned and looked at her, winking. She smiled and he returned it with a sensual one of his own.

Daniel returned to the table, determined to enjoy his wife and the evening. He knew this retirement dinner was the beginning of many he would attend over the next five to ten years. This fall was the twentieth anniversary of his graduation from the police academy. If he hadn't retired five years before, most of the people in the ballroom would have come to celebrate his departure from the NYPD. If everything had gone according to plan, he could have looked forward to attending law school during the upcoming fall semester.

His life hadn't gone according to plan. He had not put in twenty years on the force, and he was not going to law school, but none of that mattered because his personal life was remarkable. He'd married the first woman he'd fallen in love with, purchased the property he'd wanted on sight, and now looked forward to becoming a father.

He thought of his own father, who had called to say that he wouldn't be able to come down until Christmas. He had decided to make *all* of the furniture for his granddaughter's bedroom, and he was too busy to take off for a visit. Albert had laughed when he asked about Helen, saying she was fine. *"A little sassy, but that's the way I like her,"* had been his rejoinder. Daniel ended the call with the comment that making furniture wasn't the only thing occupying Albert Clinton's days and nights.

The table began filling up as he greeted old friends with rough embraces and heavy slaps on the back. All of the men grinned foolishly when he introduced Rebecca, while their wives and girlfriends raised facetious eyebrows and flashed false smiles. Daniel knew they were jealous and reminded Rebecca of this when he led her out to the dance floor once the band started to play.

Her protruding belly, artfully disguised under her tunic, would not permit them to dance close. The baby, who had turned head down in preparation of its impending birth, rested heavily in her womb, and Rebecca knew this social event would be her last.

"What if I go into labor now?" she said, smiling up at Daniel.

"Hush your mouth, Becky. Even though these guys may have gone through emergency medical training, and I suspect many have had more than their share of delivering babies. What I don't want is for these knuckleheads to see my wife with her legs up in the air."

She nearly dissolved into hysterics when seeing his expression. "Could you deliver a baby in an emergency?"

"Of course," he declared confidently, swinging her around and tightening his grip on her waist.

The dance number ended and he escorted her back to the table. A wide grin split his face when he saw a woman standing at his table, waiting for him.

"Valerie."

"Hello, handsome. It's been a while."

Daniel nodded. "Ten years."

"Eleven," she corrected.

Valerie smiled at Rebecca, winking. "Once you reach middle age the memory is the first to go."

"Must I remind you that you're older than me, Val."

"Only by an hour." She extended a hand to Rebecca. "Valerie Kent."

Rebecca took the proffered hand. "Rebecca Clinton."

"You managed to hook the best of what was New York's Finest. I hope you don't mind if I take a turn around the dance floor with your husband. I doubt if I'll be able to talk to him later because I'll be on the dais."

"Not at all. It's nice meeting you, Valerie."

"My pleasure, Rebecca."

Daniel seated Rebecca, then led Valerie out to the dance floor. He curved an arm around her waist, holding her close, though not too close.

His sharp gaze had catalogued everything about Valerie Kent in one sweeping motion. She hadn't changed much. There were a few strands of gray in her short coifed hair and she'd gained weight since he last saw her. But the over-all result was still a very attractive African-American female who had risen quickly through the ranks of the NYPD. At forty, Valerie Kent had become the first female Deputy Inspector and commanding officer of the Queens and Brooklyn Public Moral Division, under the Organized Crime Control Bureau. Her quick ascent had not been without casualties. Valerie was a two-time divorcée.

"You're looking wonderful, Daniel."

He stared down at her from under half-hooded lids. "What can I say, Val. Life is good."

"So I see. You didn't waste any time marrying Michael's widow and getting her pregnant."

He wanted to tell her that Michael had gotten his own wife pregnant, but swallowed back the words. Only Albert,

Rebecca's family and her close friend Selma knew the child in her womb wasn't his.

"You know that I was seeing Rebecca at one time."

"The same way you knew that I'd dated Michael in high school, Valerie countered. She managed a wry smile. "Out of all of the men I ever thought I might be in love with, Michael was the only one I truly ever loved. What I can't accept are the rumors circulating about him being dirty."

Daniel decided not to discuss the rumors about his former partner being a rogue cop. "If you loved him, why didn't you marry?"

Valerie's clear brown eyes were fixed on Daniel's mouth. She missed a step and he steadied her. "Because I wanted what Michael couldn't give me. There were only three things that I'd ever wanted and I managed to get them all. I wanted to get married, become a police officer and have children."

Daniel frowned. "Michael could've offered you two of the three."

Valerie shook her head. "No, he couldn't. Michael couldn't father children. Apparently he had contracted mumps as an adolescent and it left him sterile."

It was Daniel's turn to miss a step. He felt cold, icy cold. If Valerie spoke the truth, then the child in his wife's womb was his, not Michael Williams'.

"Are you certain?" He hardly recognized his own voice once he asked the question.

"Of course I'm certain. When Michael told me I ran to his aunt, crying my heart out. She confirmed it, warning me never to speak of it again. She said Michael went through a difficult period of adjustment after the doctor told him he would never father children. When I asked her why he'd told me, she said that he loved me enough not to deceive me. I left it at that. I got over Michael once I met and married Richard Patton. Then I got over Richard when I married Charles."

Daniel nodded, only half-listening to Valerie. Why hadn't Rebecca told him she was carrying his baby instead of Michael's? Why had she lied to him? Had she deliberately seduced him to get pregnant?

The questions bombarded him until, instead of feeling joy and relief that his own blood flowed through the tiny baby in wife's womb, he was enraged at her duplicity. She had deceived him! He could not trust her!

The last thought that twisted in his mind like a piece of heated steel was Rebecca probably was aware of Michael's illegal undercover activities. Who had he married? Was the woman he shared a roof and bed with an accomplice to a man who'd broken the very laws he had sworn to uphold?

Thanking Valerie for the dance, he led her back to her table, then returned to his own. His gaze met Rebecca's as she smiled sweetly at him.

Deceiver! Liar! He cursed her silently, wondering how he could have fallen so much in love with a woman who had blinded him to the truth.

What he wanted to do was run out of the room and never see her again. Her deceit cut deep, deeper than the knife that had almost severed his left arm. He wanted to hate her, but how could he hate someone he had spent nearly half of his life in love with? How could he stop loving a woman who, without saying a word, had made him want her more than anything in the world.

CHAPTER SIXTEEN

The celebrating continued with the predictable speeches and an occasional wiping of tears, followed by numerous toasts. The speeches ended, and with the constant flowing of champagne from more than a dozen silver fountains, the sound of escalating voices was almost deafening.

Daniel, more than subdued by Valerie's revelation, was relieved when Rebecca whispered that she was tired and wanted to return home.

He retrieved her coat and led her to the expansive lobby of the catering hall. "Wait here where it's warm while the valet brings the car around."

It wasn't until after he'd made the suggestion that he realized he was still protecting and taking care of her. Despite her deceit he could not turn his feelings off and on like a faucet.

The valet pulled up in front of the entrance with a squealing of tires, grinning. He stepped out of the Porsche, shaking his head. "It's awesome, man."

Daniel handed him a tip, smiling at his youthful enthusiasm. "Did you save me some rubber, man?"

His head bobbed up and down. "Yup!"

Retreating to the entrance, Daniel opened the door, extended his hand, and led Rebecca slowly to the car. There was no doubt that she was exhausted.

Her eyes closed soon after she secured the seat belt over her chest, and Daniel was relieved that he did not have to pretend that all was well between them. There would be time for questions, but not now. What he wanted to do was sort out everything Valerie had told him, while trying to recall his conversations with Michael and Rebecca when they discussed adopting a child.

She had to have known that Michael couldn't father children. Why else would they nave considered adoption?

The fingers of his left hand tightened on the steering wheel when he shifted savagely into fifth gear with his right, maneuvering expertly around a slower-moving van.

"What are you doing?" Rebecca asked softly, not opening her eyes.

"Going home," he snapped angrily.

"If you don't slow down we'll end in a hospital or in the morgue." His jaw snapped loudly as he increased his speed, prompting Rebecca to open her eyes. "What's going on, Daniel?"

"I should be the one to ask what the hell is going on." He took his gaze off the road for a second and glared at her.

Sitting up straighter, Rebecca leaned forward and braced her hand against the dashboard. "Get off at the next exit and let me out."

"To do what!"

"To call a taxi, that's what. I will not ride with a drunken maniac who's bent on committing suicide."

"I'm not drunk." He'd only had one drink. He accelerated, the powerful sports car speeding over the winding road like a dizzying rush of wind.

"Then you're crazy."

"I'm as sane as you are."

"Let me out." The three words were pushed out through clenched teeth. "I will not let you kill me and my baby."

The mention of the baby snapped the fragile, tenuous hold on his self-control. "*Our baby*, Rebecca McDonald-Williams-Clinton," he ranted. "Don't ever forget that the child you carry is *our baby!*"

Clamping a hand over her mouth, Rebecca stared numbly out the windshield, the deep, booming angry sound of Daniel's voice echoing around the interior of the car.

She wanted to scream, scream at the top of her lungs. It hadn't mattered what set Daniel off; what she wanted to do was retaliate in kind.

Slowly she dropped her hand, staring straight ahead. "If you ever use that tone with me again, Daniel Albert Clinton, you will forget what I ever looked like, because I will walk away from you with just the clothes on my back."

There was something ominous in her tone that communicated to Daniel that she was not issuing an idle threat. His right foot eased off the accelerator, slowing the car. Once he and Rebecca wed he had thought there would never be a time when they wouldn't be together; but now she threatened to leave him.

He shook his head. No, she wasn't ever going to leave, not when he had waited almost half his life to make her his. He would not lose her.

The remainder of the drive home was accomplished in complete silence. Daniel deactivated the security system and, when he opened the door leading from the garage into the kitchen, Rebecca brushed past him and made her way across the living room and up to their bedroom. He stood at the bottom of the staircase listening to the solid slam of the door. Before he could ask her about Michael's sterility, she'd shut him out.

Taking the stairs two at a time, he walked down the carpeted hallway to their bedroom and flung open the door. The soft light coming from a bedside lamp highlighted the figure of his wife on the bed, sobbing softly. Her shoulders shook uncontrollably as she clamped a hand over her mouth to cut off the strangled cries.

The hot, blinding pain he'd experienced when the rapist's knife sank deep in his shoulder blade returned, this time in his gut. He was bleeding again, hot flowing invisible blood that threatened to drown him.

He'd hurt her—deeply. And he had vowed never to hurt her. All he'd ever wanted to do was love and protect her. Now, who was going to protect her from her own husband? And in his fit of rage, who was going to protect him from himself?

Moving slowly over to the bed, he sat down and pulled her against his chest. He rocked her gently until her sobbing subsided. Surveying her swollen lids and tear-stained face, Daniel felt like an ogre. He had attacked her without giving her the opportunity to defend herself. In that moment he promised he would not tell her what he'd learned—that he, not Michael was the biological father of the child in her womb.

He would wait—wait until after their daughter's birth.

Rebecca awoke alone in the bed, not remembering undressing herself and knew Daniel must have done it. She wore a nightgown she had put away weeks before because it had become too tight across the bodice.

Rolling onto her back, she stared up at the ceiling. Bits and pieces of the confrontation with her husband came rushing back. What had happened? What had happened to make him shout at her as he had?

Michael! It had to be something about Michael and the investigation surrounding his undercover activities. The possibilities that he may have been corrupt whirled around in her head until pressure in the lower part of her body forced her from the bed. It was time that she get up and prepare to open The Golden Needle.

Business had picked up so that she now stayed open a fourth day. The shop was normally closed for business on Sundays, Mondays, and Thursdays, and she had talked at length with Catherine Cunningham about coming in a fourth day. Catherine agreed when she decided to open on Saturdays between the hours of ten and three.

She completed her morning toilette quickly, and twenty minutes later she walked into the kitchen. She spied a note, cellular phone and beeper immediately on the counter top.

Picking up the single sheet of paper, she recognized slanting script. *Carry the phone and beeper with you at all times. If you need to contact me in an emergency, call the following numbers:*

She repeated the numbers to herself, inhaling deeply and shaking her head. So their marriage had dissolved to a point that he left the house before she woke up, and would communicate electronically with her.

Shrugging nonchalantly, Rebecca went through the motions of eating breakfast and preparing lunch. She slipped a plastic container filled with a tuna salad and accompanying side dishes of chick peas and sliced pickled beets in a canvas bag. Slipping on a wool jacket, she left the house to open The Golden Needle.

She unlocked the door, switched on the lights, and adjusted the thermostat for the heat. Gray clouds and a biting chill was indicative of snow, but Rebecca prayed it would hold off for another month. It was the last day of October, Halloween, and much too early for winter to make its appearance. There were times when she imagined going into labor during a snow storm. Three weeks. She had another three weeks before she claimed the status of a mother.

She did not feel very much like a wife after her tiff with Daniel. What she still could not understand was what made him lash out at her? What had she said or done?

She knew married life was not all ups and no downs, and knew occasionally they would disagree. But to have him attack her without provocation,, that was totally unacceptable. And she had meant every word of her threat; she would leave him if he ever raised his voice to her again.

The tiny bell tinkled lightly over the door as Catherine walked in, rubbing her hands together. She was a tall, thin woman with salt and pepper gray hair, a flawless peaches and cream complexion, and kind hazel eyes. Classically fashionable, she favored tailored skirts, slacks and conservative white blouses.

"It's not even Thanksgiving and it feels like snow."

Rebecca glanced up from filling a coffee urn with freshly ground beans. "Tell me about it."

Catherine glanced at the large refreshment table covered with a variety of black and orange decorations. Her lively hazel eyes crinkled attractively with her dimpled smile. "You remembered it was Halloween."

"I remember all of the holidays. I suppose I kind of miss teaching."

Catherine shrugged off a wool-lined raincoat and hung it up in a narrow closet. "You haven't been away long enough to miss it."

"But I do. I miss the cafeteria noise and activity. I miss the classroom instruction, as well as the look on the faces of my students when they finally grasp a concept."

"Once your baby arrives you won't have time to miss school," Catherine reminded her.

"That's what my sister and mother keep telling me."

"Who's scheduled to come in this morning?"

Rebecca glanced down at the appointment book spread out on her desk. "Mrs. Symthe needs help finishing a baby sweater. She's coming in at eleven."

"I'll help her," Catherine volunteered.

"And I'll work with Mrs. Kravitz on piecing her afghan. She's not due in until one."

Having an hour to themselves was a luxury Rebecca and Catherine had come to treasure. It left time for them to work on their personal projects. Rebecca completed several knitted sweater sets and had to put the finishing touches on a crocheted blanket for the baby's crib.

Sitting down on the cushioned rocker, she raised her feet to the footstool, then leaned over to pull a crocheted coverlet from the large wicker basket beside the rocking chair. She had crocheted the lacy-look blanket in a soft pistachio-green using two strands of the same color in a silk and a cotton. The green matched the borders on the wallpaper in the bedroom she had set up for the baby's nursery; it would also pick up the color in a quilt her grandmother had made for her own birth.

At her request, Daniel had had the room repainted a white that reminded her of aged parchment. It took her three days to select a deep pile carpet in a pale yellow. She wanted a color that would compliment the furniture Albert had promised his granddaughter. Albert did not show her his designs, but hinted that he intended to use rosewood and a bleached pine for the bed's head and foot boards.

Winding the thread around her forefinger, she slipped a steel hook in a stitch at the corner of the blanket and pulled the thread through, working a series of stitches for a scalloped border. She concentrated on setting up the foundation row, counting the number of chains and double crochets in each stitch. The delicate shells took shape quickly as she executed rapid yarn overs, pulling the thread up and around her forefinger in a smooth rhythmic motion.

The bell chimed and she and Catherine glanced up. A counter clerk from the bakery left two trays of butter cookies and miniature pastries on the table with the coffee and carafe of hot water for tea.

"Good morning, ladies. Happy Halloween."

"Happy Halloween," the two women replied in unison.

Rebecca had a standing order for baked goods for her customers on the days The Golden Needle opened. Future plans included adding a television, VCR and movie videos to liven up the shorter winter days. She wanted to wait for an increase in her clientele and for the warmer weather before expanding from four to five days with the store open.

"The sugar-free tray is labeled, Mrs. Clinton," Kyle called through the partially closed door as he rushed back to the bakery.

"Thank you, Kyle."

Both women worked furiously on their projects while listening to the music from a soft-listening station before the arrival of their first customer for the day.

The Saturday afternoon was as busy as it was lively. Instead of closing at three, Rebecca remained opened until five. She thought about calling Daniel to let him know that she was staying open later than her regularly scheduled hours, but changed her mind. He knew if she wasn't at home, he would find her at the shop. The additional two hours, spent on her feet, played havoc with her legs and lower back. She shooed Catherine home after closing and locking the door behind the last customer, lingering behind to clean up and put away the many skeins of yarns and magazines scattered around the shop.

By the time she turned off the lights, adjusted the thermostat and locked the door for the last time it was nearly six. Only a few of the stores were still open in the small shopping center. Most closed early because the shopkeepers anticipated the annual pranks perpetrated by the local adolescents, who threw eggs and sprayed shaving cream on every surface they could find.

Rebecca walked around to the parking lot, sighing in relief when she saw that her car had escaped the shaving-cream-on-the-windshield craze that most adolescents found hilariously funny. She adjusted her shoulder bag, leaning over to put her key in the lock.

She felt the presence before she swung around. A man stood over her, his arm raised high above his head. She couldn't make out his face, nor was she given the chance to scream as he pushed her violently. She fell, holding onto the front of his jacket and bringing him down with her. The weight of his body knocked the air out of her lungs, as she struggled vainly to free herself.

"Hel…" Her cry for help was cut off abruptly when she felt a sharp pain rip through her belly, radiating from front to back. She inhaled sharply with the next pain. Then came a gush of liquid, and she knew. The attack had precipitated labor. She waited for the man to hit her again, but the blow never came.

Rebecca lay onthe ground in the parking lot behind the stores, listening to the sound of her car driving away. She had been carjacked!

Crawling slowly over to a lamppost, she struggled to stand. Her shoulder bag slipped off her arm, spilling its contents. The pains were coming faster and harder, and she knew that if she did not get to a hospital she would lose her baby.

She heard a beeping sound. It continued incessantly. Glancing around wildly, she searched the parking lot. It was nearly empty of cars. She opened her mouth to call for help, but couldn't as another wave of pain gripped her. Moaning, she slipped down to the cold cement.

A gentle ringing joined the beeping, and she realized the sounds were coming from the beeper and phone in her bag. Searching the depths of the bag, she found the phone and pressed a button. The ringing stopped. She had disconnected the call.

Biting down hard on her lower lip, she steadied her hand and dialed nine-one-one. She managed to tell the operator where she was before blackness descended on her, shutting out the pain and the fear that she would lose her baby before it was given the opportunity to draw its first breath.

Daniel paced the floor in the family room, cursing violently under his breath. Where the hell was Rebecca? He'd called The Golden Needle and got the answering machine. He had beeped her *and* called the number to the cellular phone he'd left for her, but the call was disconnected.

Was she that angry that he'd raised his voice to her? Had she changed her mind and left him?

The possibility that she had walked out of his life frightened him more than anything else in the world. He would willingly face down someone pointing a loaded gun at him than not have her with him.

He thought of calling her sister. Maybe she'd driven down to New Jersey. Or maybe she'd gone to see Selma. What if she had gone to her parents in Florida?

The what-ifs and maybes pounded him relentlessly until the telephone rang. Taking two steps, he swooped up the receiver.

"Clinton residence."

"Daniel Clinton?"

He went still, unable to identify the male voice. "Speaking."

"Mr. Clinton, I'm Doctor Cushing from Mid-Island Central Hospital. You wife was brought in a few minutes ago. We need you to come and sign some papers before we can…"

"I'm on my way," Daniel interrupted, slamming down the receiver on its cradle.

Not bothering to grab a jacket, he raced from the house, picking up his keys off a counter in the kitchen. He didn't remember getting into his car or exceeding the fifty-five-miles-per-hour speed limit until he pulled into the hospitals parking lot.

The papers he needed to sign were waiting for him at the front desk. A nurse escorted him down a corridor and to an elevator that would take him to the operating room, where his wife was prepped for surgery.

Another nurse helped him into a green hospital gown, whispering that he could hold his wife's hand. Daniel walked over to where Rebecca lay on a table, eyes closed.

"Becky?" She shifted her head, opening her eyes, and he saw the bruise on her chin for the first time. He wanted to ask her what had happened, but didn't. There would be time later for explanations, for pleading for forgiveness.

A tired smile touched her mouth. "Daniel."

Daniel blinked back the tears filling his eyes. "I love you, darling."

"I know you do," she sighed heavily.

Those four words were the last she uttered as the team in the operating room administered general anesthesia, then began the Cesarean procedure which would bring the Clinton baby girl into the world.

CHAPTER SEVENTEEN

Daniel sat outside the recovery room, waiting. The operation was successful; his daughter, tiny and wrinkled, emerging from her warm, dark safe world mewling like a kitten once she was cleaned and weighed. She topped the scales at five pounds, two ounces. It took another half hour to stitch up Rebecca's incision before she was wheeled into the recovery room.

The doctor explained that she had lost a lot of blood before she was brought in, and that her recovery would take longer than the usual patient who had undergone a C-section.

Daniel counted the hours—one, two. Finally a nurse emerged and told him that Rebecca had come out of recovery, and she would take her to her room.

He took the time to retreat behind the doors to a washroom, where he closeted himself in a stall and uttered a prayer of thanks and forgiveness. When he emerged he splashed cold water on his face. Patting his damp face with a towel, he returned the grin of another man who stared into the mirror while washing his hands.

"I'm a father," he stated proudly. "My wife just delivered a boy."

"Congratulations," Daniel returned. "I have a daughter."

"Congratulations to you, too."

"Thanks." Tossing the towel into a waste basket, he nodded at the other new father and walked out of the rest room, whistling. He would stop at the nursery to see his daughter, then go see his wife.

Rebecca couldn't keep her eyes open. She heard people entering and exiting her room, but did not recognize who they were. Placing a hand over her middle, she realized it was flatter than it had been in months. Her baby! She had had her baby.

"Hello, beautiful."

This voice she recognized and she fought against the weight pressing against her eyelids and opened them. "Daniel."

He sat down on the chair beside her bed. "Thank you."

"For what?"

"For a daughter who is as beautiful as her mother."

Her gaze widened. "You saw her?"

Daniel nodded. "Of course I saw her. I saw her being born, and I saw her again a few minutes ago."

Rebecca reached for his hand, holding it tightly. "Is she all right? Who does she look like?"

"She's in remarkably good health, given her early arrival." He hesitating, forming the answer to her other question. "She looks just like her father, Becky. She looks like *me*."

A frown creased her forehead as she shook her head. "Don't you mean Michael?"

Sitting down on the side of the bed, Daniel smoothed back the curling hair falling over her forehead. "No, I don't. I'm her father, Becky. I'm the one who got you pregnant, not Michael."

Rebecca tried sitting up, but Daniel put a hand on her shoulder, gently pushing her down to the mound of pillows cradling her back.

Capturing her stunned gaze, he told her about his conversation with Valerie Kent, leaving nothing out. When he saw the tears well up in her eyes, he gathered her to his chest and held her.

"Why, Daniel? Why wouldn't he tell me he was sterile?"

"I don't know, darling. Maybe because he'd lost one woman when he told her the truth, and he didn't intend to lose out again with you."

Rebecca sniffled against her husband's hard shoulder. "Now I know why he would never consent to a fertility test. He knew what the results would be." Pulling back, she stared up at Daniel. "Didn't he know that I would've married him anyway?"

"I don't think he was willing to take that risk. Valerie wouldn't marry him, and he had no way of knowing whether you would also reject him." Holding her chin between his thumb and forefinger, Daniel studied her face. "What happened to your face? Why didn't you return my beep or phone call?"

"I was carjacked."

He didn't move, only his chest rising and falling. "What?"

"Some man attacked me as I was getting into my car," she explained, watching disbelief sweep over Daniel's features. A muscle ticked noticeably along the left side of his face.

"He hit you?"

"No, he pushed me."

"Did you see his face?"

She shook her head. "There wasn't enough light in the parking lot." Daniel released her, easing her down to the pillows. In one smooth motion, he was standing. "Where are you going?"

"I'm going to call the police and report the car stolen." What he didn't say was that the carjacker would be safer in police custody than if he found him first.

"Daniel?"

He stared at his wife, forcing a smile he did not feel. "Yes, Becky?"

"We have to name our daughter."

"We still have some time to come up with one that is fitting our little princess." Bending over, he pressed a kiss over each eyelid. "Relax, darling. I'll be right back."

Rebecca waited until Daniel walked out of the room before she closed her eyes. The enormity of what he had revealed hit her full force for the first time. She had conceived only hours after she had buried her husband. In her grief she'd reached out to her first lover for comfort, and together they had started a new life.

Despite her joy of thinking that she was carrying Michael's baby, there had been the underlying guilt that she had slept with Daniel. But with the knowledge that the baby was Daniel's she felt that she had been given a second chance to throw off the mantle of guilt.

She had fallen asleep by the time Daniel returned to the room, his arms filled with a vase of long-stemmed red roses. Placing the vase on the table beside the bed, he sat down on a chair and waited, waited for his wife to wake up so they could name their child and plan for their future.

A gentle smile touched his mobile mouth. He had it all. Everything he'd yearned for had become his.

EPILOGUE

Two months later—Christmas Eve

The pungent smell of firewood mingled with the tantalizing aroma of roast turkey, and the distinctive scent of live pine needles.

The melodious chiming of the doorbell echoed repeatedly throughout the large house known as Wind Watch as Daniel Clinton opened the door to family members who had come to celebrate Christmas Eve together, while meeting Mistress Michelle Eunice Clinton for the first time.

He greeted his in-laws, taking their coats and escorting them into the living room; making certain they were comfortable, he excused himself and made his way up the curving staircase to the second floor bedrooms.

He halted his determined stride as he walked slowly into the nursery. Rebecca sat on a rocker, holding Michelle as she fed hungrily from her breast.

A slow smile deepened the attractive creases along his lean jaw. He would never get used to seeing the miracle of his daughter. There were times when he stood at her crib, watching her sleep the same way he continued to rise early to watch Rebecca as she slept.

The horror of the Halloween Night when Rebecca was carjacked was over. The car was recovered, along with the man who had stolen it. The police discovered he was a college student who had taken the car as a prank. The local district attorney was not amused, and had charged with him a felony which carried a sentence of us to five years in prison.

The rumors surrounding Michael Williams' criminal activities were also put to rest. The Internal Affairs Bureau had closed the case, citing insufficient evidence. He saw an expression of relief on Rebecca's face when he told her the news. A veil of suspicion had been lifted, allowing them to proceed with lives unfettered.

Leaning against the door, he crossed one ankle over the other, while crossing his arms over his chest. Michelle had gained a pound and had taken to sleeping five hours between feedings, allowing her parents to catch up on their much needed sleep.

Rebecca had lost all of the weight she'd gained during her pregnancy, regaining her former slimness, at the same time acquiring a lushness that she hadn't had before. There were times when he stared at her with a hunger she had no problem interpreting as lust.

"Tell her to leave some for Daddy."

Looking up from her nursing baby, Rebecca stared at the tall, imposing figure dressed in black. "There will be plenty for you."

"When, Becky?"

Her eyes darkened with her own rising desire. It had been a long time, too long, since she had shared her body with her husband. Her doctor had given her a clean bill of health, telling her that she could resume having sexual intercourse. That had been two days ago. But she wanted to do was wait, wait until Christmas before she gave Daniel his gifts.

"Tonight, my darling."

He straightened from his leaning position. "At what time, darling?

"At the stroke of midnight." Her voice was the low, cloaking fog that sent shivers up and down his spine.

"Is that a promise?" he queried, making his way across the room.

She met his stare, holding it with hers. "Yes."

He arched an eyebrow. "What if I set my watch ahead and pretend that it's midnight and we disappear for an hour."

"To do what?" she asked, repeating the same question put to him on their wedding day.

"Crawling into bed together."

The sucking motion on her breast stopped, and she glanced down at her sleeping child. Easing the nipple from Michelle's mouth, she handed her to Daniel, along with a cloth diaper.

Daniel tossed the diaper over one shoulder and cradled the baby with one hand, his fingers supporting the tiny, round head. He waited for the sound of her expelling air, then shifted her to the crook of his arm.

Looking down at the sleeping infant, he smiled. There was no doubt that the child was his. Everything about her tiny face was a miniature copy of his mother's face, with the exception of her eyes. The soft dark-gray color was Rebecca's. She thought that Michelle's eyes would probably change, but he doubted it.

Lifting the child, he placed a tender kiss on her forehead, inhaling the clean smell exclusive to infants. "Your grandfathers, grandmother, aunts, uncles and cousins are waiting for your grand entrance. Are you ready, princess?" Michelle yawned, smiled a toothless smile, but did not open her eyes. She was very full and very sleepy.

Rebecca glanced at her husband and daughter, then at the exquisite furniture gracing the nursery. Albert Clinton had crafted a sleigh bed, chest-on-chest, double dresser, rocking chair, toy chest, and a delicate crib in rosewood and bleached pine. The furniture had arrived the day she brought Michelle home from the hospital.

The sound of raised voices and laughter drifted up from the living room, and Daniel extended his free hand. "Let's go see to our guests."

She took his hand, rising on tiptoe to press her mouth to his. "I love you, Daniel Albert Clinton."

"Not as much as I love you, Rebecca Clinton."

They walked out of the nursery and down the staircase to present their love, their special gift of life, to their families.

They'd decided to wait a year, then do it all over again, joking and praying Daniel wouldn't have to experience the nausea that had plagued Rebecca the first three months she had carried Michelle.

A satisfied smile curved Rebecca's full lips as she walked into the living room beside her husband. The next time she conceived it would be as Rebecca Clinton.

ABOUT THE AUTHOR

A native of New York, **Rochelle Alers** is now residing in a quaint fishing village on Long Island with her family where she draws the inspiration to write her sensual novels and short stories. Formally a pre-school teacher, she changed her career for the corporate world. Rochelle holds a degree in sociology and psychology. Both help her to create the sophisticated, sexy characters who, in her novels, dare to risk everything for love.

January

A Lover's Legacy
Veronica Parker
1-58571-167-5
$9.95

Love Lasts Forever
Dominiqua Douglas
1-58571-187-X
$9.95

Under the Cherry Moon
Christal Jordan-Mims
1-58571-169-1
$12.95

February

Second Chances at Love
Cheris Hodges
1-58571-188-8
$9.95

Enchanted Desire
Wanda Y. Thomas
1-58571-176-4
$9.95

Caught Up
Deatri King Bey
1-58571-178-0
$12.95

March

I'm Gonna Make You
    Love Me
Gwyneth Bolton
1-58571-181-0
$9.95

Through the Fire
Seressia Glass
1-58571-173-X
$9.95

Notes When Summer
    Ends
Beverly Lauderdale
1-58571-180-2
$12.95

April

Sin and Surrender
J.M. Jeffries
1-58571-189-6
$9.95

Unearthing Passions
Elaine Sims
1-58571-184-5
$9.95

Between Tears
Pamela Ridley
1-58571-179-9
$12.95

May

Misty Blue
Dyanne Davis
1-58571-186-1
$9.95

Ironic
Pamela Leigh Starr
1-58571-168-3
$9.95

Cricket's Serenade
Carolita Blythe
1-58571-183-7
$12.95

June

Cupid
Barbara Keaton
1-58571-174-8
$9.95

Havana Sunrise
Kymberly Hunt
1-58571-182-9
$9.95

July

Love Me Carefully
A.C. Arthur
1-58571-177-2
$9.95

No Ordinary Love
Angela Weaver
1-58571-198-5
$9.95

Rehoboth Road
Anita Ballard-Jones
1-58571-196-9
$12.95

August

Scent of Rain
Annetta P. Lee
158571-199-3
$9.95

Love in High Gear
Charlotte Roy
158571-185-3
$9.95

Rise of the Phoenix
Kenneth Whetstone
1-58571-197-7
$12.95

September

The Business of Love
Cheris Hodges
1-58571-193-4
$9.95

Rock Star
Rosyln Hardy Holcomb
1-58571-200-0
$9.95

A Dead Man Speaks
Lisa Jones Johnson
1-58571-203-5
$12.95

October

Rivers of the Soul-Part 1
Leslie Esdaile
1-58571-223-X
$9.95

A Dangerous Woman
J.M. Jeffries
1-58571-195-0
$9.95

Sinful Intentions
Crystal Rhodes
1-58571-201-9
$12.95

November

Only You
Crystal Hubbard
1-58571-208-6
$9.95

Ebony Eyes
Kei Swanson
1-58571-194-2
$9.95

Still Waters Run Deep –
  Part 2
Leslie Esdaile
1-58571-224-8
$9.95

December

Let's Get It On
Dyanne Davis
1-58571-210-8
$9.95

Nights Over Egypt
Barbara Keaton
1-58571-192-6
$9.95

A Pefect Place to Pray
I.L. Goodwin
1-58571-202-7
$12.95

Other Genesis Press, Inc. Titles

Other Genesis Press, Inc. Titles (continued)

Breeze	Robin Hampton Allen	$10.95
Broken	Dar Tomlinson	$24.95
By Design	Barbara Keaton	$8.95
Cajun Heat	Charlene Berry	$8.95
Careless Whispers	Rochelle Alers	$8.95
Cats & Other Tales	Marilyn Wagner	$8.95
Caught in a Trap	Andre Michelle	$8.95
Caught Up In the Rapture	Lisa G. Riley	$9.95
Cautious Heart	Cheris F Hodges	$8.95
Chances	Pamela Leigh Starr	$8.95
Cherish the Flame	Beverly Clark	$8.95
Class Reunion	Irma Jenkins/	
	John Brown	$12.95
Code Name: Diva	J.M. Jeffries	$9.95
Conquering Dr. Wexler's Heart	Kimberley White	$9.95
Crossing Paths, Tempting Memories	Dorothy Elizabeth Love	$9.95
Cypress Whisperings	Phyllis Hamilton	$8.95
Dark Embrace	Crystal Wilson Harris	$8.95
Dark Storm Rising	Chinelu Moore	$10.95
Daughter of the Wind	Joan Xian	$8.95
Deadly Sacrifice	Jack Kean	$22.95
Designer Passion	Dar Tomlinson	$8.95
Dreamtective	Liz Swados	$5.95
Ebony Butterfly II	Delilah Dawson	$14.95
Echoes of Yesterday	Beverly Clark	$9.95
Eden's Garden	Elizabeth Rose	$8.95
Everlastin' Love	Gay G. Gunn	$8.95
Everlasting Moments	Dorothy Elizabeth Love	$8.95
Everything and More	Sinclair Lebeau	$8.95
Everything but Love	Natalie Dunbar	$8.95
Eve's Prescription	Edwina Martin Arnold	$8.95

Other Genesis Press, Inc. Titles (continued)

Falling	Natalie Dunbar	$9.95
Fate	Pamela Leigh Starr	$8.95
Finding Isabella	A.J. Garrotto	$8.95
Forbidden Quest	Dar Tomlinson	$10.95
Forever Love	Wanda Y. Thomas	$8.95
From the Ashes	Kathleen Suzanne	$8.95
	Jeanne Sumerix	
Gentle Yearning	Rochelle Alers	$10.95
Glory of Love	Sinclair LeBeau	$10.95
Go Gentle into that Good Night	Malcom Boyd	$12.95
Goldengroove	Mary Beth Craft	$16.95
Groove, Bang, and Jive	Steve Cannon	$8.99
Hand in Glove	Andrea Jackson	$9.95
Hard to Love	Kimberley White	$9.95
Hart & Soul	Angie Daniels	$8.95
Heartbeat	Stephanie Bedwell-Grime	$8.95
Hearts Remember	M. Loui Quezada	$8.95
Hidden Memories	Robin Allen	$10.95
Higher Ground	Leah Latimer	$19.95
Hitler, the War, and the Pope	Ronald Rychiak	$26.95
How to Write a Romance	Kathryn Falk	$18.95
I Married a Reclining Chair	Lisa M. Fuhs	$8.95
Indigo After Dark Vol. I	Nia Dixon/Angelique	$10.95
Indigo After Dark Vol. II	Dolores Bundy/	$10.95
	Cole Riley	
Indigo After Dark Vol. III	Montana Blue/	$10.95
	Coco Morena	
Indigo After Dark Vol. IV	Cassandra Colt/	$14.95
	Diana Richeaux	
Indigo After Dark Vol. V	Delilah Dawson	$14.95
Icie	Pamela Leigh Starr	$8.95
I'll Be Your Shelter	Giselle Carmichael	$8.95

Other Genesis Press, Inc. Titles (continued)

I'll Paint a Sun	A.J. Garrotto	$9.95
Illusions	Pamela Leigh Starr	$8.95
Indiscretions	Donna Hill	$8.95
Intentional Mistakes	Michele Sudler	$9.95
Interlude	Donna Hill	$8.95
Intimate Intentions	Angie Daniels	$8.95
Jolie's Surrender	Edwina Martin-Arnold	$8.95
Kiss or Keep	Debra Phillips	$8.95
Lace	Giselle Carmichael	$9.95
Last Train to Memphis	Elsa Cook	$12.95
Lasting Valor	Ken Olsen	$24.95
Let Us Prey	Hunter Lundy	$25.95
Life Is Never As It Seems	J.J. Michael	$12.95
Lighter Shade of Brown	Vicki Andrews	$8.95
Love Always	Mildred E. Riley	$10.95
Love Doesn't Come Easy	Charlyne Dickerson	$8.95
Love Unveiled	Gloria Greene	$10.95
Love's Deception	Charlene Berry	$10.95
Love's Destiny	M. Loui Quezada	$8.95
Mae's Promise	Melody Walcott	$8.95
Magnolia Sunset	Giselle Carmichael	$8.95
Matters of Life and Death	Lesego Malepe, Ph.D.	$15.95
Meant to Be	Jeanne Sumerix	$8.95
Midnight Clear	Leslie Esdaile	$10.95
(Anthology)	Gwynne Forster	
	Carmen Green	
	Monica Jackson	
Midnight Magic	Gwynne Forster	$8.95
Midnight Peril	Vicki Andrews	$10.95
Misconceptions	Pamela Leigh Starr	$9.95
Montgomery's Children	Richard Perry	$14.95
My Buffalo Soldier	Barbara B. K. Reeves	$8.95

Other Genesis Press, Inc. Titles (continued)

Naked Soul	Gwynne Forster	$8.95
Next to Last Chance	Louisa Dixon	$24.95
No Apologies	Seressia Glass	$8.95
No Commitment Required	Seressia Glass	$8.95
No Regrets	Mildred E. Riley	$8.95
Nowhere to Run	Gay G. Gunn	$10.95
O Bed! O Breakfast!	Rob Kuehnle	$14.95
Object of His Desire	A. C. Arthur	$8.95
Office Policy	A. C. Arthur	$9.95
Once in a Blue Moon	Dorianne Cole	$9.95
One Day at a Time	Bella McFarland	$8.95
Outside Chance	Louisa Dixon	$24.95
Passion	T.T. Henderson	$10.95
Passion's Blood	Cherif Fortin	$22.95
Passion's Journey	Wanda Y. Thomas	$8.95
Past Promises	Jahmel West	$8.95
Path of Fire	T.T. Henderson	$8.95
Path of Thorns	Annetta P. Lee	$9.95
Peace Be Still	Colette Haywood	$12.95
Picture Perfect	Reon Carter	$8.95
Playing for Keeps	Stephanie Salinas	$8.95
Pride & Joi	Gay G. Gunn	$15.95
Pride & Joi	Gay G. Gunn	$8.95
Promises to Keep	Alicia Wiggins	$8.95
Quiet Storm	Donna Hill	$10.95
Reckless Surrender	Rochelle Alers	$6.95
Red Polka Dot in a World of Plaid	Varian Johnson	$12.95
Reluctant Captive	Joyce Jackson	$8.95
Rendezvous with Fate	Jeanne Sumerix	$8.95
Revelations	Cheris F. Hodges	$8.95
Rivers of the Soul	Leslie Esdaile	$8.95

Other Genesis Press, Inc. Titles (continued)

Rocky Mountain Romance	Kathleen Suzanne	$8.95
Rooms of the Heart	Donna Hill	$8.95
Rough on Rats and Tough on Cats	Chris Parker	$12.95
Secret Library Vol. 1	Nina Sheridan	$18.95
Secret Library Vol. 2	Cassandra Colt	$8.95
Shades of Brown	Denise Becker	$8.95
Shades of Desire	Monica White	$8.95
Shadows in the Moonlight	Jeanne Sumerix	$8.95
Sin	Crystal Rhodes	$8.95
So Amazing	Sinclair LeBeau	$8.95
Somebody's Someone	Sinclair LeBeau	$8.95
Someone to Love	Alicia Wiggins	$8.95
Song in the Park	Martin Brant	$15.95
Soul Eyes	Wayne L. Wilson	$12.95
Soul to Soul	Donna Hill	$8.95
Southern Comfort	J.M. Jeffries	$8.95
Still the Storm	Sharon Robinson	$8.95
Still Waters Run Deep	Leslie Esdaile	$8.95
Stories to Excite You	Anna Forrest/Divine	$14.95
Subtle Secrets	Wanda Y. Thomas	$8.95
Suddenly You	Crystal Hubbard	$9.95
Sweet Repercussions	Kimberley White	$9.95
Sweet Tomorrows	Kimberly White	$8.95
Taken by You	Dorothy Elizabeth Love	$9.95
Tattooed Tears	T. T. Henderson	$8.95
The Color Line	Lizzette Grayson Carter	$9.95
The Color of Trouble	Dyanne Davis	$8.95
The Disappearance of Allison Jones	Kayla Perrin	$5.95
The Honey Dipper's Legacy	Pannell-Allen	$14.95
The Joker's Love Tune	Sidney Rickman	$15.95

Other Genesis Press, Inc. Titles (continued)

The Little Pretender	Barbara Cartland	$10.95
The Love We Had	Natalie Dunbar	$8.95
The Man Who Could Fly	Bob & Milana Beamon	$18.95
The Missing Link	Charlyne Dickerson	$8.95
The Price of Love	Sinclair LeBeau	$8.95
The Smoking Life	Ilene Barth	$29.95
The Words of the Pitcher	Kei Swanson	$8.95
Three Wishes	Seressia Glass	$8.95
Ties That Bind	Kathleen Suzanne	$8.95
Tiger Woods	Libby Hughes	$5.95
Time is of the Essence	Angie Daniels	$9.95
Timeless Devotion	Bella McFarland	$9.95
Tomorrow's Promise	Leslie Esdaile	$8.95
Truly Inseparable	Wanda Y. Thomas	$8.95
Unbreak My Heart	Dar Tomlinson	$8.95
Uncommon Prayer	Kenneth Swanson	$9.95
Unconditional	A.C. Arthur	$9.95
Unconditional Love	Alicia Wiggins	$8.95
Until Death Do Us Part	Susan Paul	$8.95
Vows of Passion	Bella McFarland	$9.95
Wedding Gown	Dyanne Davis	$8.95
What's Under Benjamin's Bed	Sandra Schaffer	$8.95
When Dreams Float	Dorothy Elizabeth Love	$8.95
Whispers in the Night	Dorothy Elizabeth Love	$8.95
Whispers in the Sand	LaFlorya Gauthier	$10.95
Wild Ravens	Altonya Washington	$9.95
Yesterday Is Gone	Beverly Clark	$10.95
Yesterday's Dreams, Tomorrow's Promises	Reon Laudat	$8.95
Your Precious Love	Sinclair LeBeau	$8.95

ESCAPE WITH INDIGO !!!!

Join Indigo Book Club©
It's simple, easy and secure.

Sign up and receive the new releases
every month + Free shipping
and
20% off the cover price.

Go online to www.genesis-press.com and click on Bookclub
or
call 1-888-INDIGO-1

Order Form

Mail to: Genesis Press, Inc.
P.O. Box 101
Columbus, MS 39703

Name _____
Address _____
City/State _____ Zip _____
Telephone _____

Ship to (if different from above)
Name _____
Address _____
City/State _____ Zip _____
Telephone _____

Credit Card Information
Credit Card # _____ ☐ Visa ☐ Mastercard
Expiration Date (mm/yy) _____ ☐ AmEx ☐ Discover

Qty.	Author	Title	Price	Total

Use this order form, or call 1-888-INDIGO-1

Total for books	_____
Shipping and handling: $5 first two books, $1 each additional book	
Total S & H	_____
Total amount enclosed	_____

Mississippi residents add 7% sales tax